"You and your feelings." Tanzi gave him a teasing glance.

"You and your lack of feelings." He returned the look. *Careful, Malone.* This was starting to feel a lot like flirtation.

"I've been discovering lately that I might be able to feel more than I believed I could." Her sidelong glance was a combination of invitation and confusion.

To hell with caution, Lorcan thought as he pulled Tanzi into his arms. He'd never know which of them was the most surprised. All he knew was that the action was long overdue.

D0493640

OTHERWORLD RENEGADE

JANE GODMAN

MILLS & BOON

First Published in Great Britain 2016
By Mills & Boon, an imprint of HarperCollins*Publishers*
1 London Bridge Street, London, SE1 9GF

© 2016 by Amanda Anders

ISBN: 978-0-263-92172-4

89-0516

Jane Godman writes in a variety of genres including paranormal, gothic and historical romance and erotic romantic suspense. She also enjoys the occasional foray into horror and thriller writing. Jane lives in England and loves to travel to European cities, which are steeped in history and romance—Venice, Dubrovnik and Vienna are among her favorites.

A teacher, Jane is married to a lovely man and is mum to two grown-up children.

This book is dedicated to Denise Zaza,
who believed in me.

Chapter 1

"Trust me, Tanzi. If you need me, I will know."

Those words, spoken by Lorcan Malone in the heat of battle, must have been a bit of Irish blarney. He probably didn't even remember who she was, let alone recall their strange encounter on that fateful day. So why, in this moment—when she was in more trouble than she could ever have imagined possible—was she suddenly experiencing a fierce longing for the bad-boy necromancer with the twinkling blue eyes?

It's called clutching at straws, she told herself. *It's what you're doing right now instead of facing reality and finding your own way out of this madness.*

"What are you thinking, my daughter?" Moncoya, exiled King of the Faeries, watched her face.

"I'm thinking that defeat has unhinged you. That you have finally done what others have whispered of for years and taken leave of your senses." Never before had Tanzi spoken so boldly to him. Defiance was the trait her twin sister, Vashti, proudly exhibited. Tanzi had always been the acquiescent one. Until now. There were some things she could not bow down and agree to. This was one of them.

Moncoya's perfect features hardened with fury. His blue eyes, so like her own with their sidhe ring of fire encircling the iris, lit with a brighter inner blaze. His fingers tightened on the arm of his chair so that his knuckles gleamed white in stark contrast to the black polish that decorated his perfectly manicured nails. Tanzi braced herself. His retribution would be swift and merciless. She couldn't hope to match him in strength, but she might be able to outrun him.

The outcome hung in the balance for seconds that stretched into minutes. Then Moncoya laughed. It was a brittle, mirthless sound that set Tanzi's teeth buzzing. She knew that laugh well. It had never boded well in her childhood. She didn't imagine things had changed. Unexpectedly, he relaxed back into his seat.

"My child, you are overwhelmed by the honor I have arranged for you. I should have foreseen this." He rose, draping a deceptively casual arm about her shoulders. "Walk with me awhile."

They stepped through a set of double doors straight onto a sand-and-shingle beach. The entire island, known locally as the Silver Isle, seemed to be made up of sand. Even the ocher-hued cliffs looked ready to crumble into grit at the touch of a fingertip. Ferns, wild fennel and coarse bamboo grasses clung determinedly to soil that was a combination of granule and dust. Tanzi thought of her father's palace, of the precisely laid-out gardens leading down to the elegant lake. She glanced back over her shoulder at the beachside villa they had just left. Sea breezes and salt water had taken their toll on its elegance so that it had a faded charm she doubted her father would acknowledge. In comparison with the soaring, white marble palace she had called "home" for all her life, it was a shack. Moncoya was as out of place here as a diamond in a dung heap.

"You made sure no one followed you?" Moncoya withdrew his arm from about her shoulders as they walked along the water's edge. Secrecy surrounded this hiding place. If he was discovered, he faced trial and inevitable execution.

"Of course." Tanzi was offended at the question. Would he have asked Vashti the same thing? She doubted it. *Yet we both trained with the Valkyrie. We are equally astute when it comes to warfare and subterfuge.* It came back to the same weary argument. The same reason Tanzi had been summoned to be the recipient of his latest piece of "good news" instead of her twin. Moncoya viewed Vashti as the son he had never had. Tanzi's only value to her father was as a pawn in the marriage stakes. *Not this marriage, Father. The sacrifice you are asking of me is too great.*

"Tell me what has been happening at the palace in my absence." Three months had passed since the cataclysmic battle that had forced Moncoya into hiding. It felt like three years.

"There is a peacekeeping council known as the Alliance in place. Each of the Otherworld dynasties has representation on it. The Alliance itself is led by Merlin Caledonius."

Moncoya's expression hardened further at the name. "That half-blood cur will pay dearly for his part in this."

Merlin, the greatest sorcerer the world had ever known, was Moncoya's half brother and the man who had brought about his exile. Cal, as he preferred to be called these days, had widened the existing gulf of hatred between the two men further by falling in love with and marrying the woman Moncoya had hoped to make his queen.

Tanzi paused, looking out across the turquoise waters toward the horizon. She drew a deep breath. "My father, you wrong him. He is man of conscience who is doing a fine job of uniting the dynasties..." Moncoya's growl of rage told her she had gone too far.

"Am I, the greatest leader Otherworld has ever known, to be forced into hiding while *he* lives in luxury in my royal palace? Am I to endure the knowledge that he has stolen the necromancer star, the woman I chose as my own, from under my nose? Must I kick my heels in this backwater while you, my own daughter, take the seat that should be mine at this pathetic council table—" He broke off, his voice ragged. When he spoke again, his tone was softer, the words a caress. "But you know nothing of these things, my child. It is wrong of these men to ask you to involve yourself in their political machinations. They seek to trick you."

Tanzi bit her lip. How could she explain it to him when he insisted on viewing her as a helpless dupe? Being part of the Alliance had brought her new life. Oh, she had been regarded with suspicion initially by many of the council members. She was Moncoya's daughter, after all. They saw her as the spoiled brat sidhe princess who had been his consort—his puppet—in the past. Together with Vashti, she had blindly carried out his wishes. But things had changed three months ago on that battlefield. *She* had changed.

A pair of laughing Irish eyes came into her mind once more and she determinedly dismissed them. Cal and his wife, Stella, treated her as their equal, and with their help she was learning how to be the voice and conscience of her people. She was developing an understanding of compassion and democracy. Tanzi cast a sidelong glance at her father. She was learning that there was a way to rule other than Moncoya's iron-fisted style.

"Let us leave this talk of the mongrel sorcerer for another day. I look forward to dealing with him when the time comes. This marriage I have arranged for you is the highest distinction ever to be bestowed upon a woman. Through this union, I will not only be able to come out of this undignified hiding and return to my palace, I will be the undisputed ruler of all Otherworld." Moncoya's lips thinned into a smile. "There will be no need for their puny Alliance when that day dawns."

"And what of me, Father? While you become all powerful, what will I become?"

He paused then, perhaps considering for the first time the true implications of what he was asking of her. Such was his arrogance, she might have known he would not allow her feelings to influence him for long. "You will be revered above all others."

She shook her head. "I will not do it."

His face was set. The silken note in his voice made the threat even more menacing. "You have no choice."

"By all the angels, Father, you cannot intend to force me into this!"

Moncoya's lips smiled but Tanzi's heart quailed at the look in his eyes. "Given the bridegroom I have chosen for you, might I suggest you refrain from speaking of angels in the future?"

Lorcan Malone narrowed his eyes against the harsh blast of sand that swept off the golden beach. He was seated on a cliff top looking across the stretch of blue Mediterranean Sea from Tangier to Gibraltar and wondering what the hell he was doing there. He knew why he had come to Morocco. Of course he did. The same reason that led him anywhere had brought him to this place. But that had been two days ago. The job was done and yet he was still hanging around, waiting for... Well, what was he waiting for, exactly?

"Damned if I know," he muttered, kicking a pebble and watching it bounce down the steep slope.

His sources had been insistent when they persuaded him of the need to stay on. There was more work for him here, they had maintained. There were others in danger, men who needed his help. All that urgency and secrecy. Then silence. He was beginning to suspect a trap. Moncoya might be out of action, but he wasn't the only evil bastard in Otherworld. He certainly wasn't the only one who would like to see the anti-Moncoya resistance movement wiped out.

If it was a trap it meant Lorcan's cover was blown. Someone had seen through the aimless veneer he worked so hard to preserve. The Irish wanderer guise had slipped somewhere along the way. Lorcan shrugged. *I'm surprised it's lasted this long.*

A movement on the hillside caught his attention and he turned his head. A car so battered it looked as if it was held together with string and candle wax screeched to a halt, throwing up clouds of red dust in its wake. The head that thrust through the open driver's window wore a battered fez and a grin as wide as the Strait of Gibraltar itself.

"Taxi for Malone?"

"Ali!" Lorcan sprang up from the scrubby grass. "Tell me it's not yourself who has kept me kicking up my heels in this sorry place. Because if it is you're a dead man, my friend."

"Get in and save your bluster for someone who cares." Ali threw open the passenger door. Tossing his backpack in first, Lorcan slid into an interior that smelled of cheap tobacco and cheaper aftershave. Before he could even close the door, Ali screeched off again in the direction of the city. Lorcan had been in Tangier long enough to become acquainted with the rules of the road. There were no rules. There were no seat belts either. Not in this car, anyway.

"Out with it. What's going on?" If Ali was involved, at least Lorcan could be reasonably confident this wasn't a trap. Ali was a prominent member of the resistance movement and as fiercely anti-Moncoya as Lorcan himself.

Ali turned soulful brown eyes, made even darker by their sidhe ring of fire, toward him. Lorcan wished he'd keep them on the road, particularly as they were navigating a narrow cliff-top bend, but he kept his thoughts to himself. "There are friends of yours imprisoned in the catacombs beneath the Kasbah."

Lorcan shook his head. "That's not possible." At Ali's inquiring look, he elaborated. "I have no friends."

"Be serious, necromancer. Unless you can get them out, these two men are finished come sunset tonight."

"Why me? Why can't the resistance here in Tangier do it?"

"You will see." They had reached the center of the town now and Lorcan fell silent as all of his energy was required to regulate his breathing and cling to his seat. They tore across lanes of oncoming traffic, squealed around bends and finally slammed to a halt, narrowly missing oncoming cars, camels, pedestrians and several goats.

"Do your roads have lanes, traffic signals, *anything* that might give a clue about who has right-of-way?" Lorcan pried his fingers off the dashboard.

Ali grinned. "Scared, necromancer?"

"No. Bloody terrified."

It seemed they were abandoning the car in the middle of the road. Unwinding his long frame from the tiny vehicle, Lorcan followed Ali into the crowded streets of the ancient Kasbah. His sidhe companion moved with confidence through a series of increasingly narrow alleyways while Lorcan shrugged off offers of food, watches, livestock and sexual favors. They passed stalls selling pungent spices and colorful woven carpets until Ali ducked through a mosaic-encrusted arch into a sandstone courtyard.

"This is the oldest part of the Kasbah." Ali indicated the castellated fortress walls. "This building was a prison many thousands of years ago."

"What is it now?" Lorcan's voice echoed oddly in the confined space. Or perhaps it was just the effect of the silence after the bustle of the Kasbah.

Ali licked his lips and cast a glance over his shoulder. "A dark house."

A dark house was a very specific portal, one that led directly to the darkest, seediest underbelly of Otherworld. There were other portals—harmless ones—all over the world. Some of them, like Stonehenge, made grand statements. Most were quieter. It was the dark houses that the resistance fought a relentless battle to close down. From the outside, this place didn't have the feel of a dark house. Lorcan should know. He had been in more than his fair share over the years.

He glanced at the tiny square of blue sky that was still visible between the high sandstone walls. The sun was sinking from late afternoon into evening. Otherworld was closest at dawn and dusk. He should go, get out of here while he still could. Ali had said the two men had until sunset. Being a good guy never brought him easy choices.

He sighed. "Take me inside."

The interior of the fortress was cool after the heat of a Moroccan summer day. Dust tickled Lorcan's nostrils and caught in the back of his throat while something unpleasant crawled along his spine. And there it was. That dark house feeling. It was unmistakable. This one probably wasn't used much anymore, which was why he hadn't felt it instantly. They traversed empty corridors and passed ancient cells, their footsteps echoing in silence. The suffering of thousands of years hung heavy in the air.

"Down here." Ali indicated stone steps hewn into the floor.

Lorcan gestured for the sidhe to go first. He might trust Ali, but he had done this sort of thing too many times. There was trust and there was gullibility. Lorcan knew which he preferred. They descended into total blackness. Lorcan extended a hand and light flickered around them.

Ali gave an appreciative whistle. "I like the way you necromancers do that."

"We aim to please."

They reached a circular dungeon and Ali stepped back, allowing Lorcan to move into the center of the room. On one wall two men, both naked from the waist up, were suspended by manacles around their wrists. One was so badly beaten Lorcan could barely make out his features. He hung unconscious between his restraints. The other man raised his head as Lorcan approached. His lips curved into something that was almost a smile.

"They promised you would come. It is too late for me,

but there is still time to save my master." His voice was heavily accented.

"My God, Dimitar, what the hell has happened here?" Lorcan hurried forward. He was brought up short as Dimitar turned his head, revealing the telltale marks on his neck. There was no mistaking the puncture marks made by repeated vampire bites, even in the gloom of the catacombs.

"Prince Tibor never forgave me for deserting him and choosing Jethro as my master instead. This is his revenge." Until the recent battle, Dimitar had been the human slave of the all-powerful Prince of the Vampires.

"Has he also been bitten?" Lorcan jerked a thumb in the direction of the unconscious man. He could see now, from his height and muscular physique, that it was Jethro de Loix, his fellow sorcerer. The mercenary who gave necromancing a bad name by selling his skills to the highest bidder. When he told Ali he had no friends, he wasn't being entirely honest. He had Cal, and these two men had saved his life in the heat of the battle to reclaim Otherworld from Moncoya's bloodthirsty ambitions. Some things went even deeper than friendship.

"Only once. He is stronger than I. After the first time, he resisted and used his powers against the vampires. They chained him and brought their human servants to beat him each night. They promised me I would watch him die tonight."

"I don't understand. A mortal has to willingly invite the vampire's first bite."

"There was a woman…" Dimitar cast a sorrowful glance in Jethro's direction.

Lorcan laughed. "Say no more. Where Jethro is concerned, there is always a woman. Ali, can we get these manacles open?"

"Yes. That is what we have been waiting for these past two days. One of our fighters stole the keys and made a copy." He produced the keys from the pocket of his robes and handed them to Lorcan.

"No." Dimitar shook his head as Lorcan reached up to place the key in the lock at his wrist. "I told you it is already too late for me." As he spoke, Lorcan could see his canine teeth lengthening. Darkness must be falling already outside. "Save my master."

Lorcan didn't hesitate. There was no room for sentiment in a situation like this. Leaving Dimitar in his restraints, he turned to Jethro. "Unlock the manacles while I hold him." He spoke over his shoulder and Ali hurried to do his bidding. Once free, Jethro slumped into Lorcan's arms with a groan that indicated he was coming round.

"That's a relief. I didn't fancy carrying you out of here, my large friend." Lorcan eased Jethro's long body down so that he was resting in a near-sitting position against the wall.

"Lorcan? What the...?" Jethro sat up straighter, his half-closed eyes widening as they took in something behind Lorcan's shoulder. "Watch out, she's the one who got to me."

Lorcan rose to his feet as a stunningly beautiful, voluptuous woman entered the dungeon. She wore the traditional garments of a belly dancer, and her honeyed skin had a sheen that cried out to be touched. Thick ebony hair hung to her waist, and above the half veil that covered the lower part of her face, her huge almond-shaped eyes were enough to melt any man's heart. It might almost be worth eternity as a vampire just for a bite from her. Lorcan shook the temptation away quickly, aware that she was already getting inside his head.

"You are new." She had shimmied across to him be-

fore he even noticed the movement. "And so very pretty."
Her grasping little hands reached for him.

"Sorry. I prefer blondes." No sooner had he spoken the
words than his wayward mind decided to dwell on the
one blonde he knew for sure he could never have. It was
amazing how often it managed to do that. Resolutely, he
turned his thoughts away from Princess Tanzi and back
to the matter before him.

"Oflinnan." Lorcan issued the halt command and the
vampire's eyes flickered briefly with surprise before she
froze, becoming a statue of loveliness.

"She has some nasty friends." Jethro was struggling to
his feet. "And they won't be far behind. Let's free Dimitar and get out of here."

He turned to where Dimitar hung in his manacles.
The halt command had worked on him as well and he
was frozen in position, his mouth open, revealing new,
fully formed fangs. Even behind the mask of blood that
covered Jethro's swollen features, Lorcan could see the
pain on his face.

"They did this to him because of me. He lost his immunity when he switched allegiance. I won't leave him
here for them." The words were wrenched from Jethro.

"We can't risk taking a vampire with us. He will want
to feed." Ali's voice echoed high and panicky around
the dungeon.

"I want to get him out of here so I can stake and de-
capitate him. That way he can rest in peace instead of
being in torment for all eternity." Jethro's response was
hard, flat and—some might have said—uncaring.

Lorcan gestured to Ali for the keys and, once the manacles were opened, Jethro hoisted Dimitar's stiffened
frame onto his shoulder.

"These tunnels will take us beneath the city and closer

to the coast." With Ali in the lead, they made a silent, cautious trek through the tunnels. Some time later they exited out into the mimosa-scented Moroccan night.

"There is a fishing boat waiting near the lighthouse. It will take you to Barcelona. Until we meet again, necromancer." Ali clasped Lorcan's hand. The little sidhe gave Jethro, who still carried Dimitar's body, a wide berth. Lorcan began to walk toward the beach. He was halted in his tracks when Ali called out softly. "I almost forgot! You asked us to let you know if anything happened to Princess Tanzi."

"Yes?" Lorcan's heart gave an uncomfortably loud thud. Just when he thought he'd trained it *not* to do that at the mention of her name. "What about her?"

"Word came from Otherworld earlier today. She has disappeared."

Chapter 2

Running away from home. Surely more the action of an angst-riddled teen than a mature adult? And certainly not one upon whom the political future of her dynasty depended. But Tanzi had agonized over her options before making this decision. There was no one in whom she could confide.

Vashti was recovering well from the injuries she had sustained during the battle, but she was still weak. And could her sister be trusted not to share Moncoya's feelings in this matter? Although they were twins, they had never been close. *We are too different. She sees black and white, I see color. We both choose the fast lane, but she focuses on the road ahead, while I enjoy the scenery. Vashti is our father's daughter. I am said to take after the mother we never knew.* No, Tanzi could not share her plight with Vashti.

Her instincts told her she could trust Cal and Stella. Intuition and certainty were two very different things, however. Did she want to give them more proof of her father's depravity, even if it might lead to protection from the marriage he planned for her? The faeries were in turmoil, unsure of their loyalties, their confidence in tatters. Every day further proof of atrocities under Moncoya's leadership emerged, yet he was still revered by his people. Tanzi felt the weight of her responsibility to the faerie dynasty and her sidhe heritage. She could not publicly denounce her father, no matter how villainous his latest scheme might be.

That left her with only one option. If she was to avoid this marriage, she had to get away from Otherworld. She must put her trust in Cal to do the right thing for the faeries in her absence. There was only one person she could turn to. As crazy as it seemed, Tanzi was going to put Lorcan Malone's promise to the test.

The decision to seek refuge with him, once made, brought her a whole new set of problems. How would she find him? He had told her he would know if she needed him. But that must have been bravado. Something to impress the girl he had just rescued. Necromancers did not possess psychic powers. No, she would have to go in search of him. It was a daunting prospect. She knew little of the mortal realm. The only times she had interacted with humans in their own world had been when she was sent by her father to attack, assassinate or kidnap them.

There was talk of a place in Barcelona, a resistance safe house. So well guarded it was impossible to gain entrance unless you knew the right people. Cal was known to be a resistance sympathizer, so perhaps his best friend also had links with the freedom fighters. La Casa Oscura, the dark house that led from the mortal realm to her father's Otherworld palace, was also a conduit in the opposite direction. It would take her directly to the mortal city of Barcelona. If she went there and asked for Lorcan, perhaps she could get a message to him. It wasn't much of a plan, but it was all she had.

Moncoya had always forbidden his daughters from using the portal. He had instilled in them a fear of the mortal realm that remained strong in Tanzi, teaching them that the earth-born were the enemy of the fae. Those thoughts persisted as she made her plans to leave. Not that she did much planning. She didn't have time. Moncoya would act swiftly. Tanzi must do the same.

That was how, two days after her meeting with Moncoya, she came to be standing on the Barcelona quayside, surrounded by a growing crowd of interested sailors, dock workers and one or two tourists. Patiently, Tanzi repeated the message she had rehearsed.

"I need Lorcan Malone."

"Is it a publicity stunt? A trailer for a new film, maybe?" a passing tourist asked her husband. "I'm sure I know her face. Isn't she that American actress, the one who won all those awards recently? She's just as stunning in real life, and that outfit she has on must be worth a fortune."

Damn. She hadn't thought the wardrobe aspect through. Hadn't thought anything much through. Once she had decided to go she had done just that and gone, pausing only to stuff a few items of clothing into an overnight bag. Until now, she hadn't given what she was wearing a second thought. The delicate lemon lace dress with its full, knee-length skirt and layers of petticoats was perfect for the dinner she had been about to attend with Cal, Stella and a number of Otherworld dignitaries. Her nude heels, piled-up hair, and understated makeup and jewelry were all precisely matched to the dress. It was what people expected of Princess Tanzi, Otherworld fashion icon. Instead of going to the dinner, she had thrown a soft, calf-skin jacket over the dress and marched out of her old life forever. With hindsight she should have taken the time to match her outfit to the new location.

"*Necesito* Lorcan Malone." Was she pronouncing his name wrong in their language? Did he use an alias when he was here? The faces of those around her remained blank.

A sailor staggered close. "You can call me Lorcan Malone, *querida*. Before, during and after." The eye-watering alcohol fumes on his breath caused Tanzi to take a step back. He followed, reaching out a hand to grip her arm. When she shrugged him off, he lost his balance and staggered, cursing. Tanzi didn't dare hit him. One blow and she'd break his neck. She couldn't risk drawing that sort of attention to herself. Unfortunately.

There were too many people around her, and anywhere in this city was too close to La Casa Oscura. Her father's spies were everywhere. *Walk away, head down. Find somewhere quiet to come up with a better plan. Whatever you do, don't draw any more attention to yourself.* All good advice. Putting it into practice wasn't going to be easy. The heels were not designed for a swift getaway. *Note to self...if you find yourself in this situation again, raid Vashti's street-inspired wardrobe before leaving.*

As Tanzi left the quayside—acutely aware of the small group of men following in her wake—the sheer magnitude of her error became instantly apparent. Barcelona wasn't just a big city. It was enormous. Crowds thronged the pavement and traffic was bumper to bumper in the street. Noise, life, color and smell all assailed her senses at once, stunning her into immobility. Buildings spread out around her, stretching high onto the hillsides as far as the eye could see. A laugh rose in her throat and met a gurgle of panic coming the other way. Her sheltered lifestyle hadn't prepared her for this. In the past, each time she left her father's palace, she had been surrounded by sidhe bodyguards. They had shielded her from harm and, she now appreciated, had hidden reality from her view, while she completed her assignments. Then they had escorted her back to safety. The substance of life in the mortal realm had never once been allowed to intrude into her carefully ordered existence. But had she really been naive enough to believe that she could step out of La Casa Oscura, simply speak Lorcan's name and that the first person she came across would know whom she meant?

"I truly did," she murmured to herself, using the sound of her own voice to calm her nerves.

The crowds flowed around her, but most seemed to be heading toward a wide, tree-lined street. She allowed herself to be drawn along with them. When she reached the mosaic-tiled thoroughfare, she paused. Leaning against a low wall, she gave herself a few minutes to assimilate her surroundings. Thankfully, there was no sign of her pursuers. Nearby, a youth was propelling himself across the street on a board on wheels. When he noticed Tanzi watching him, he performed a series of tricks for her benefit, finishing by flipping the board up into his hand, catching it and coming to join her. His smile was infectious and, in spite of her plight, she returned it.

He held the board out to her in invitation. Tanzi indicated her clothing and he laughed. "Yeah, right. Not really dressed for skateboarding."

"How many people live here?"

Her abrupt question made him blink and he shrugged. "In Barcelona? One and a half million, maybe? Probably more."

And she was looking for one man. The sad truth was that she had no idea if Lorcan was in this city at all. Even if he was in the country. Or this world. He had told her he was a wanderer. That meant he could be anywhere and that he was constantly on the move.

Her attention was drawn back to her companion. He was regarding her with undisguised admiration. "You have the most amazing eyes I've ever seen. I don't suppose you're looking for someone to show you around?"

She shook her head, softening the gesture with another smile. "Do you know Lorcan Malone?"

"No. Is he your boyfriend?"

"I need him." Tanzi looked along the bustling boulevard. Darkness was falling now and lights from the bars and coffee shops spilled out onto the mosaic tiles. Street artists played several competing musical styles and a flamenco troupe nearby danced an intricate routine. Mortals. They were a mysterious lot.

The youth picked up his skateboard. "Then he's a lucky guy. Be careful, senorita. Stay on the Ramblas, some of the side streets can be dangerous at night." He waved a hand before speeding off into the crowds.

Dangerous? In Tanzi's experience, limited though it was, mortals were troublesome rather than hazardous. There were certainly a lot of them crowded onto this one street, but that didn't make them a threat. Sighing, she picked up her bag. The heels were definitely her biggest mistake. She would ditch the shoes, find Lorcan… Tanzi halted her stride abruptly, much to the vocal annoyance of a girl on a bike just behind her. A frown furrowed Tanzi's brow. What then? After she found Lorcan, what would happen next? It didn't matter. Nothing mattered other than the fact that she was free. Even if she didn't find the necromancer tonight, there was no way she was going back to Otherworld to face the fate her father had in store for her.

"Lost, *querida*?" One of the street entertainers called across to her. His blue-black hair was spiked so high that he resembled a cockatoo and he was dressed as a toreador. His partner was a bull.

"I need Lorcan Malone."

"Lorcan?" The toreador abandoned his bullfighting routine and came over to her. She didn't like the way his narrowed eyes wandered over her body as though he was assessing her, but she did like his next words. "I know him."

Relief flooded through Tanzi's veins. "Can you take me to him?"

"Cierto!" Although his Spanish was heavily accented, Tanzi thought she recognized the same Irish intonation that lilted through Lorcan's voice. It reassured her. "You're in luck. Follow me."

He walked quickly, dodging in and out of the crowds, and it was a struggle to keep pace with him in heels and on the uneven surface of the tiles. Tanzi was so comforted at the thought that he was taking her to Lorcan that she'd have walked across hot coals. With only the occasional glance over his shoulder to check that she was following, the man led her into a side street and then down a narrow alley. There were no lights here and the walls rose uncomfortably high on each side, closing in on her.

"Are you taking me to the safe house?" Tanzi called out, but the man ahead of her didn't answer. The skateboarder's warning came back to her and she glanced over her shoulder just in time to see a flash of movement. Something struck the side of her head. She felt a crushing pain and the slippery cobbles came up to meet her as she fell to her knees. Greedy hands grabbed at her bag.

Tanzi tried to fight back. To her horror, there was no strength in her limbs and her head swam alarmingly. The bag was wrenched from her grasp. She managed to get into a sitting position with her back against the wall and was able to kick out at her assailant's groin. A grunt of pain greeted this action. She knew a moment's satisfaction before a fist connected with her face. Seconds later a heavy boot thudded into her ribs.

"Stop wasting time." Through the haze of pain, she recognized the toreador's voice.

"The bitch kicked me in the balls. She'll pay for that."

"The clothes are expensive. Get them and the shoes and get out of here. She knows Lorcan Malone. That renegade bastard will take no prisoners if he hears about this."

The resistance sidhes hauled the fishing boat ashore onto the beach. Dawn was stirring the Catalan skies above Barcelona, and Lorcan heaved a sigh of relief. He didn't have a home, but this city was as close as it got. After more than thirty hours of being thrown about in a tiny boat on the open sea, he was looking forward to some sleep. Jethro stepped ashore beside him, yawning and stretching.

"Will you come and stay a while at the safe house?"

Jethro shook his head. "Places to go, people to see." It was his standard response. It meant he had some risky dealings lined up that he was not prepared to discuss with anyone. Not even Lorcan.

"Take care, my friend. Lie low for a while. Vampires are not to be messed with." Lorcan waved a farewell to the fishermen as they set off again.

Jethro's hand strayed to his bruised cheekbone. "Tell me about it. But I owe Prince Tibor." His expression hardened and Lorcan recalled the look of anguish in Jethro's eyes as he drove the stake into Dimitar's heart. The two men had buried their friend's body in a shady spot on the Tangier cliff top before setting off on their journey across the Mediterranean.

"Why did Dimitar switch his allegiance from Prince Tibor to you? He was the prince's human slave. You're not a vampire. You can't command the same sort of devotion."

"I don't understand it any more than you do. As soon as Dimitar set eyes on me he was adamant about it. The gist of what he said seemed to be that I was more deserving of his servitude than Prince Tibor." Jethro scanned the expanse of blue sea. "What was the Romanian word he used to describe me? *Maiestuos.* I asked him what it meant and he said the closest translation was 'imposing' or 'stately.'"

"And yet he'd met you?" Lorcan raised an incredulous eyebrow.

Jethro grinned. "Fuck off, Irishman."

"Gladly." He held out a hand and Jethro clasped it. "You know where to find me."

"Likewise. And thanks. For clothing me as well as saving my life." Jethro plucked at the T-shirt that strained across his muscular chest.

Lorcan watched him walk away before hauling his backpack onto his shoulder and making his way up the beach toward the port. The resistance safe house was within walking distance, and he drank in the early morning sights and sounds of the city as he made plans. Shower and sleep were fairly high on his list of priorities. Then he had to get to Otherworld and find out what had happened to Tanzi. If anyone could tell him what was going on within the dysfunctional sidhe royal family, it would be Cal.

The safe house was in a decidedly seedy area close to the famous promenade known as the Ramblas. Lorcan followed a series of narrow lanes that led him behind a fish market, dodging prostitutes, drunks and rough sleepers as he went. The location of the safe house was a closely guarded secret and Cal himself had overseen the web of detailed spells that had been woven around it to ward off intruders. Lorcan was one of the few people who could walk up the steep steps and knock on the scarred panels of the door without hindrance. He was conscious of hidden eyes observing him for several minutes before the door creaked open just wide enough to allow him to slip inside.

"Hola, Pedro." The sidhe caretaker spoke very little and, when he did, only in Spanish. Fortunately, Lorcan had become fluent in that language over the years. Pedro had a reputation for never sleeping. During all the years he had been coming here, Lorcan had certainly never known a time, day or night, when the door was opened by anyone else. "How goes it?"

Pedro shrugged, closing the door behind him. From the expression on his face it might reasonably be construed that the world was about to come to an end.

"I'm going straight to my room." Lorcan placed his foot on the first stair. Pedro and his wife, Maria, tried to keep one of the tiny attic bedrooms free for him. At times like this he was eternally grateful for their consideration.

"No, Senor Lorcan. *No es posible.*" Pedro's voice halted him before he could advance any farther.

"Why isn't it possible?"

"The house is full. We gave your room to the girl."

"What girl might this be?"

"The one they found beaten and half-naked in an alley behind the Ramblas." Conversing with Pedro was like wading through treacle at the best of times. Now, when he was bone tired, dirty and hungry, it was like having to wade there and back again.

"Pedro, try to remember I haven't been here for weeks. I know nothing about any girl."

Pedro's smile was mildly triumphant. "No one does. She won't speak. All she will say is your name."

"*My* name?"

"*Sí.* 'I need Lorcan Malone.' Two days and this is all she will say."

Two days. He had left for Tangier five days ago. "I will go up and see this girl for myself."

Pedro returned no reply and Lorcan made his way up the familiar staircase with its worn carpet and peeling paintwork. Money was always tight and renovations were a luxury of which the resistance could only dream. *How the hell did I end up in charge here?* No one else wanted the job. That was the obvious answer. Being bloody good at what he did was the other. Hating Moncoya enough to want to bring down his network of evil was probably closest to the truth.

Moncoya represented the Celtic sidhes. The opposing Iberian sidhes formed the main backbone of the resistance. Ancient animosities still burned deep. Even with Moncoya in hiding, his network of evil remained in place. The work of the resistance was more important than ever now that Moncoya's allies had been driven underground. Every penny was needed for the fight.

Lorcan paused with his hand on the attic room's door-knob. He had no wish to startle this girl, whoever she might be. Most of the people who sought refuge in the safe house had traumatic stories to tell. Moncoya's mortal residence, La Casa Oscura, was the most well-known of the dark houses. It was a portal to Otherworld, leading to the sleaziest side of the beautiful kingdom. Trafficking of substances and beings was rife, and La Casa Oscura was the conduit for much of this illegal trade. If this girl had been trafficked and used in ways Lorcan did not care to dwell upon, she would be disturbed. And rightly so.

A man bursting into her room in the early hours was not going to help her recovery.

Yet this girl was asking for him by name, and he had no idea why. He needed to discover who she was in order to solve that riddle. Perhaps he could enter the room and get a glimpse of her without waking her? Gingerly, he turned the doorknob. It was locked. He felt a proprietorial sense of pride toward the unnamed girl who had the sense to protect herself against intruders. Feeling slightly furtive, Lorcan fished his own key out of his pocket. As the unofficial leader of the resistance, he was the only person with his own room, and his own key. After a moment's hesitation, he unlocked the door.

There was enough early-morning light sneaking through the thin curtains to allow him to assess the scene. The girl was lying on her side, facing away from the door. She appeared to be sleeping peacefully. Frowning, he entered the room and closed the door behind him, leaning his shoulders against its battered panels as he gazed down at her. Two things alerted him immediately to her identity.

It was the bright mass of wavy blond locks spilling over the pillow almost to the floor together with her unmistakable scent—a subtle floral mix of violets, lily of the valley and jasmine that smelled natural and was probably wildly expensive—that told him who she was.

Why would the Crown Princess Tanzi—spoiled brat sidhe royal, Moncoya's darling daughter, Valkyrie-trained warrior, Otherworld fashion icon—have turned up at this run-down resistance safe house? And why would she be asking for Lorcan when at their last encounter she had spent all her time looking down her dainty, aristocratic nose at him?

Chapter 3

Tanzi came awake slowly, blinking as she took in the shabby, vaguely familiar surroundings. Consciousness wrapped itself around her like a warm blanket. She was in the safe house. *Safe.* That was the essential word. Her head still ached. Her knees, face and ribs were a rainbow of bruises, but at least Moncoya couldn't get to her here.

It must have been very early because the room was semidark and there were no noises, voices or footsteps echoing around the rambling house. She yawned, turned and stifled the startled cry that rose to her lips as her gaze took in a pair of long, denim-clad legs stretched out in the chair near the window. The lower body was all she could see. Whoever it was had fallen asleep with his upper half in shadow. It was definitely a he. She did a double check, and the larger-than-average bulge in the crotch of his jeans confirmed it. A blush burned her cheeks. *When there is an unknown man in your room, does size matter?*

But I locked that door. I know I did! Carefully, she felt under the pillow for confirmation. There was the key. Next to it was the carving knife she had stolen from Maria's kitchen drawer on her first night in the safe house. Her hand closed gratefully around the handle. Wincing as the movement triggered a sharp pain in her injured side, she slid stealthily from the bed with the knife extended in front of her. The only time in her life Tanzi had been caught unawares was in that alley two days ago. It would never happen again. This intruder was going to wish he had finished the job when he first broke in instead of taking time out for a nap. The thought jolted her. If he intended to harm her, why *had* he fallen asleep?

She paused, inches from him, trying to get a look at his face. *Hesitation. Bad mistake, Tanzi.* She could hear the words spoken in the voice of the Valkyrie mentor her father had employed to train his daughters. The intruder's hand snaked out and caught Tanzi by the wrist. There was a blur of movement and he was on his feet, his body colliding hard with hers. The knife went spinning across the room. With her weapon gone and her opponent so much taller than her, Tanzi resorted to street-fighting tactics. Keeping her head low, she aimed for his eyes with her nails, missed and pulled out a chunk of his hair instead. When he grunted in pain and responded by pinning her arms at her sides, she attempted to knee him in the groin.

Within seconds, it was all over. With no very clear idea of what had happened, Tanzi was sprawled on her back on the bed with her opponent straddling her and pinning her hands above her head.

"Considering you've been going around telling everyone how much you need me, this is not quite the welcome I was expecting."

The words, and the Irish accent, acted like a spell on

Tanzi and she stopped struggling. Following his naked, muscular torso upward, her gaze encountered the very pair of smiling blue eyes she had been seeking. Lorcan studied her face, his head on one side. There was a flash of something in his eyes that she had never seen before. It drove the laughter away, replacing it with a cold, hard fury that made her shiver.

"Christ, Tanzi, you look like shit."

"So do you."

It was true. His good looks always had a dangerous edge to them, as if he should be a bad-boy rock star or a Byronic hell-raiser. Today he was taking the cynical, world-weary look to extremes. His eyes were bloodshot, his chiseled jawline darkened with stubble. He didn't even bother to brush away the characteristic flop of dark blond hair from his brow. Clearly deciding she was no longer a danger to him, Lorcan risked letting her go and moved to sit on the side of the bed.

"I haven't slept in—" he paused and clearly had to think about it "—two nights."

"So why did you break in here and sleep in the chair?"

A corner of his mouth lifted into a smile. "You were in my bed."

"Oh." She bit her lip. "I'm sorry."

"Don't be. Your need was greater than mine."

Tanzi felt at a disadvantage lying down. She was also conscious that she was wearing nothing but her underwear and a very old, faded T-shirt that Maria had unearthed for her. She shuffled into a sitting position, wincing as the movement caused more pain in her ribs.

"Did I hurt you?" Lorcan's tone was apologetic.

"Yes. But I was going to kill you so I suppose it can be forgiven."

He started to laugh. "Always so literal. Why are you here, Tanzi?"

"Pedro and Maria gave me this room."

"You know that's not what I meant. Tell me why I shouldn't immediately suspect this is one of your father's tricks to infiltrate the resistance."

She fiddled with a loose thread on the bottom of the T-shirt. It meant she could keep her head down and avoid looking at him. "On the battlefield that day, when you rescued me, you made me a promise. That you would be there for me if I needed you." Suddenly the words were hard to say. Why hadn't she anticipated this? She took a deep breath and looked up. Lorcan's steady blue eyes gave her the confidence she sought. "I need you now."

He didn't hesitate. "Then you have me. I'm all yours."

An emotion she had never felt before tugged hard at Tanzi's chest. Was it gratitude? Tenderness? Empathy? They were all new to her. Moncoya discouraged mortal emotion, particularly where his daughters were concerned. Tanzi and Vashti were his finely tuned weapons. Their hearts should be encased in steel. It was an odd sensation to discover that her own steel casing might have a flaw. Tanzi's voice was husky when she spoke again. "Aren't you going to ask me why?"

"If you want me to know, I expect you'll tell me in your own time." Lorcan stretched his arms above his head. "Right now, if I don't shower and then get some breakfast, I'll be no use to you or anyone."

The square was crowded with students. Competing music blared from open dormitory windows and from the bars around the outer edge. Lorcan skirted around skateboarders, impromptu dancers and chattering groups, carrying beer and pizza to where Tanzi was sitting on the steps of the university building waiting for him. She wore leggings and a sweatshirt that was at least three sizes too big. Her hair was tied back and hidden under a black baseball cap, and her face was still swollen and bruised. Even so, when she looked up with a smile as he approached, he felt the full impact of the effect she had on him. It hit him somewhere just south of his abdomen. Whom was he kidding? The feeling began well south of his abdomen. He told himself it was what faeries did best. Their ability to enchant was legendary. Faerie glamor, his mother would have called it. The old-fashioned term and the memory of his mother made him smile. Moncoya's dislike of the phrase was well-known. The faerie king preferred to believe it was his personal charm that drew others to him. Dismissing the unwelcome intrusion of Moncoya into his thoughts, Lorcan joined Tanzi on the step.

"I thought you wanted to talk to me in private?" Tanzi leaned in close so that he could hear her above the noise. Her breath brushed tantalizingly close to his ear.

"I do." He pointed with his beer bottle at the teeming square. "No one here is remotely interested in us or anything we have to say. They are all too busy having their own good time."

She laughed, taking a slice of pizza from the box on his knee and biting into it with very white, very even teeth. He remembered another thing his mother used to say. "Are you claiming me for your own?" He nodded at the pizza. "Sharing food with me? In faerie terms, doesn't this mean I belong to you now?"

Tanzi blushed and glanced down at the slice of pizza in her hand. "I didn't think. I never meant…"

"I'm teasing you. In a way, I'm already yours to command. I told you that three months ago, on the day of the battle for control of Otherworld."

She drew in a deep breath and, for a moment, he thought she was about to say something more. Instead, she nodded at the crowded square. "Is this what you mortals do?"

So she bought in to the pretense that he was mortal. Most people did. He was good at it and it was half-true, anyway. He didn't contradict her. "Have fun? Yeah, we try. Sometimes we even succeed."

They ate and drank in companionable silence.

"What did you wish to say to me?" Tanzi turned to face him and Lorcan thought again how amazing her eyes were. The bright blaze of sidhe fire around her irises made the blue of her pupils appear darker. There was something slightly feline in the slant of her eyes and the finely arched brows above them. A man could drown in those eyes. Unless he was very careful.

"If you are to remain in the safe house, we must take great care not to let anyone know who you are." The long lashes swept down, shadowing her cheeks, but not before he caught a glimpse of the pain his words had caused her.

"Because of my father."

"Yes." What else could he say? There was no way to soften the blow. She was Moncoya's daughter. If she was recognized, she'd be lucky to get out of the safe house in one piece. Moncoya had wrecked too many lives for anyone to forgive and forget. And Tanzi was no innocent. She had played a willing part in her father's villainy.

"Was I wrong to come here?"

"No. You were right to come to me. I will keep my promise and take care of you, but you need to face facts. Your name isn't going to win you any popularity contests among the Iberian sidhes."

"So what story shall I tell? What must my name be?"

Lorcan frowned. He hadn't thought of her name. But there was only one Tanzi. She was as well-known as her father. The name had to go. "Keep it simple. You have no story because you have no memory. You don't even remember your own name."

"I can't be nameless. You will have to call me something."

He stared into those endless eyes. "I will call you *Searc*."

Tanzi wrinkled her nose. "I'm not sure I like that. What does it mean?"

"Ah, some old Irish words have lost their meaning in the mists of time," he lied. "Now, if you are to stay at the safe house, you must earn your keep."

Tanzi started to laugh, the action bringing her shoulder into contact with Lorcan's arm. A warm feeling spread from his chest to his stomach. She was addictive. Perhaps he should allow himself these small doses of her touch now and then. Just to develop immunity and test his own strength. "I have not been trained to cook or wash dishes."

"You should offer to help Maria with both. She'll refuse, but it will endear you to her. No, I think your fighting skills will prove more useful than your domestic talents." How would she respond? He was asking her to take up arms against her father. It was the ultimate test of how serious she was.

Tanzi's face told him she understood. For a moment her expression was open to him and the anguish he read in her eyes shocked him. What had Moncoya done to her?

"Agreed."

That single word said it all. Whatever had caused her to run to him, it was so bad she was prepared to change

sides. Lorcan knew how that felt. It was the hardest decision in the world. Without thinking, he took her hand
in his. Tanzi looked down in surprise. Briefly, she let her
hand rest passively in Lorcan's palm. Then she turned it
and twined her fingers between his. It was a touching,
trusting gesture. They sat together for a long time, hand
in hand, watching the lively display of life unfolding in
the square in front of them.

"Tell me about the men who hurt you." Lorcan broke
the silence at last.

She let go of his hand, and it felt as if a spell had been
broken. Perhaps it had. "I was foolish."

"You trusted me enough to come looking for me. You
can tell me about this." Pedro said they had found her
half-naked and beaten. That was bad enough. Was it even
worse? His mind made a connection he didn't want. "Tell
me they didn't—?"

"No." She interrupted quickly. Her cheeks flamed.
"They didn't rape me. Is that what you meant?" He nodded. "They were street performers. Dressed as a bull-
fighter and a bull. I suppose they thought I was just a
naive tourist flaunting my expensive clothes. I think it
could have been much worse, but I'd told them I was
looking for you. They knew your name. They seemed
to be afraid of you."

"So they bloody should be." His jaw muscles tightened.

"They called you a renegade. What did they mean
by that?"

Lorcan didn't answer at first. *Renegade*. It was a word
he hadn't heard in a long time. A word he had hoped
never to hear again. When he did speak, it wasn't in answer to Tanzi's question.

"I know who they are."

* * *

Tanzi regarded Lorcan thoughtfully. "You take your old room, I can sleep in here."

She indicated the cramped space in which they were standing. It was the only other room on the top floor of the house and, until an hour ago, it had been used by Maria as a linen closet. After returning from the square, Lorcan and Tanzi had cleared it of its contents and carried a foldaway bed up the winding stairs all the way from the cellar. It just fitted into the cramped space. Maria, after eying the arrangement in disgust, was making her way—with much huffing and complaining—down the stairs with laden armfuls of bedding.

"Sure, isn't this the height of luxury after some of the places I've been forced to get my head down in my time?" He grinned and Tanzi's stomach responded by doing a strange little flip-flop movement. She wondered briefly if it might be some sort of necromancer spell. If it was, its purpose eluded her. "Go to bed, *Searc*."

It must be a spell, she decided later. Why else would she be drifting aimlessly around her room in a giddy trance, listening to the sounds of Lorcan getting into bed in the room next door? Smiling to herself as she heard him bump his head on the low ceiling and curse? Picturing the tanned torso she had seen that morning and imagining running her fingers lightly over those interesting ridges of muscle? Discovering that she was not, as she had always believed, immune to the pull of sexual attraction that others found so enticing?

Flopping down onto her own bed, Tanzi thought about what Lorcan had said. If she stayed here, she was changing sides. She would join the fight against her father. To even contemplate such an action should make her weighed down by her own duplicity. So why did she feel—her mind searched for the right word—*liberated*? It was as though her subconscious had been seeking this decision all along and, now it was made, every part of her felt lighter and freer.

This all-enveloping sense of relief was not just a result of Moncoya's behavior toward Tanzi herself. The preceding three months had provided her with more than enough proof of his corruption and viciousness. Even though she was his daughter, the faeries had started to come to Tanzi with their stories. She was gaining a reputation for fairness and action. They were beginning to trust her. Tanzi herself no longer had any faith in Moncoya. Finally, she could accept that she had never loved him. Her life had been ruled by her fear of him.

So I will proudly turn my coat. I will become a renegade like you, Lorcan Malone. Tanzi had seen the wretchedness in his eyes when she said the word, and her curiosity had spiked in response. *I know why I am crossing the line, and I will do so with my head held high. What was your reason, necromancer?*

The third stair from the top had a creak that sounded like a strangled cat. When it came, it was the signal Tanzi had been waiting for. The noise had either been caused by someone coming up the stairs, or, as she suspected, by Lorcan sneaking down.

Slipping fully dressed from her bed, Tanzi pulled the hood of her dark sweatshirt up so that it hid her hair. Leaving her room, she closed the door carefully behind her and leaned over the banister. She could see Lorcan on the flight of stairs below her. He was carrying his shoes. Avoiding that telltale third step, Tanzi made her way down, hiding in the shadows of the landing as Lorcan paused to pull on his boots.

The night air was crisp as she followed him outside.

Lorcan's long stride made him hard to keep up with, but the streets were thankfully quiet. Tanzi found herself running from one corner to the next, peeking around buildings before tiptoeing on. *Like a cartoon caricature of a sleuth,* she thought in annoyance. *Are all men this obstinate? Why couldn't he have just offered to take me with him?*

Lorcan made his way out of the winding lanes around the safe house and into a wider promenade near the Ramblas. There were more signs of life here. Neon lights cut through the darkness and a few revelers were trying to maintain the daytime carnival atmosphere. The smell of beer and fried onions hung heavy in the air. Tanzi kept her hands in her pockets and her head down, glancing up only now and then to check that Lorcan was still in her sights. That was how she almost missed it when he ducked into a narrow alley between a bar and a strip club. Doubt assailed her. Maybe she had this all wrong. Was he actually planning a nocturnal visit to seek comfort in one of the district's seedier establishments? These advertised their services with red lights hung over their doors. Although the prostitutes loitering on the doorsteps might also have been a clue.

Tanzi hung back, watching by the light of a single streetlamp as Lorcan followed a short cobbled passage, then turned left. When she sprinted after him, she found herself in a walled courtyard, with a church at one end. The building was abandoned. Even in the darkness it was clear that half the roof had fallen in and there was no glass in the windows. There was no sign of Lorcan. Tanzi spun round. There hadn't been time for him to scale one of the ten-foot-high walls that enclosed the square yard and, while she knew that his friend Cal had the power to make himself invisible, it was not a common trait among necromancers.

A shout of laughter from inside the church drew Tanzi's attention and, clinging to the shadows, she made her way in that direction. As she approached, she noticed Lorcan's tall figure to one side of the door. He was hanging back, observing what was taking place inside. Presented with a dilemma, Tanzi considered her options. If she went any closer, Lorcan would notice her. If she remained where she was, she would be unable to see what was going on. Curiosity won, which was probably what prompted her next action.

When Tanzi was a child, she and Vashti used to sit spellbound while their old nurse, Rina, told tales of faerie folklore. Of a time when mortals understood that the wee, fae folk were part of their heritage, accepting the decisions of the Seelie and Unseelie Courts, even referring to Otherworld as "Faeryland." There were no divisions then between the faerie factions. No separation between faerie and sidhe, no fighting for prominence between Iberia and Celt for who would rule the faerie dynasty. Now, of course, Tanzi understood Rina's hidden message. She spoke of a time when there was no Moncoya. Rina would tell them of the powers of the ancient faeries. Faeries of the Seelie Court could bestow good fortune upon mortals, change the landscape, control the weather and the crops, levitate or fly and shape-shift. These powers were frowned upon by Moncoya because, in him and other descendants of the Unseelie Court, they were weak or nonexistent. Gradually, over the centuries of sidhe rule and as the distance between Otherworld and the mortal realm grew wider, the faeries had become a fighting race and their benign powers faded.

Nevertheless, Tanzi and Vashti had been determined

to put their own skills to the test. Tanzi had never mastered levitation, although, after much practice, Vashti had been able to hover a few feet above her bed. Beyond all others, the one faerie power that had fascinated them throughout their childhood had been shape-shifting.

"I will be a cat," Tanzi had declared.

"Panther." Trust Vashti to go bigger, bolder, meaner and keener.

With no clear idea of how to go about the necessary transformation, they had spent hours concentrating on the feline forms into which they wished to change. Tanzi recalled a whole day during which she had followed the kitchen cat around the palace grounds, emulating its movements and imagining herself inside its skin. No matter what they did, neither twin sprouted so much as a whisker. Dispirited, they had questioned Rina about the problem.

"Your father would not like it if he knew I talked to you of the old ways." Their nurse had cast a nervous look over her shoulder as though expecting Moncoya to emerge from the very walls. "It would be worse if he thought I was encouraging you to try them."

"We won't tell if you don't," Tanzi had assured her. "But we want to know *how* to shift."

"I don't understand how it works," Vashti, a stickler for detail, had grumbled. "Even if we could work out what to do, what happens to our clothes when we shift? And how do we come back into our own form again?"

Rina had shaken her head, clicking her tongue indulgently. "Ah, my princesses, you are thinking about this in the wrong way. This is what happens when the old traditions are allowed to die. You are faeries, not were-creatures. Your bodies do not change in the way theirs do."

Spellbound, Tanzi and Vashti had gazed at her. "Go on."

"The faerie skill lies in the ability to weave an illusion. We are creatures of magic. Changing shape is part of our glamor. All you have ever needed is the desire to create your disguise. If you believe, you will make others believe with you."

Round-eyed, the twins had watched each other in delight as they shifted easily into their chosen animal form. From that day on, Tanzi's go-to shift throughout her childhood had been a black cat. Mercurial Vashti chose a different animal each day, depending on her mood. It had remained their secret, one they had never revealed to anyone else. Their father's response to their newfound skill was not one they cared to predict.

It had been a while since she had donned her feline disguise, Tanzi conceded. But, if she wanted to see what was going on over at that church, it was her only option. Her mind was made up when Lorcan moved out of the shadows and pushed open the wooden door. Dropping into a crouch and then onto all fours, Tanzi padded into her cat form. She crossed the square and then sprang lightly onto one of the window ledges so that she could look down through the broken glass and onto the scene below.

Chapter 4

The interior of the ruined church was lit by two branches of flickering candles set on a table near the altar. Upon this were piled numerous items, including bags, wallets, clothing and shoes. From her vantage point looking down on the scene, Tanzi immediately spotted her own belongings. She also knew the toreador from his spiky hair and distinctive street performer's clothing. She didn't recognize his companion, but he wore dark clothing that could easily have been the bull's costume. The discarded bull's head lying on one of the lopsided pews was the final giveaway. Tanzi's injured ribs ached in acknowledgment of the second man's identity.

"Raimo and Ronab." Lorcan strolled into the church, coming up behind them. He lit a path before him in the way that was unique to necromancers. "It's been a while, guys."

They swung around, matching expressions of comical incredulity on their faces. The toreador attempted a sneer. It didn't quite work. "Not long enough."

Even from a distance, Tanzi could hear Lorcan's exaggerated sigh. "Raimo, will you lose the attitude? Is that any way to greet a fellow countryman?"

Lorcan was standing next to them now, and Tanzi noticed that the other two men had a tendency to hunch over with their backs curved forward and their heads hanging almost below their shoulder line. Maybe it was just because Lorcan was so tall and straight in comparison. Perhaps it was even a trick of the shadows or a distortion caused by her viewing angle. It was disconcerting because when she had first arrived the two men had looked completely normal. They had also appeared to be individuals, completely different from each other. Now, only minutes later, when she looked from one to the other and back again, they had become almost identical, like indistinguishable mirror images.

Lorcan ran a casual hand over the hoard on the table. "Busy night?"

"What's it to you, necromancer?" The one who had been dressed as a bull adopted a belligerent tone. It was the same one he had used in that alley when he'd stolen her clothes and kicked her in the ribs. It made Tanzi arch her back and unsheathe her claws.

Lorcan's hand shot out and grabbed him by the front of his shirt. Effortlessly, he lifted the other man off the ground. "A friend of mine was attacked in an alley just off the Ramblas a few nights ago. If I remember rightly, beating up girls is your specialty, Ronab. Would you know anything about this incident, by any chance?"

Before Ronab, who seemed to be struggling for breath, could speak, Raimo moved closer to Lorcan. His gait was odd, almost gamboling, and his arms appeared much longer and thinner than Tanzi remembered. Why had she not remarked upon these very noticeable traits when she first saw him? *I might be naive, but even I would not have will-ingly followed one whose appearance was so clearly odd.*

"You wrong us, Lorcan." The combative note in Rai-mo's voice had been replaced by a high-pitched wheedle. "It would not be the first time."

Lorcan laughed, letting go of Ronab so quickly that the other man stumbled and fell to his knees. "I have never been wrong about you."

Tanzi almost lost her grip on the window ledge as she caught a glimpse of Ronab's face, as he turned fully in her direction for the first time. There was no longer anything left of his human features. It was as if he had donned a mask of polished bone. Roughly triangular, his head narrowed from a wide top to a sharp, pointed chin. Small, downward-curving horns protruded from the upper corners, and bright red slits glowed in place of his eyes. Ronab blinked once and, as Tanzi watched in fascination, his eyelids moved from side to side in-stead of up and down. As far as she could see, he had no nose or mouth.

"We have to earn a living. Ever since we were cast off…"

"Don't give me that old sob story. We all know you were cast off because of your thieving ways."

"To our sorrow. If we could go back, start again, ex-plain what happened." Raimo sighed. "Too late. We miss her."

"You should have thought of that while you still had her protection." Lorcan's voice was colder than the ice on the mountains surrounding Valhalla. "The question is, what shall I do with you now?"

"Speak sternly and make us promise never to do it again?" Ronab got to his feet. With the change in their appearance, the demeanor of the two men had also altered. They had become skittish, almost fawning over Lorcan. They were subservient to him now. Any suggestion of confrontation was gone.

"I could do that," Lorcan agreed. "And five minutes after I left here, you'd be back out on the street doing a number on the next unsuspecting tourist you came across."

"There is one way to ensure our eternal obedience." The creatures that had once been men arranged themselves on each side of Lorcan, gazing up at his face. "Become our master."

Before Lorcan could respond, Ronab turned his head to slowly gaze at all four corners of the church. Despite his lack of nostrils, he appeared to be sniffing the air. "Faerie," he grunted, when he had completed the circle.

Raimo crouched lower in a defensive attitude. "I cannot feel it but you are better at detecting the fae ones than I. Where?"

"Very close."

Was it Tanzi's imagination, or did Lorcan actually look directly at her? She tried to draw back into the shadows, but it was difficult on such a narrow perch. "Can we get back to the matter in hand? You know very well I cannot be your master. Even if I wanted the job, I lack the necessary credentials."

"You changed once, you can go back again. It is what she would want." Raimo, who was clearly the spokesperson, hovered somewhere between pleading and desperation.

"I'm a patient man." Tanzi decided that she loved listening to Lorcan speak. Even now, when there was a slight edge to his tone and danger in the air, those lyrical notes in his voice reassured her that she was safe. "But if you speak of her again, I swear I will raise her from her grave so that she can punish you herself."

"You would not!"

"Try me." Evidently deciding that he meant business, the creatures subsided into an aspect of supplication at his feet. Lorcan turned back to the haul of stolen goods. "Here's the deal. You will take these to the Santa Maria homeless shelter tonight. Then you can take yourselves off home and find a new master."

"If we say no?" Ronab scurried out of reach as he asked the question.

"Then I'll beat you to within an inch of your miserable lives," Lorcan told him cheerfully. "And, when I've done that, I'll take you home myself and hand you over to someone who'll know how to keep your light-fingered tendencies in check."

Needing no further encouragement, the two creatures began to gather up the items from the table. "Not these." Unerringly, Lorcan picked out Tanzi's property. "I'll return them to their owner. Oh, and guys?" They paused, looking at him inquiringly. "You might want to go to the homeless shelter in your mortal guise. No point frightening the volunteers by showing them the real you."

Muttering under their breath, Raimo and Ronab scurried out of the building, loaded down with their haul of goods. After they had gone, Lorcan stood very still in the center of the aisle.

"You can come down now, *Searc.*"

Surprised, Tanzi sprang lightly down from the window ledge, shifting back to her own form as she landed. "How did you know it was me?"

His grin lit up the gloom. "Sure, even the luck of the Irish wouldn't be enough to get me followed by more than one cute faerie."

She came to stand beside him. "What were those beings? I haven't seen their like before."

"You wouldn't. They are imps. Faeries are their worst nightmare. They'd run a mile across hot coals to avoid you."

"They weren't doing much running in that alley." Tanzi ran reminiscent fingertips over the bruises on her cheekbone.

"Imps are generally loyal to their masters. This pair—Raimo and Ronab—are a rarity. They proved to be subversive and disobedient to the point where their master disowned them. When that happened, they were forced to become wild and fend for themselves. They did so by donning a mortal form and taking to that which they do best...robbery and violence. I'd heard what they were up to, but I didn't know they were in Barcelona until you told me what had happened to you. One of their favorite insults for me is 'renegade.' That was how I knew who they were. That and the fact that your experience had all the hallmarks of one of their attacks. In their mortal guise they lose their impish traits. They wouldn't have recognized you as a faerie."

"Who was the master who disowned them?" The imps had spoken of a mysterious "she." Tanzi sensed that, whoever "she" was, it caused Lorcan pain to speak of her.

"My mother." He shook himself slightly as though ridding himself of a memory. "Let's get your stuff and go."

"How did you know which was mine?" Tanzi gathered up her dress, jacket, shoes and bag.

He looked surprised and then shrugged. "They looked like your style. Which means you can't wear them in the safe house. You'll stand out too much."

"Maybe so, but at least I'll have more than one change of underwear."

They walked out into the darkened square. Overhead, the sky was midnight blue sprinkled with silver stardust.

Even though they were in the heart of the city, it was quiet as they strolled back the way they had come.

"So, the cat thing. Do you do that often?"

Tanzi cast a glance up at Lorcan's profile. It was impossible to read his expression. "It comes in handy now and then."

His smile was teasing as he looked down at her. "I imagine it would. Come on, let's get you home. I'll get you a saucer of milk. That'll make you purr."

A tummy rub from you would make me purr more. Tanzi almost tripped over her own feet in surprise. Where did *that* thought come from? Could she say it out loud? Did she dare? She opened her mouth to try but the words wouldn't come. Flirting. It was something she had never considered important until right now. They reached the steps to the safe house and the moment was lost.

Camaraderie. Laughter. Teasing. Fun. Tanzi was developing a new vocabulary. Sitting around the table in the ramshackle kitchen late into the night with Lorcan and his resistance friends had initially been a frightening experience.

"What if they recognize me?"

"Then we're in deep shit."

Lorcan's response had been to pull her into the room with him. Although their entrance halted the noisy conversation that had been taking place, no one had denounced Tanzi. To be fair, no one had taken much notice of her. Apart from one or two curious glances thrown her way, there was no doubt Lorcan was the main attraction. He was hailed with noisy delight by the group of two women and five men. From then on, he was the one they consulted and deferred to. He was in charge, and Tanzi saw a different side of him in this new role. Oh, he was still the blue-eyed charmer. He still had a laugh and a smile for every occasion, but there was something deeper in his expression when the group around the table spoke of their work. She saw the fire and passion of belief in what he was doing and felt a burning sense of shame. These people had been brought together to fight evil. And the evil they fought was her own father.

Most of the time, she let their conversation wash over her. The persona she had donned when they carried her into the safe house, half-conscious, terrified and pleading for them to find Lorcan, stood her in good stead now. No one but Lorcan knew that her voice and her memory were back to full capacity. Tanzi was happy for it to stay that way. She was content to curl up in an ancient armchair near the fire with one of Maria's cats on her lap and to let them ignore her.

"Every time we close one of the brothels down, they open another." The young faerie who spoke was called Aydan. He looked mortal, except for a faint ring of fire around his irises. He hid his eyes behind tinted glasses and wore his hair in long dreadlocks.

"So why do we bother?" A girl called Lisbet spoke up. "It costs us so much each time we challenge them. We are lucky if we come away with every life intact. There are always injuries. If all we do is cause them a minor inconvenience, is there any point?"

"There is always a point," Lorcan stated, and Tanzi noticed the way every head turned his way. He was their undisputed leader, even if he made light of his own skills. "If we save only one person from a life of degradation in one of Moncoya's hells, it is worth the risk."

Tanzi was aware of Aydan looking at her with sympathy, and a blush stained her cheeks. He thought that she had escaped from one of these brothels of which they spoke. She loathed, yet needed, the pretense in which their assumptions cloaked her. Their kindness and compassion was misplaced and she hated herself for accepting it. *What would they do if they knew that in reality I was part of all they work so tirelessly to destroy?* She pressed her cheek against the cat's silken fur, turning her burning face away from gentle Aydan's stare.

"Why are these brothels so much worse than the ones run by mortals?" The man who spoke was a recent recruit called Iago. He was slightly older than the others around the table, and his eyes were an unusual pale green color, made even lighter by their bright ring of fire. He reminded Tanzi of one of the medieval knights in Rina's tales. With his dark beard and courtly manners, she could imagine him slaying dragons or rescuing maidens. "Some of them can get pretty nasty."

"The beings in Moncoya's brothels are slaves, stolen from their homes—sometimes as children—and forced to work there. They have no choice. Often they are beaten, starved or drugged into compliance. The services they offer are not only illegal, they are deadly. These brothels cater for the basest desires, both mortal and nonmortal. Moncoya's henchmen provide a personalized service. They will kidnap a being to order. You've seen a teenage were-cougar you like the look of? Hand over the cash and she's all yours. You have a fantasy about an underage male witch imprisoned in your own torture chamber? As long as the price is right, consider it done." Somehow, Lorcan's lilting accent made the horrors he described sound even worse.

"Is La Casa Oscura one of these brothels?" Iago asked.

Lorcan shook his head. "No. La Casa Oscura is unique. The darkest of the dark houses."

"I don't understand."

"La Casa Oscura was designed to be a well-disguised portal to Otherworld."

"Until Moncoya made it into something more." Aydan's pleasant features hardened.

"Yes." Lorcan continued his explanation. "I'm not going to pretend that before Moncoya there were never those who exploited the border between Otherworld and the mortal realm for nefarious purposes. Of course it happened. But until Moncoya, it was never done on this scale. This is organized crime that would make the gangs of Eastern Europe gnash their teeth with envy. This is people trafficking to an extent that the mortal realm cannot conceive. Yet, because it takes place between worlds, the law enforcement agencies of this world have no idea it even goes on. The Alliance has sworn to stamp it out, but they have enough problems at present bringing the dynasties around the table, and Moncoya is flexing his muscles from his hiding place. In the last few days, there have been faerie terrorist attacks in some of the major Alliance strongholds." This was the first Tanzi had heard of this, and she sat up straighter. Lorcan, noticing her movement, threw her an apologetic glance.

"You said La Casa Oscura is more than just a portal." Iago drew Lorcan's attention away from Tanzi and back into the conversation.

"In addition to the day-to-day portals, there are other ways of gaining entry into Otherworld. These are the dark houses. They are a very specific portal, leading to the darkest reaches of Otherworld. Those who wish to gain entry without attracting attention do so by using a dark house. Smuggling, trafficking, anything illegal is done through the dark houses."

"Were the dark houses created by Moncoya?" someone else asked and Tanzi closed her eyes, leaning back in her chair. Even though, since the battle, she had seen concrete evidence of her father's vile deeds for herself, it still hurt her to hear of more.

"No. They have always existed. For as long as mortals have spoken of heaven and hell or of Otherworld and Underworld. Moncoya was not even the first to exploit their unique properties." Lorcan looked tired. Tanzi wanted to go to him and brush back the errant lock of hair that flopped onto his forehead. When did these odd, protective feelings toward him start developing? And, more important, how was she going to get rid of them? "What Moncoya brought to the equation," Lorcan continued, "was his organizational skills and his manpower. The dark houses are now used systematically and efficiently as a means of transporting—well, anything really—between Otherworld and the mortal realm. La Casa Oscura has been Moncoya's greatest and darkest accomplishment."

"How so?"

"It has served him well in many ways. Firstly, Moncoya is one of the few Otherworld leaders to develop a fully fledged mortal persona. He has been forced to abandon that guise since his defeat, of course, a fact that has led to intense press speculation here in the mortal realm. Just what *has* happened to celebrated electronics billionaire Ezra Moncoya? His disappearance is the news story of the decade. La Casa Oscura was his mortal base. Its next purpose was as a genuine portal to Otherworld. Enter La Casa Oscura and you may also, if you so choose and if you believe it to be true, enter Moncoya's royal Otherworld palace. Finally, it is the ultimate dark house. The treasury of Otherworld's grim secrets." Lorcan's beautiful mouth turned down slightly at the corners.

"Moncoya may not be at home anymore, but his legacy lingers on in the very bricks and mortar."

"So why don't we destroy La Casa Oscura?" Aydan spoke up suddenly, his voice excited and eager. "Just blow the place sky-high?"

Without thinking, Tanzi jumped to her feet. The cat's howl of rage drew everyone's attention in her direction. "No..." She thought of her beautiful childhood home. Of her sister. Of the servants who had served her so loyally and who played no role in Moncoya's dark deeds. Words bubbled up to her lips, but Lorcan was at her side in an instant, sensing her distress and calming her before she could give herself away. His arm around her shoulders steadied her, and she leaned gratefully against his side. Tanzi held out her hand, showing him blood welling in the lacerations where the cat had scratched her when she disturbed its slumber. It was a feeble excuse, but it was for the benefit of the others. She knew Lorcan already understood the real reason for her distress.

"It's okay." How was it, that as soon as he said the words, she was soothed by them? "If that was an option, sure, wouldn't we have done it long ago? For the reasons I've already outlined, it can't be done. La Casa Oscura is the cover for Moncoya's mortal enterprise. Blow it up and we destroy the home of the world's leading electronics firm, we kill Moncoya's mortal employees. We draw the wrong kind of publicity to ourselves. It is also the portal to the royal palace, now the headquarters of the new Otherworld Alliance. Innocent staff work in the palace itself but, most important of all, it is now the meeting place of the peacekeeping council. Are you willing to risk the lives of the dynasty leaders? To risk Cal and Stella on the chance that we might succeed in destroying the dark house?"

Shamefaced, Aydan begged pardon for his foolishness. "But we can close down this latest vile brothel?"

"Of course we can. In fact, I'm surprised you haven't done it before now." Lorcan scanned Tanzi's face as if assuring himself that she was really okay. In response, she nodded slightly. He seemed satisfied at what he saw and released her. She felt oddly bereft as he returned to table. *How foolish! Is it your goal to keep him at your side for all time?*

"We were waiting for you, Lorcan. We need your necromancer prowess."

Lorcan sighed. "Why do all the worst jobs always start off with that sentence?"

Chapter 5

"I don't see why Lorcan has to bring *her* along." Lisbet made no attempt to lower her voice, and Tanzi stiffened slightly as the words reached her through the open kitchen door. "Her only use seems to be decorative."

"Hush." Aydan's quieter tones carried into the hall, where Tanzi was sitting on the bottom stair, waiting for Lorcan to lead them all to the brothel. "She will hear you. We may not know who she is, but we know she has been through a great trauma."

"For that reason alone she shouldn't come. What possible good will she be to us if there is any fighting?"

"We must trust Lorcan. If he wants her with us, then she comes."

There was a definite huffing noise from Lisbet, but no further argument. Pedro was hovering near the front door and, when there was a knock, he hurried to see who it was. Once the sidhe caretaker had satisfied himself that there was no threat, he opened the door and Lorcan strolled in. He was accompanied by Iago.

"Don't we need to wait for dark?" Lisbet asked as the five of them prepared to depart. It was late afternoon.

"The ideal time for a surprise attack is under cover of darkness, when the brothel's activities will be in full swing. That's when we'll take the place. But for now we want to reconnoiter and get an idea of what we're up against. This is the best time to do it. They won't be on their guard and we can get an idea of what sort of security they have in place."

The site of the brothel was in the medieval Gothic quarter of the city in a cloistered *placa*, or square, dating back to the days of the Inquisition. It was like stepping back in time. Once they were within the decorative tiled walls, it had the feel of a country village with geese and ducks wandering freely and vines rambling wild. The vast city might have been a million miles away. Tanzi, still adjusting to the difference between her mystical Otherworld home and the harsh realities of the mortal realm, was thrust slightly off balance by another change of scene. They hung back in a side alley, surveying the *placa*.

"They chose this for the location of such debauchery?" Iago cast a disbelieving glance around at the peaceful setting.

"That building was an Inquisition torture chamber." Lorcan's face was grim as he pointed to a Gothic structure with curved walls and high, arched slits in place of windows. "Many of the original features have been preserved."

Everyone fell silent as they contemplated the building and the implication of Lorcan's words. It was Aydan who broke the silence. "What do we do now? We can't go and knock on the door, can we?"

"There isn't a door," Tanzi pointed out. It was only when they all turned to stare at her that she realized she had spoken aloud.

"Found your voice?" Lisbet's eyes narrowed into suspicious slits.

"Pedro has plans of most of the old areas of the city. There are two underground entrances to this building. One is through another *placa* to the rear of the building. That is the one the sidhes currently use. The other is through an underground crypt in the cloisters over there." Lorcan pointed. "The inquisitors took their victims straight from the altar to the torture chamber."

"It strikes me as odd." Iago viewed the strange structure again. "Surely the point of running a brothel is to make money? Isn't the fact that there is no obvious way of getting into it something of a disadvantage from a business point of view?"

"On the contrary," Lorcan responded. "The exclusivity of this place is its selling point. Passing trade would be a hazard. And let's not forget Moncoya's human guise. He is the mortal realm's electronics virtuoso, internet supremo, master of the dark web. Those mortals who want to know what is offered here—so long as they can pay the going rate, of course—will learn of it. There is no need to tout for trade."

Tanzi shuddered. How little she had known of the man whose genes she shared. And yet she never doubted that Lorcan was speaking the truth about her father. She accepted Moncoya's ability to lead a double life as readily as she accepted his evil tendencies. Perhaps she was more like him than she cared to believe. She was hiding her true personality from these people, after all, and doing it very effectively. *I am not evil. Please let me not have inherited his destructive traits.* She shivered again at the thought.

Lorcan, sensing the movement, glanced down at her. "You okay with this?" His voice was low enough for her ears alone. "You don't have to do it."

"You will never know how much I do."

He studied her face, then nodded decisively. "Very well. Aydan, wait here with Iago and Lisbet. Watch out for any activity. *Searc*, come with me."

They followed the shadowy outer edge of the *placa*, following in the footsteps of ancient cruel inquisitors. When they were at a right angle to the building that housed the brothel, Lorcan paused. "According to the plans Pedro showed me, the entrance to the crypt should be around here."

The marble wall that marked the outer edge of the *placa* was smooth, with decorative arches set at regular intervals along its length. Tanzi pointed to one of these. "There."

Camouflaged within the dappled gray surface of the marble there was a small iron ring, slightly rusted with age. Lorcan lifted it and, with a groan of protest, the marble panel slid inward, revealing gaping darkness beyond. A scurrying sound indicated that they had disturbed the creatures lurking within.

Lorcan raised a hand and the darkness vanished. The light he cast revealed a narrow corridor and the disappearing shapes of several large rats. "The entrance to our crypt, I believe. Can you cope with the rodents?"

"Have you forgotten my preferred choice of shift?" Taking the hand he held out to her, Tanzi followed him into the narrow space.

"Hadn't I just? Don't you be off chasing rats and leaving me to fend for myself, will you now?" Lorcan pulled the marble panel closed behind them.

They were in a narrow corridor just wide enough for Lorcan to walk along and lead Tanzi behind him. It smelled of damp and decay, and thick dusty cobwebs brushed their faces. Nature had made an attempt to reclaim it, and dark moss covered the walls, while green tendrils stretched down through cracks in the roof. As they followed the twists of the passage, it led them sharply downward until it opened out into a cavernous space. Here the rocky walls were lined with shelves. Lorcan kept Tanzi's hand in one of his, but he held his other hand high to illuminate the scene. Each shelf was stacked high with coffins in varying states of repair.

"The crypt."

There was something different about Lorcan's voice when he said the word. Tanzi studied his face. His expression was serene, almost dreamy, as his eyes scanned the coffins. It was as though an inner peace had descended upon him. Should it surprise her that he was at home here among the dead? He was a necromancer, after all, one of those rare and magical beings who were born with the ability to communicate with those who had gone beyond life. She just hoped he wasn't going to start doing it now.

As if he sensed her unease, Lorcan drew his eyes back to her face. "If Pedro is right, we should be able to enter the other building from here. The inquisitors used this crypt to hide the true number of their dead from the outside world."

"There doesn't seem to be any way out, other than the way we came in." Tanzi looked around. It was a manmade cave with rough stone walls and a high, rounded ceiling. "It's a dead end."

Lorcan groaned and rolled his eyes. "Less of the dead jokes, please. I've heard them all before."

"I didn't mean—" Tanzi's protest was cut short by a scraping noise from one of the coffins. It was soft but unmistakable. Nervously, she drew closer to Lorcan. "What was that?" Even though she whispered, her voice sounded unnaturally loud in the echoing space.

"One of them needs to tell me something." Lorcan started to move toward the shelf from which the noise was becoming louder and more insistent. Tanzi gripped his hand tighter, keeping him at her side.

"Just like that? Do dead people often feel the need to tell you things?"

"If it's important they do. They can sense my presence." He turned to face her. "You're trembling." He drew her to him, running his hands up and down her arms. *Soothing me as he would a frightened animal,* Tanzi told herself, even as she gave herself up to the sensations his touch provoked. *Just as if I really am the kitten he jokes about me being.* "There is nothing to fear from the souls who lie here. Even if they wished us harm—and I doubt they do—the dead cannot hurt a necromancer." He slid his fingers under her chin, constraining her to look up at him even though her instinct was to burrow her head into his chest. "I'll look after you, *Searc.*"

Releasing her, Lorcan went over to the stack of coffins. The noise was coming from the casket on the top shelf. It was newer and less elaborate than the others, little more than a plain box compared with their wrought iron–encrusted grandeur. Placing his hands on the lid, he bent his head as if in prayer. "*Asprecan.* Speak to me." His voice was gentle, offering a world of sympathy to the coffin's occupant.

The coffin began to rock back and forth on its shelf

as the noises from within became frantic. Muffled cries from inside tugged at Tanzi's heartstrings and she hurried to Lorcan's side, forgetting her earlier fear. "What can we do?"

"Help me get this top off."

Lorcan produced a serviceable-looking army knife from his back pocket and, flicking out the blade, began to unscrew the coffin lid. When it was free, Tanzi helped him to lift it clear of the casket and place it on the ground. The young girl who instantly sat up and regarded them with huge, petrified eyes didn't look dead. Her skin was creamy, her hair lustrous, and her lips retained a cherry bloom. The only telltale sign that she might have relinquished her hold on life was the dagger embedded in her chest and the splash of bright crimson that bloomed around it.

She looked at Lorcan in surprise, then lifted a hand to point at Tanzi. "Faerie."

"Yes, but she will not hurt you," Lorcan reassured her.

"Faeries is deadly."

"I mean you no harm." Tanzi stepped forward, but the girl shrank away from her.

"She is a dryad," Lorcan said. "Or she was in life. They fear your race. Although she can see you, you cannot interact with her now that she is dead. Nothing you say or do will comfort her. It's best if you stand to one side while I discover what she wishes to say to me."

"Does she know she's dead?" Tanzi whispered.

"Possibly not." There was a trace of regret in his smile. "She'll find out soon enough. It's my least favorite part of the job description."

Tanzi moved away slightly, casting a wary glance at the other coffins. What if one of the other occupants of this crypt suddenly discovered a burning desire to converse with Lorcan while he was otherwise engaged? She decided to stay far enough from the walls not to find herself on the receiving end of a bony hand reaching out from one of the shelves. The dryad stared around her with wide, startled eyes.

"What is your name?"

"Iphae." It seemed she was compelled to answer Lorcan. "What place is this?"

"You are in the mortal realm, in a city called Barcelona. Do you remember how you got here?"

She began to shake her head. Then she raised a hand to cover her lips, and the shaking turned to nodding. The hand dropped, her lip trembled and tears filled the gray-green depths of her eyes. "Sidhes did come to our forest and hunt us down like animals. Only the youngest girls did they want. I was fearful for my little sister so I helped her to hide deep in the woods. Took me instead, didn't they?"

"What happened when they brought you here?" Lorcan's voice was gentle.

Iphae hung her head. "Cannot say it. Not to make me, please."

"Did they make you work for them? In their brothels?"

She nodded and fat, glistening tears rolled down her cheeks. "Mortal men pay good money for no-good dryad bitches, sidhes do say. Keep us in chains until our masters come, don't they?"

"Who hurt you, Iphae?"

She gazed up at him blankly. Then her hand went to her breast, seeking the hilt of the dagger. "Oh!" Iphae's breath hitched in shock and Tanzi wanted to go to her and cradle the lost girl in her arms. Sympathy was another new emotion she had learned through her contact with Lorcan. What a pity a faerie's touch would terrify the sad little dryad even further. "Big mortal took a liking to me. Cruel, and getting worse each time, wasn't he? In fear for my life, I was. Stole this knife from one of the sidhes, didn't I? This time when he got too rough, I cut him. Wasn't going to take that from a cheap dryad whore, was he? Paid me back, didn't he?"

"Is that what you wished to tell me?"

She frowned as though concentrating hard. "No. I hear them talk, don't I? Saying the great Moncoya is set to rise again stronger than ever and return to his rightful place. Time to put these resistance dogs down, isn't it? Set a trap for them. Their leader is back in town, isn't he? Get him and slit his cursed throat." Her hand reached out suddenly and gripped Lorcan's. "Beware."

Tanzi glanced apprehensively over her shoulder. Was it possible her father knew who the resistance leader was? Worse, could he know that she had joined them? If so, his revenge against Lorcan would be absolute and vicious. For her—his daughter—death could not be any worse than the marriage plans he had already made for her.

Iphae was speaking again. "Moved the dryad money spinners on, didn't they? Gone from here, my friends are now."

Lorcan placed a hand on the girl's head and her eyelids fluttered. "You have done well, Iphae. It is time for you to rest now."

"Not to go, sir. Not yet, please…" For a moment her face was a mask of fear. Gradually, she relaxed under Lorcan's touch and her expression lightened. "Sleep, shall I?"

"Yes, Iphae. You've earned it."

"Thank you, sir." She lay down again in her casket, her eyes closing like a tired child who had fought slumber for too long.

Lorcan signaled for Tanzi to help him replace the coffin lid. She watched his face as he performed the task. "How do you stand it?" Her voice was husky. She wanted to hold him, but she didn't know how he would react. Instead, she settled for placing her hand on his forearm.

Lorcan glanced down at her slender fingers where they rested on the sinewy muscles of his arm, but made no comment about the gesture. "It's what I have to do for them. Listening to them, comforting them, allowing them to share their secrets and unburden their fears. It's an obligation that was placed upon me when these powers were bequeathed to me. It's a great responsibility but also a privilege. The final dignity I can bestow on them is to get this part right."

"You did," Tanzi said quietly. "Today, for Iphae, you got it absolutely right."

"Thank you." A corner of his mouth lifted briefly. "What now?"

"Now? We steer clear of that bloody place." He nodded at the blank wall at the end of the crypt. "Whatever their trap is, we're not walking into it."

"What about Iphae's friends?"

"We'll find them and free them, of course."

The talk around the table that night was of the plan to rescue the captured dryads. Pedro was charged with discovering any likely places to which the girls might have been transported. Tanzi, from her habitual seat by the fire, kept her eyes on Lorcan's face. She thought his eyes revealed his fatigue, but his expression remained determined.

"This is too dangerous for you," Lisbet insisted. "It seems they know of your presence here. They know you are our leader."

"How can they know it?" Aydan asked.

"There is only one way." Lorcan looked at each of the faces around the table. "We have an informer in our midst."

There was an outcry at that. Perhaps it was her imagination, but Tanzi thought that, in the ensuing series of furious protests, Lisbet cast one or two suspicious glances her way. Eventually, when the matter had been discussed several times over with no clear conclusion reached, they all departed for their separate rooms.

"I know how difficult it is for you to hear of the things his followers have done." Lorcan paused outside Tanzi's bedroom door. Even though they were alone, he was careful not to make any direct reference linking her to Moncoya.

"You mean it is hard for me to hear what he has instigated." He inclined his head in acknowledgment and she continued. "Will I develop immunity over time, do you think?"

"Do you want an honest answer?" She nodded. "Probably not."

Tanzi sighed. "I fear you may be right. Can I ask you something? About what happened with Iphae?"

"Only if I can sit down while I answer." His devastating grin dawned. "I'm knackered."

She wrinkled her nose. "Knackered?"

"An Irish expression. It means done in. Worn-out. Exhausted." He followed her into her bedroom and sat on the bed.

"Is it practicing your craft that tires you so?" Tanzi glanced around, trying to decide where to sit. The bag containing her clothes—what she now thought of as her "princess kit"—was on the chair. With a feeling somewhere between apprehension and euphoria, she joined

Lorcan on the bed, primly maintaining a distance of about twelve inches between them.

"Yes. The mental energy required to commune with the dead drains my strength, and then there is the emotional toll. What did you want to ask me?"

Even though his eyelids were drooping with tiredness, he still managed to look utterly adorable. It was very unfair of him. It made concentrating on anything else extremely difficult. "I thought that when the dead were raised they became zombies preying on human flesh. Yet Iphae returned to her coffin peacefully and, in the end, accepted—even welcomed—her death."

"It's a common misconception. Zombies are undead who are raised against their will. Iphae came to me of her own free choice and, although I suggested she should return to the other side and even exerted some pressure on her to do so, it remained her decision."

"Do you ever raise the dead against their will?"

"I try not to. Inevitably sometimes I have to, but it's a messy business. Zombies are a bugger to deal with. My turn to ask you something now." His eyes were probing on her face. "What was so bad back in Otherworld that this is better?"

The question was so unexpected that Tanzi gasped. Yet she *should* have been expecting it. Especially now that they suspected someone was passing their secrets on to the sidhes. "Do you think I am the one who betrayed you?" She tried to keep her voice level so that the hurt didn't show.

"Funnily enough, that never even occurred to me." He closed the distance between them, catching hold of her hands. "I trust you, Tanzi, truly I do. I just thought perhaps it was time to tell me. Because, and maybe I'm wrong, I sense it eating away at you. I know we've been over the fact that I'm a lowly necromancer, you're a royal princess, and we're worlds apart many times, but I want to help you if I can."

Her throat felt suddenly tight, as though his kindness had triggered a warm emotion that was threatening to choke her. She nodded. "Let me get a drink and I will tell you." She owed him the truth.

Rising, she went over to the dresser and poured a glass of water from the bottle Maria had placed there. She kept her back to Lorcan as she drank, attempting to restore some of her lost equanimity. When she felt that her composure had returned sufficiently, she turned around. A slight smile touched her lips at the sight that greeted her. There would be no confidences tonight. Lorcan was stretched full-length on her bed, sound asleep.

Chapter 6

Lorcan woke in the middle of the night with a feeling of well-being, which was soon explained when he realized his arms were full of Tanzi. It was a situation that did nothing for someone with an overactive imagination and a currently underactive cock. Ascertaining that they were both fully clothed and, from his memory of the previous night, being fairly certain that nothing had happened between them, he eased himself regretfully away from her. She gave a soft little murmur of protest in her sleep, and his erection responded to the sound by jackhammering uncomfortably against the restraining cloth of his jeans.

Why couldn't he do the uncomplicated thing for once in his life and lust after a nice, straightforward girl? Someone he could actually have? The troublesome thing was, he was fairly certain he *could* have Tanzi. He sensed that the intense physical attraction he felt for her was mutual. But that wouldn't make it right. It was wrong on

so many levels. His internal mantra started to kick in…
Moncoya's daughter, sidhe princess, Valkyrie warrior.
The words had become tired and meaningless so he silenced them. Yes, she was still all of those things. This
rift with her father didn't change what she was, it only
made her vulnerable. A sweet, vulnerable killing machine. *You don't want to mess with one of them, Malone.*

He thought of all the things he'd heard about Tanzi
and her sister, Vashti, over the years. Setting aside their
reputation as Moncoya's ruthless weapons, it was said
that the King of the Faeries viewed his daughters as his
stepping-stone to even greater power. He boasted that
through them he would forge alliances to make the faerie dynasty invincible. In order for that to happen, the
sidhe princesses must remain pure until such time as
their father would choose a mate for them. Woe betide
the man who touched one of Moncoya's daughters before she reached her marriage bed. *I'm not afraid of yon
faerie feller, but I'll not put his daughter at risk from his
wrath. Not for the sake of a one-night stand.*

Because that was all it would ever be. A one-night
stand. Or maybe a series of them. A brief fling. *I haven't
got it in me to offer her more.* The thought brought with it
a pang of regret. Lorcan made jokes about being a wanderer, the implication being he never settled. Love 'em
and leave 'em Malone. It was a myth he didn't deny. On
the contrary, he cultivated it. Only Lorcan himself knew
the truth. Something in his heart had been damaged beyond repair way back in the dim and distant past. That
capacity others had for sustained emotion—he supposed
it was called commitment these days—wasn't part of his
makeup. It had burned at the stake, while he had sobbed
and pleaded for help that never came.

Why was he thinking of commitment in relation to

Tanzi, anyway? Just because she happened to be bloody gorgeous and, at this precise moment, deliciously inviting. His inner nice guy—and, yes, he did have one—was attempting to justify the crushing desire he felt to draw her back into his arms, wake her with a kiss and then let his fingertips glide up between the silken flesh of those slender thighs. *Stop being such a bloody hypocrite. You're not fooling anyone. You are trying to defend the fact that you want to fuck this gorgeous girl by making it into something more than mere lust.* It didn't help that Tanzi was wearing some sort of elongated T-shirt that had rucked up as she slept, revealing the very thighs that were fueling his imagination in an erotic and interesting way. Determinedly, Lorcan gritted his teeth. Sliding from the bed, he pulled a blanket over Tanzi's prone form. Out of sight, out of mind. That was the theory.

Feeling very virtuous—but oddly bereft—he tiptoed out the door and made his way to his own room. Despite his tiredness, he was unable to sleep. The dawn light saw him pulling on his clothes and taking out his frustrations by jogging the length of the Ramblas before following the harbor toward the Barceloneta Beach. He ran until the ache in his muscles drove every other thought from his mind. This was better. He couldn't afford any distractions.

The house was still quiet when he returned. He headed for the shower, then spent a long time letting the jets of cool water drive any lingering traces of heat and temptation from his body. He stayed there so long that the ancient pipes creaked and groaned and threatened to tear the old house apart. When he emerged, drying his hair on a towel, Tanzi was standing framed in the open door of her room, blinking sleepily in the early-morning sunlight. The elongated T-shirt skimmed her thighs and the bright mass of her hair tumbled wildly about her shoulders. She smiled when she saw him and then stretched her arms lazily above her head. The T-shirt rose precariously higher.

"I was disturbed by strange clanking noises," she explained.

Shit. The run and the shower hadn't worked one bit. Her presence hit him like an injection of carnal longing direct into his bloodstream. It fizzed into his nerve endings, making him feel alive in a way he couldn't remember ever having felt before. Whatever Tanzi was, she wasn't a mere distraction. She was something far more dangerous and disturbing, and it was going to take more than physical exertion and cold water to flush her out of his system.

"This is definitely the house where the girls are being held." Aydan had been the one to survey the building identified by Pedro as the most likely place for the sidhes to keep their dryad prisoners. "But it is closely guarded."

Of course it was. The sidhes would take no chances with their lucrative prisoners. "By what?" Lorcan asked with no expectation of liking the answer. *Let it be something simple like a pack of rabid attack dogs.*

"Zombies." Aydan's throat gave an audible click as he swallowed. He attempted a brave smile. "Just as well we have a necromancer with us, eh?"

"I hate to disillusion you. If I didn't summon these zombies, I can't command them." That wasn't strictly true. Zombies were undead, so Lorcan could exercise a measure of control over them. As long as their true master wasn't around. If he or she was close by, then things could get very messy.

Aydan was moving forward now, beckoning for Lorcan to follow. With a resigned sigh, Lorcan accompanied him along the outer edge of the high, rugged wall that marked the border of the property. The others in the group were in the truck under the shade of a nearby copse of olive trees awaiting their instructions. Aydan led the way to a gap in the wall, through which they had a clear view of the house. The building was a rambling, seemingly uninhabited farmhouse. Built on two floors, it had a wide, paved porch running all the way around the outside. The walls were built from the rough terra-cotta stone that was common throughout the area, and the windows were tiny squares set in heavy dark wood frames. It was impossible to tell what was going on behind their blank stare. According to the resistance sources, and from what Aydan had gleaned on his reconnoiter, there were five dryads being held captive inside. Five innocent, frightened girls like Iphae. Lorcan felt his lips thin into a determined line. An encounter with zombies would be a small price to pay if they could get those girls home to their families.

Aydan pointed to the building. "The dryads are all together in one room at the back of the property. Yesterday I counted four sidhes coming and going at different times. Things are fairly low-key. They probably don't imagine these girls are going to cause them many problems."

"To be fair, if they have zombies as watch dogs they don't need much additional manpower." Lorcan looked around at the rolling countryside. There were no other buildings in view and they had driven their ancient open-backed truck over a dusty track for at least half an hour after they left the main road. "And this place is so isolated no one is going to stumble across it by chance."

"Could it be a trap?"

"How will we know unless we walk into it?" Lorcan

laughed at Aydan's horrified expression. "Let's get the others over here. Go over the plan of attack."

Aydan left him and returned a few minutes later with Iago, Tanzi, Lisbet and two young Iberian sidhes, Sam and Iker, who were active resistance members. Lisbet's face wore a sour expression. Tanzi gave Lorcan one of her dazzling smiles and the reason for Lisbet's bad mood become clear. The two young faeries were clearly smitten with Tanzi, although the object of their interest appeared oblivious to their admiring gazes.

"Aydan and I will go in through the front door. *Searc*, you come with us. Iago and Lisbet will take the back entrance." Lisbet opened her mouth as if she was about to protest, but Lorcan turned away to talk to Sam and Iker. He didn't have time for a debate. "You guys stay outside and act as lookout. Warn us if anyone comes."

Without any further discussion, he followed the wall, gesturing for the others to follow him. When they reached an arched gateway, Lorcan paused. The wooden gates hung loosely on their hinges and several of the scarred panels were missing or damaged. The gates swung inward with a protesting groan when Lorcan pushed against them. He was about to step through when Tanzi's hand on his arm forestalled him.

"Let me go first." She kept her voice low so that the others couldn't hear.

"Like there's a chance in hell of that happening."

"Think about it," she urged. "If there are any of my—" she broke off, biting her lip "—any of Moncoya's sidhes in there, I am the last person they will be expecting to see. Whatever else they do, they certainly won't attack me."

Reluctantly, he was forced to acknowledge the truth of what she was saying. Sending Crown Princess Tanzi in through that gate was the best possible diversion they

could throw at a group of Moncoya's sidhes. So why
was he hesitating? Why was he standing here trying to
find reasons not to do as she asked instead of putting the
safety of the whole group first? And why was he tempted
to come up with an excuse to send Tanzi back to the
truck to wait it out until the danger was over when she
was probably the most experienced and deadly fighter
of them all?

"Lorcan? Is there a problem?" Lisbet's strident voice
brought him back down to earth.

"No problem," he called back over his shoulder. "As
for you...we'll go together." He held out his hand to Tanzi.

"I don't need you to protect me, necromancer." It was
her stubborn, haughty-princess voice. The one she had
used to try to squash him during their first encounter on
the battlefield. The one that always turned him on a little
bit, even in this situation.

"Have you ever considered that *I* might be the one who
needs *you*?" Taking advantage of her look of surprise,
he grabbed her hand and marched through the gates,
keeping Tanzi close by his side. Steeling himself for any
eventuality, he got the last one he had anticipated. Nothing. Only silence, stillness and a pervading air of menace greeted them.

Once inside the boundary walls, the property looked
even more run-down and neglected. Nature had reclaimed the garden and run riot among the flower beds.
The path that led to the front door was only just discernible through the weeds that had crept between the flags. If
anyone was watching from behind those blank windowpanes, they made no move to stop them as Lorcan and
Tanzi made their way along the path and approached the
shallow steps of the porch. Aydan followed close behind,
with the rest of the group bringing up the rear.

"The door is open," Tanzi pointed out as they mounted the steps.

"Which means they've either gone, or they are expecting us." Lorcan moved to one side of the door, keeping Tanzi with him, while Aydan took the opposite side.

Wet shuffling sounds and the smell of rotting flesh indicated that the zombies were within. Of all the undead beings he dealt with, zombies were Lorcan's least favorite. Mindless, soulless and flesh-eating, they had no redeeming qualities. Vampires were charismatic, werewolves loyal, ghosts often kindly and sometimes humorous. Zombies didn't even have their own personal hygiene sorted out.

Lorcan nodded and the three of them entered the house together. They were in a large, old-fashioned farmhouse kitchen, devoid of all but the most basic items of furniture. Half a dozen zombies were gathered around the edge of the room and, at the sight of the intruders, they began their distinctive stumbling walk toward them, hands extended and heads down.

"Oflinnan." Lorcan issued the order for the zombies to halt. To his relief, with much snuffling and grunting, they stopped. You just never knew with zombies. If the necromancer who raised them was close by, they would remain under the influence of their master and refuse to obey the commands of another. Behind Lorcan, Aydan exhaled loudly with relief. Tanzi wrinkled her nose and drew closer to Lorcan.

Although the zombies halted, they continued to mutter and scuff their feet, like images paused on an old TV screen. From elsewhere in the house the sound of several loud crashes indicated that Iago and Lisbet might not have found it so easy to gain access to the property.

"Let's find the room where the girls are being held."

Something about the whole setup—even beyond that of the zombies and the accompanying scent of putrefaction—was making Lorcan uneasy. For someone who had spent most of a very long life denying his intuition, he found it had a tendency to surface at the oddest moments. However much he might dislike and try to ignore his inner voice, it was unerringly right. And it was telling him now to get out of this place.

Aydan led the way out of the kitchen and into a gloomy hallway. This was dominated by a wide staircase that looked as though time and woodworm had done their worst. From somewhere beyond the hall, Lorcan heard Lisbet's voice raised in a sudden, panicky cry. Without conferring with his companions, Aydan threw open a door on the opposite wall and dashed across a large, empty room. Keeping a firm grip on Tanzi's hand, Lorcan followed. Beyond this room, he could see a gallery running the length of the rear of the house. Seated on the floor, with their backs to the wall, their hands tied behind them and their feet bound, were the five young dryads. In front of them, Iago lay on the floor, apparently unconscious, with Lisbet kneeling beside him.

"What happened?" Lorcan glanced quickly around for any sign of an assailant. There was no one else around. The dryads, who were gagged, gazed up at him with large, frightened eyes.

"I don't know." Lisbet rose to her feet, allowing Aydan to take her place. He felt for a pulse in the other man's neck, nodding a confirmation to Lorcan when he found it. "He had to kick down the door to get in at the back. When we came in here and saw the girls, Iago just toppled forward. It was as if he fainted."

"You didn't see or hear anything?"

"Nothing at all. He's breathing normally, but he's been out cold for a few minutes."

The crawling feeling of unease was stronger now, as if icy fingers were tracking teasingly up and down his spine. "Start untying the girls," he directed Tanzi and Lisbet. They hurried to do his bidding.

"We need to get Iago some air." Aydan turned his head to look at Lorcan and, as he did, his eyes widened in terror. It was this, together with a warning scream from one of the newly freed dryads, that caused Lorcan to duck. The samurai sword that should have sliced through his neck caught him a glancing blow on his right shoulder instead. Even so, it was enough to send him staggering backward.

The zombies, all of them armed now with swords and knives, lumbered into the gallery. Clutching his shoulder, Lorcan blinked away the dark spots that were threatening to obscure his vision as he struggled to stay upright. His mind reeled as he weighed their options. From the sticky heat in his shoulder, he knew he was bleeding. Iago was still unconscious. The zombies were blocking their exit. They had walked into a trap.

Before he could fully process what was happening, a blur of movement drew his attention and Tanzi was in front of him, facing the zombie that had struck him. It had raised the sword over its head and was poised to attack again.

"No." The word hadn't even left his lips before Tanzi's foot connected solidly with the center of the undead monster's chest. The zombie tottered, its balance uncertain.

"Keep talking to them." As she spoke, Tanzi brought her elbow up and jammed it full force into the zombie's windpipe. It let go of the sword and fell to its knees. "Make them stop."

"Their master must be close by. My commands will not be as strong as his." Lorcan winced as she picked up the sword and, taking a two-handed grip, swung it into the zombie's neck. You couldn't kill a zombie, but cutting its head off, as Tanzi had just done, was a fairly effective way of slowing it down.

"You can dilute their master's control." Tanzi was striding forward now, the bloodied sword extended in front of her.

She was right, of course. He might not be able to counteract the orders of whoever was controlling the zombies, but, by issuing his own, contrary instructions, he might be able to confuse them. At the very least, he should be able to slow them down. Ignoring the pain in his shoulder, he stepped forward so that he was just behind Tanzi. "*Oflinnan.* Stay where you are."

In response to his words, the zombies paused, resembling clockwork toys that were winding down. Their shambling forward momentum slowed and became unfocused.

"*Fŷrwylm.*" Lorcan raised his left hand, wondering how his injury would affect his capability. Although flames shot from his fingertips toward the nearest of the zombies, showering them with sparks, Lorcan felt the reduction in his powers caused by his inability to use both hands. The zombies' grunts held a note of confusion. Turning their heads, the creatures appeared to be listening to instructions from an invisible voice.

Lorcan took advantage of their disorientation. "Aydan, move Iago out of the way. Lisbet, as soon as you get the chance, take the dryads outside. Get them into the truck." He kept his voice even.

Tanzi didn't need any guidance. She was taking advantage of the bewilderment Lorcan had caused their undead opponents and had started systematically slashing her way through the zombie ranks. Because she was so much smaller and faster than the zombies, she was able to wade into them before they had even noticed her. It wasn't a pretty sight. Zombie limbs and blood littered the room within seconds. Lorcan wished he could take a measure of comfort from that fact, but he had seen zombies hacked into tiny pieces and each piece continued to attack its target. That was how they were programmed. They had no brain to speak of. Each cell within their body simply followed its master's command.

Aydan dragged the inert Iago to one side of the gallery. Leaving him there, he pried a machete from the severed hand of a zombie and joined Tanzi. Repeating his commands regularly, Lorcan armed himself with a discarded ax and the three of them cleared a path through the bewildered zombies so that Lisbet could lead the dryads to safety. The frightened girls scurried gratefully past the bloodbath into the other room and beyond.

"My influence over them is waning," Lorcan warned the others, as, ignoring the damage inflicted upon them, the zombies began to advance again. "Their master must be incredibly powerful to be able to control them from a distance."

"You and Aydan get Iago while I deal with them." He wanted to protest at Tanzi's words, but she was right. Again. Her combination of martial arts and ruthless swordplay were by far the most effective means of holding back the zombies. She whirled in and out of the lumpish figures like a deadly ballerina, leaving them blundering blindly in her wake.

Hoisting Iago to his feet, Lorcan and Aydan draped his arms over their shoulders and began to drag him between them. Tanzi followed, keeping the zombies at bay with her sword. Even burdened by Iago's weight, Lorcan and Aydan were faster than the shuffling creatures. When they burst out of the house and into the open, Lorcan gulped fresh air gratefully, driving the stench of decay from his lungs and nostrils. With profound relief, he saw that Lisbet had brought the truck up to the front of the house. Sam and Iker, keeping watch outside, had been oblivious to the carnage going on inside the house and regarded them in horror. He caught a glimpse of the frightened dryads peering out from the back of the vehicle and took a moment to picture himself and his companions from the perspective of an observer. His lips curved into a wry smile. They looked like extras in a horror movie. Tanzi had fared the worst. She was unrecognizable beneath a covering of zombie blood and other unmentionable gunk. Aydan didn't look much better and Lorcan guessed he must appear about the same.

"I smell of zombie," Tanzi grumbled as they loaded Iago into the back of the truck.

"We can't drive into the city like this." Aydan plucked at his bloodstained clothing.

Lisbet poked her head out of the driver's side window. Her expression was disapproving. "There is a lake nearby. If you get in instead of standing around chatting, I'll take you there first so you can get cleaned up."

Obediently, they piled into the back of the truck while Sam and Iker climbed in next to Lisbet. Lorcan draped his good arm around Tanzi's shoulder, drawing her close against his side. "You make a pretty awesome zombie slayer, *Searc*."

The dryads were regarding Tanzi and Aydan with even more consternation. "Be they faeries?" one of them whispered to her companions.

"Be hard to tell beneath the muck, wouldn't it?"

"Yes, we are faeries, but don't worry...we've done our random act of deadliness for today." It wasn't funny, but for some reason Aydan starting laughing at his own joke and Tanzi joined in.

The dryads turned wary eyes to Lorcan, who gave them a helpless, I-got-nothing shrug. "It's a faerie thing," he said, indicating his chortling, blood-encrusted companions.

One or two of the dryads managed polite smiles in sympathy, but they all edged as far away from their rescuers as they could in the cramped confines of the truck bed as it rocked wildly over the uneven road surface.

Chapter 7

They waded into the lake fully clothed. Who knew zombie blood could prove so difficult to wash out? Tanzi's new life was proving full of difficult lessons. While Lorcan and Aydan stripped down to their underwear, Tanzi shook her head primly at their invitation to join them and remained fully clothed. Ducking under the water, she scrubbed at her skin and tried to clean the blue vest and faded jeans that were among the few things Maria had found in her size. Her efforts were partially successful. When she emerged, the stains on her clothing had faded to rusty-brown blotches so that she looked less like a serial killer and more like the victim of an overzealous paintballer.

Lorcan had his back to her so she was able to enjoy the view without fear of discovery. Her eyes lingered on his wide shoulders—the right one of which now bore a deep gash—and trim waist, moving lower to appreciate his toned buttocks and powerful legs. Giving herself a mental shake, she waded over to him. Her wet clothes weighed her down so that she sloshed through the shallow water and, hearing her approach, he turned to face her. If she thought the rear aspect was enticing, full frontal was even more glorious.

"My hairdresser would break down in tears if he knew I was trying to get zombie entrails out of my hair using nothing but lake water." *That's it. Keep it light and, while you're at it, keep your eyes fixed on his face.*

"I won't tell him if you don't." Unaware of her "keep it light" vow, Lorcan drew her close to him, sliding his fingers through the length of her curls. *Oh, well...* Tanzi closed her eyes, reveling in the sensation his touch provoked. She gave herself up to the feeling and rested her forehead against his chest, feeling his breath hitch slightly as she did. It was a clear indication of the effect she had on him and, while she enjoyed it, she wasn't quite sure what to do about it.

Attraction. Flirtation. Seduction. All darkly tempting notions that had, until now, belonged firmly in other people's lives. Tanzi had been brought up in the knowledge that, as Moncoya's daughter, she existed within a bubble of purity that would not be penetrated until her marriage to the Otherworld leader chosen by her father. She was above such things. It had given her a security and superiority that she had never questioned. Not until the day of the battle when Lorcan had pulled her out from the chaos and turned her world upside down with one look from those denim-blue eyes.

Now she was forced to question everything she had once believed about herself. Had she ever really developed a royal immunity to temptation? Or was it simpler than that? Was it just that she had never met anyone for whom she felt even the slightest pull of physical attraction? Until Lorcan. And there was nothing slight about what she felt for him. She was in a constant state of restlessness. Or readiness. If she was with him, she was acutely aware of him, of herself and how she appeared to him. When they were apart, too much of her time was spent wondering what he was doing or rehearsing conversations she might have with him. Was this what people meant when they talked about a "crush"? Surely such a mundane thing was beneath her. Tanzi nearly laughed aloud. If that was the case, why was she quivering with anticipation as Lorcan raised his hand and ran it through her hair once more?

In the period after the battle, she had surreptitiously gleaned as much information as she could about the Irish loner who had rescued her from certain death on the battlefield. It wasn't an easy task. Necromancers were usually solitary and private, and Lorcan was no exception.

"Best friend to Merlin Caledonius." That was the most widespread piece of useless information about him.

"Irish." Equally unhelpful.

"Bit of a heartbreaker, that's what I've heard." Tanzi had pricked up her ears at that comment from one of the vampire envoys to the new Alliance. In answer to her look of inquiry, the female vampire had tossed her head. There was a hint of hurt pride in the gesture. "Love 'em and leave 'em, that's what they say. A new girl in every town, all trying to hold on to him. They say that's why he's always on the move. He can't be held."

Tanzi had even swallowed her own pride and managed to bring Lorcan's name into a conversation with Stella. "Lorcan?" Stella's green eyes had held an affectionate smile. "He's a good friend."

Tanzi had bent her head over the papers she was supposed to be reading for the next Alliance meeting. Her voice had been gruff when she spoke again. "I have heard that he is not to be trusted."

"I would trust Lorcan with my life." Stella's initial quick-fire defense of her friend had been followed by a laugh. "Well, I suppose it's true that, while I'd trust him with the big things, I wouldn't count on him turning up when he said he was going to for dinner or a movie. And if he swore undying love, would I be entirely sure he hadn't said the same thing to another girl just last night? Probably not. I guess that's all part of his charm."

"So he is a cheat where women are concerned?"

"I wouldn't say that exactly. Cheating means you don't tell the truth, and Lorcan is honest about the fact that he's a player. You don't get that from many men." Stella laughed again, this time reminiscently. "He once told me he's terribly shy around women. But a man with Lorcan's looks couldn't expect to make that claim and be taken seriously, could he?"

So Tanzi had been forewarned about him. She knew what he was and had been able to give her heart—an organ that seemed determined to embark on a new and interesting course—plenty of warnings. Yet standing waist-deep in the crystal clear lake water, with her head resting against the solid muscle of Lorcan's naked chest while he ran those magical fingers through her hair, it was proving hard to remember why she must keep her distance.

She wasn't the only one feeling the effect of Lorcan's legendary charm. Tanzi had seen the glances Lisbet gave Lorcan when she thought no one else was looking. It was a look that explained everything. *She is in love with him. No wonder she doesn't like it when he pays me attention.*

Several other thoughts flitted through Tanzi's head, none of them logical. She reassessed her first impres-

sion of Lisbet and found her opinion of the other woman
greatly improved. *She could do worse than to bestow
her devotion on a man like Lorcan,* she decided. Tanzi
wondered if anyone would be prepared to tell Lisbet that
she was setting her sights hopelessly high. With her unusual coloring, the girl was not unattractive. Some might
even consider Lisbet's sharp features, light hair and coal-
black eyes pretty. *Of course, she is not good enough
for Lorcan.* Surely someone would tell her that? Finally,
Tanzi wondered why the thought of Lisbet and Lorcan
together should make her own chest constrict so painfully. This was another new emotion, one she didn't recognize. Whatever it was, she didn't like it.

How did mortals cope with all these feelings raging
around inside them? It was a most disturbing condition,
quite unpleasant. And yet, when Lorcan moved his hand
down from her hair to caress the length of her arm, the
thrill that ran through her spiked out of control. *Unpleasant* was not the first word that sprang to mind. *Maddening. Agonizing. Stomach-flippingly exhilarating.* But
unpleasant? No, not that.

"Tanzi." Lorcan's voice was husky.

"Hmm?" She seemed to be enveloped in a strange sort
of languor that made any movement—even the lifting of
an eyelid—too much of an effort.

"I think it's a good idea if we move apart now and
continue what we came here for." She lifted her head, a
question forming on her lips. "Before I forget that we're
not alone. Forget completely, I mean."

There was something in his voice that did convince her
to look up then. The blaze of passion in his eyes, coupled
with the realization that the unmistakable ridge of his
erection was hard against her stomach, caused Tanzi's
breath to catch in her throat.

"Oh!" She jerked quickly away from him, feeling the blush stain her cheeks. What *had* she been thinking? Apart from how much she wanted his hands to explore other parts of her body. Hearing the splash as Lorcan dived beneath the water, she risked a glance toward the riverbank. Sure enough, she encountered the interested stares of five dryad girls plus those of Sam and Iker as they sat in a group in the shade of a few trees. Even worse than their mild curiosity was the storm of disapproval on Lisbet's face. At least Iago, who had started to come around but was still groggy, had remained in the truck and Aydan had his back to them. The audience was large enough as it was.

Tanzi was beginning to appreciate that a very important aspect of her education had been neglected. Moncoya had employed the very finest tutors for his daughters. She and Vashti were introduced from an early age to the delights of literature, art and music. Their bodies were finely honed fighting machines. Their minds had been trained to assimilate the intricacies of mathematics and science, including the complex details of reproduction. So Tanzi knew exactly what had been going on in Lorcan's body just now when she felt his cock press insistently against her. She also knew what was going on in her own body when she felt an answering rush of heat between her legs. The biological aspects of it all had been explained to her. She had seen and drawn diagrams. Moncoya had ensured that her wedding night to one of Otherworld's powerful leaders would hold no surprises. Tanzi would not disgrace her father by being ignorant of her duty. It had all been clinical and practical. *But why the hell didn't anyone tell me how wonderful physical desire is? And now that I have experienced it, how can I help craving more?*

An urgent shout from the riverbank drew her attention

away from the intensity of her thoughts. A car screeched to a halt next to the truck and four men piled out of it. Sam and Iker scrambled to their feet and were immediately subjected to a brutal attack. They were felled by vicious blows and kicked to the ground. Lisbet caught hold of the arm of one of the attackers and was flung aside. The dryads scattered into the deeper cover of the trees. Tanzi broke into a run and, hampered by her wet clothing, was overtaken by Lorcan and Aydan. Even faced with such a dire situation, she took a moment to assimilate the fact that the wound on Lorcan's shoulder already looked much better. It must be a trick of the light. It wasn't possible for such a devastating injury to heal so rapidly. And anyway, she really didn't have time to waste on hallucinations.

Hitting the riverbank slightly ahead of Aydan, Lorcan waded into the fray, fists flying. He was considerably taller than his opponents and caught two of the men by surprise, landing a hefty punch in each of their faces. By the time his presence had registered, Aydan had joined him and a full-scale fight was under way. Lisbet was also playing her part by harrying the opposition. Although Iker struggled to his feet and joined the fray, Sam remained in a worryingly motionless heap.

The four men who had attacked them were sidhes. Short of stature, fair of face and with the same unmistakable ring of fire that burned in Tanzi's own eyes. Moncoya's sidhes were always well trained in the art of combat. Although Lorcan was causing them problems, they clearly weren't wavering. With Tanzi's arrival, the balance of power shifted instantly. Weighing up the situation as she approached, she decided that Lorcan and Aydan didn't need her help. Leaving them to deal with one pair of sidhes, she turned her attention to the other two, who were facing Lisbet and Iker.

Years of martial arts training with Valkyrie meant street fighting was second nature to Tanzi. The two sidhes didn't know what hit them. One minute a slender girl in drenched clothing was approaching them. The next Tanzi had used a turning back kick to the midsection of one followed in a fluid, continuous motion by a side thrust kick to the neck of the other. Both sidhes toppled like toy soldiers flicked over by a child's careless finger. Twin clouds of red dust rising from the riverbank signaled that the fight was over before it had begun.

"What kept you?" Lorcan managed a grin over his shoulder.

The remaining two sidhes were looking distinctly worried. One of them muttered something to his companion and, casting wary glances in Tanzi's direction, they held up their hands in a gesture of surrender.

"Here's the deal, guys. You can get going with a message for your masters or I can hand you over to my friend here." Lorcan indicated Tanzi with a wave of his hand. "She's had a nice little warm-up. She'll be ready for some real action about now." Although his words were muffled because of what was clearly a broken nose, one of the sidhes indicated that he preferred the former option. "Then take this message back—and make sure they listen—the dryads are off-limits from now on. Got it? Good. Get out of here."

The sidhes made an undignified scramble toward their companions. One of them paused as he passed Tanzi, his expression undergoing a series of changes as he looked at her. Fear was replaced by recognition, then shock. The moment she had dreaded was here. Dropping on one knee before her, he placed a hand across his heart and bent his head low. "Highness."

Lorcan intervened swiftly, putting himself between

Tanzi and the kneeling man. "I thought I told you to get out of here."

"I apologize. I thought…"

"You were wrong." Lorcan's voice and expression were steely and she knew his words were for the benefit of the resistance members as well as for the sidhe who had recognized her. Nodding, but with a final bemused glance at Tanzi, the sidhe joined his companion. Lorcan sighed. "Lisbet, fetch the girls. Aydan, do you think there's any chance of you finding our pants so that we can return to town looking halfway decent? Iker, let's take a look at Sam."

"We necromancers are a rare species and I thought I knew the current whereabouts of all the greats. Stella is the most powerful of us all. She is the one Merlin—or Cal, as the big feller prefers to be known—predicted would be the means by which Otherworld would be saved. He was right, too. Her powers are second to none. Then there is Cal himself. He is a sorcerer first and foremost, but his powers of necromancy are pretty remarkable, too." Lorcan's boyish grin peeped out. "If we're going down the ranks in order, I suppose I would be next in line. Or perhaps Jethro. The two of us are pretty evenly matched."

They were seated in Tanzi's bedroom. The journey back from the lake had been a miserable one. Rounding up the dryads and persuading them to get back into the truck had been a difficult task. Sam had sustained a nasty injury, having hit his head on a rock when he fell, and Iago was still disoriented. Lorcan, Tanzi and Aydan were damp and miserable after traveling in wet clothing, and Lisbet's foul mood showed no sign of abating. All in all, it was a sorry group that Pedro had admitted to the safe house earlier that evening.

Wrapped in a blanket and sipping hot chocolate, Tanzi was still finding it difficult to get warm. Underneath the blanket she wore a thick fisherman's sweater over her underwear and a pair of Lorcan's socks. It was as if the lake water had invaded her veins. They had brought an old electric heater up from the cellar. Tanzi was seated in the chair with Lorcan a foot away on the bed and the heater whirred noisily, blowing hot air between them.

"Do you have other powers as well as necromancing?" It was something she had wondered about ever since overhearing Lorcan's conversation with the imps. Now it was even more relevant given that the devastating wound inflicted on him by the zombie sword just hours earlier had faded to little more than a deep scratch.

Lorcan had dismissed her questions about his injury with a shrug. "I've always been quick to heal."

Now he regarded her thoughtfully before answering. "I've a trick or two up my sleeve." He didn't elaborate and she sensed a distance that she'd felt before. Sometimes, behind the easy facade, there was a vulnerability about Lorcan—a torment deep within him—that placed him beyond her reach. She wondered why others appeared not to see it. He continued with his list of necromancers. "Niniane, the sorceress who was known as the Lady of the Lake, dabbled a bit in the old dark arts, but she died in the battle for Otherworld, so that's her out of the picture. Moving down the line, there is an elderly Russian necromancer called Novak, but he is a known recluse. I can't see him coming out of hiding to get involved in something like this. Then there are the twins, Darius and Nightshade, but the last I heard of them they had a very lucrative contract with the Ghost Lord sorting out some rebellious poltergeists. And that's it as far as the big hitters go. There are a few minor players on the scene, but none of them have the strength to do something on this scale."

"You are sure there was a necromancer controlling those zombies?"

"Absolutely. I could feel it. There was another force acting against mine. Whoever raised them was close by. I'd say they were in the house with us. And he or she was bloody good because those zombies were being controlled without words. The necromancer who raised them was commanding them with the power of his or her thoughts. Given that zombies don't have brains, that's some feat. I've heard of it but I've never seen it done until today."

Tanzi hesitated, reluctant to make a suggestion that involved a friend of his. Yet it seemed the most obvious solution. "Could it have been Jethro? He is a mercenary, for sale to the highest bidder, and he's worked for my father before."

Lorcan gave it some consideration. "Jethro is certainly powerful enough. But, after Moncoya locked him up for not being able to defeat Stella on the eve of the battle, I don't think Jethro is your father's biggest fan. Maybe I'm being overly sentimental, but I also like to think we've been through too much together for him to set a trap like that for me, no matter how high the price." He drained the last of his hot chocolate. "And he's got other things on his mind just now."

"So who could it be?"

He shrugged. "My best guess is that there's a new kid in town. We don't always discover we are necromancers until we are older. Look at Stella. She had all that incredible energy inside her, yet she was twenty-five before she even began to acknowledge it. Whoever did this, he or she was pretty powerful to have kept control over that many zombies at once. Sooner or later, they will surface again. Until they do, we have a bigger problem."

"Finding out who the traitor is." Tanzi said it for him. She bit her lip. "Lisbet thinks it's me. I can see it in her eyes whenever she looks my way."

He leaned forward and took the cup from her, placing it on the floor. Clasping her hands, he held them between his. "I know it's not you."

"How can you know that?" She could hear the husky edge of emotion in her own voice. "Given what you know of me, surely I must be your first suspect?"

"You asked me just now if I have other powers. It's not a power as such, but I have a strong intuition, a foresight, about people. It is something that was passed down to me by my mother."

Tanzi raised her eyes to the endless blue of his. "What does your intuition tell you about me?"

"It tells me that you are honest and good."

Her breath hitched on a gasp. Until now, in the moment of hearing those words aloud, she had no idea how much they would mean to her. She had always believed the world saw her through the warped looking glass Moncoya held up as the means by which he wanted her to be seen. To know that someone—particularly Lorcan—believed in her sent a rush of pure elation flooding through her. Unsure of her intention, she leaned closer, closing the gap between them to a mere inch.

"Tanzi…" It sounded as if it was meant to be a protest. Even a warning. Then one of his hands cupped her cheek, and that simple gesture rocketed through them both. There was no turning back from that moment, no pretense and no finesse… Their lips ground together urgently. Lorcan's hand, sliding up through her hair to the back of her head, held Tanzi to him, and she closed her

eyes, giving herself up to the commands of his mouth on
hers. Her whole body was alive and aching with instant
pleasure. Twisting her head, she fitted herself to him, and
Lorcan growled in satisfaction. He was tasting her, ex-
ploring her, his lips moving possessively over hers, then,
as Tanzi's mouth slowly opened, his tongue claimed her.
That first entry of his body into hers was so stingingly
perfect that Tanzi welcomed him with a soft moan.

One of Lorcan's hands moved below the blanket and
under her sweater, sliding over her back, tracing her
spine, and running all the way down to find the cleft of
her buttocks. With that touch, the kiss changed again, becoming laden with new purpose. Hot and heavy. Panting
slightly, Lorcan pulled away.

"I was going to say this was a bad idea…but suddenly
it seems like the best idea I've ever had. If you're sure?"

Tanzi nodded. Her own breath was suspended somewhere between her lungs and her throat. "I'm sure."

He drew her to her feet, holding her between his knees
as he gazed up at her. Before either of them could do
anything, there was an insistent pounding on the door.
Lisbet's voice was insistent. "Lorcan? We know you're
in there."

"Ah, will you listen to that? Does that sound like a
woman who'll go away if we keep quiet?" Tanzi gave
a shaky laugh and shook her head. Pausing to lift her
sweater and press a regretful kiss just below her navel,
Lorcan rose to his feet. "My head tells me to leave this,
but other, more insistent parts of me say we've unfin-
ished business here, *Searc*."

The piercing blue of his eyes burned a pathway directly into her chest as he rose and, with a rueful smile,
went to open the door.

Chapter 8

"We need to speak to you." Lisbet, accompanied by a slightly embarrassed-looking Aydan, had her hands on her hips as Lorcan opened the bedroom door. She peered round him and, taking in the fact that Tanzi was in the room, stepped back again. "In private."

"No."

Lisbet's existing frown deepened farther. "What do you mean 'no'?"

"What I said." Lorcan held the door wide-open in invitation. "If you want to speak to me you can come in and do it here."

With a huffing sound, Lisbet pushed past him and into the room. There was a suspicion of reluctance about Aydan's manner as he followed. "We know who she is. I knew it as soon as that sidhe bent his knee to her," Lisbet announced without preamble, pointing at Tanzi.

"*She* is the person who saved all our lives today." Lorcan went to sit on the bed. He drew Tanzi down next to him, announcing his allegiance. He felt the rigidity in her slender frame and wished he could do something to reassure her.

Lisbet snorted. Her coal-dark eyes dropped to where Lorcan had lifted Tanzi's hand to rest on his denim-clad thigh. "Will you be so quick to fondle her when you know she's none other than the Crown Princess of the Faeries? Daughter of the war criminal Moncoya? Hell, if it comes to that, she's committed enough crimes of her own on his behalf."

"You are forgetting one simple rule by which we work here. We don't judge those who come to us."

Lisbet's eyes narrowed. "Can it be that you have known all along who she is?"

"I have."

"My God, Lorcan. I never thought you, of all people, would make a fool of yourself over a pretty face."

Aydan spoke up, his quiet voice somehow more powerful in the small room than Lisbet's shrill volume. "Maybe we should listen to what Lorcan has to say."

Shrugging dramatically, Lisbet threw herself down into the chair Tanzi had vacated. Her expression was not indicative of open-mindedness.

"Tanzi has come here for the same reason anyone comes to us. She is escaping persecution. Her background is irrelevant."

"If that's true, why have you taken such pains to keep her identity secret?" There was a flash of triumph in Lisbet's eyes.

"Because I knew how you would react and because, more than anything, we can't risk Moncoya finding out where she is." Lorcan kept his voice calm despite the fact that Lisbet was starting to annoy him. Diplomacy wasn't his strongest point, and he was experiencing an increasing desire to tell her to get the fuck out of his face. The problem was, he didn't know quite how much damage Lisbet could do to Tanzi if she remained this wound up. So he needed to try to dredge up some tact so that he could calm her down. He was shocked at the bitterness he could see twisting Lisbet's face and couldn't for the life of him guess at its cause. Okay, so she hated Moncoya. They all did. But she'd seen what Tanzi did today. There was no way that was the behavior of someone who wasn't committed to the resistance cause. So where was all this venom coming from?

"What if Daddy knows exactly where his darling daughter is? He's probably using her to yank all our chains. You said yourself we have a traitor in our midst."

"You think I controlled those zombies at the same time I was fighting them?" Tanzi spoke up for the first time. "Thanks for the compliment, but I'm not that talented."

"We don't know what you are. That's the problem." Lisbet's expression hardened further. "This is a honey trap for Lorcan, isn't it? That's Moncoya's strategy. Get him to fall for you and rip the whole resistance movement apart from within."

Tanzi rose to her feet. Even wrapped in an old blanket, with Lorcan's socks peeping out beneath, she managed to look regal. "I should go."

"This is your room." Lorcan rose to stand beside her. "You don't need to go anywhere."

"No, I mean go away. Leave."

"Best idea I've heard," Lisbet chimed in.

"You can shut up." Lorcan decided he'd had enough of diplomacy. Lisbet opened her mouth to speak again, took note of his expression and thought better of it. "And you are not going anywhere, *Searc*. It's not safe for you to leave here. Anyway—" he glanced around to make sure everyone was listening "—if Tanzi goes, I go with her."

With an outraged huffing noise, Lisbet bounced up from her seat and flung out of the room, slamming the door behind her.

"What the hell is wrong with her?" Lorcan stared at the door in bewilderment. "This can't all be about Tanzi. We've had high-ranking sidhes change allegiance before."

He was conscious of Tanzi scanning his face. "You really don't know, do you?"

"Know what?" She shook her head, and he turned to Aydan. "Has anyone checked on Iago since we got back?"

"He said he wanted to sleep."

"That was a few hours ago. I'll go down to his room and make sure he's okay."

"I'll come with you," Aydan offered.

"I'm going to see if Maria needs help in the kitchen." To the surprise of everyone in the house, Tanzi had become something of a favorite with the irascible housekeeper. It was an unlikely friendship, but one which worked.

Iago's bedroom was two floors down and, when they reached it, Lorcan knocked on the scarred wooden panels of the door. There was no response. He tried again, louder and longer this time.

"I think we're justified in going in, given how unwell he was at the zombie house." He turned the handle and was relieved to find the door unlocked.

The first thing that struck him as he stepped inside was the smell. It reminded him of his childhood, and at first he couldn't place why. Then he remembered. He used to sit outside the smithy and watch the blacksmith at work as he shoed the horses. It was a metallic smell, like heated iron. Except this was subtly different, earthier and rawer. The next thing his heightened senses perceived was that the room was empty.

Aydan flicked the light switch on and muttered an exclamation. The whole of one wall was filled with a giant pentagram—a five-pointed star within a circle—drawn in crude black brushstrokes. On the floor next to the bed lay a headless chicken and nearby, a copper bowl was filled with bright red, viscous liquid. That explained the smell. Fresh blood always had that metallic tang. Half-burned candles of black tallow had been placed on each side of the pentagram.

"I guess we know who was controlling the zombies." Aydan's voice was shaky. "Aren't these signs of necromancy?"

"Ancient ones. Most of us have evolved beyond these." Lorcan looked around the room. Tacked onto another wall were grainy photographs of each of the resistance members, with a particular focus on Tanzi. There were also pictures of Lorcan, Cal, Stella and Jethro. "We also know who our traitor is."

Lorcan took Tanzi back to the bustling university square and sat on the same steps where they had eaten pizza when she had first arrived in Barcelona. It had been only a few weeks, but it seemed so much longer. He judged they had enough time to risk being out in the open, away from the claustrophobia of the house and Lisbet's disapproving glances. There would be time enough for running and backward glances very soon.

Lorcan studied her face as they talked. She still took his breath away every time he looked at her, but he knew now it had nothing to do with faerie glamor or enchantment. It was intrinsic to her. She enraptured him with who she was, not with any external spell. And that meant he was in bigger trouble than he'd originally thought.

"How much danger am I in?"

There was no point sugarcoating it. "It's not looking good," Lorcan admitted. "I don't know where Moncoya found him, or how Cal and I have never come across him before now, but Iago must be enormously powerful to have pulled off that stunt today."

"So it was all an act? He wasn't really unconscious at all?"

"No. He needed to be close enough to the zombies to control them, but he could do it through the power of thought. As I said, I've never seen it done before. Impressive stuff." He wondered how many other new tricks Iago had tucked away and hoped he never needed to find out.

"And afterward? When he was still semiconscious and groggy? Was that also an act?"

"Who knows? Maybe he was still playing a part or possibly the mental exertion required to control that many zombies for so long really did sap his strength. We may never see Iago again, so we might never find out, but we know he's gone back to your father with some key information about all of us and—most important of all—about where he can find you."

"If my father takes me back to Otherworld, he will make sure I never get away again." Her eyes were so dark they appeared black.

"I think the time has come to tell me why that matters so much."

She drew a deep breath. "He has arranged a marriage for me."

Lorcan looked across the square at the crowds of students milling around. Their laughter and chatter jarred with the pain in Tanzi's eyes. "On the battlefield that day, you told me it was the way of your family to arrange a marriage for its princesses. You were resigned to your fate. What's changed?"

Her lips curled in an attempt at a smile. "I didn't know then whom my father had chosen for me."

"Old and warty?"

"Oh, how I wish that was so." She closed her eyes briefly. "My father has decided that mine is to be the honor of securing his return to his home and his former position of strength. More than that, through my marriage, I am to ensure he will become the undisputed and all-powerful ruler of Otherworld."

"And whom will you have to marry in order to achieve that?" Lorcan subjected the leaders of the Otherworld dynasties to a mental review. Some of them might have egos the size of Otherworld itself, but he couldn't think of one of them who would make the sort of claims Tanzi was describing. An insidious worm of discomfort was beginning to writhe in his stomach.

"If my father gets his way, I will become the bride of Satan, Lord of the Underworld." She said it so matter-of-factly that there was no room for doubt.

Even so, Lorcan recoiled in shock. "No, Tanzi, you must be wrong. Not even Moncoya would stoop to that."

"The devil wants a son. A child who will grow up and rule the mortal realm. Many centuries ago, in a different pact, Merlin Caledonius was to have been that child. My grandfather, Cal's father, was responsible for the agreement." Tanzi studied his face. "I see you have heard that story."

He nodded. "Cal is my friend. He confided in me that his powers were bequeathed to him by Satan and how, after his birth, his mother hid him away so that his father—who was also Moncoya's father, of course—could not find him and hand him over to the devil."

"That story put the idea for a new pact into my father's head. In return for absolute power over Otherworld, he offers the devil...me." She made a gesture, indicating her body. "Young, good-looking, capable of bearing him the child he wants."

"That fucking little..." Lorcan's hands tightened convulsively as though they held Moncoya's throat between them in a death grip. But there was no time for wallowing. "We have to get you away from here. Get you to safety." Even as he said the words, his mind was working overtime trying to think where to take her. Where in the mortal realm or Otherworld could he keep her safe from her own father's evil ambition?

"There isn't anywhere." It was as if she read his thoughts. "There is nowhere in either realm where he will not find me."

"There must be somewhere."

"I can think of only one place where he will not be able to touch me."

Lorcan frowned. "Sure, aren't you a step ahead of me? I've still got nothing."

Her expression was fathomless. "My mother was a Valkyrie, one of Odin's swan maidens."

Lorcan gazed at her in dawning wonder. "Are you suggesting what I think you are?"

"It is the only place my father would never dare enter." There was a touch of regret in her voice.

"So you are seriously proposing to travel to Valhalla, Odin's great palace and hall of the fallen heroes? Fiercely guarded portal to the rainbow bridge that leads to Asgard, home of the gods?" Tanzi nodded and he ran a hand through his hair in a gesture that was midway between frustration and disbelief. "And when you get to Valhalla, what then? You'll join the Valkyrie?"

Her smile was genuine this time. "I have all the necessary qualifications." She was right about that, too. The Valkyrie were known for three things...their great beauty, their skill in battle and their unwavering bravery.

She was going to give up any other life she had and lock herself away forever inside Odin's great hall. Like a medieval nun entering a convent. But with less prayer and more blood and guts. Lorcan decided to ignore the feeling in his chest. As though something had just snapped. It was irrelevant compared with what Tanzi must be feeling. Was he going to let her do this? Not without a fight. "Setting aside the fact that you can't just walk into Valhalla, do you know how difficult that journey is? You would have to cross some of the most dangerous territories in Otherworld. My God, you'd be eaten alive. Quite literally."

"Lorcan—" she turned so that she was fully facing him, her knees touching his "—believe me when I say I would prefer that to the alternative." She took his hand and held it against her cheek. The gesture spread the pain in his chest lower so that his abdomen tightened. "I appreciate what you are trying to do for me, but I have no choice. I have to face whatever dangers the journey brings me. Valhalla is the only place I can go."

It was the look in her eyes when she said she would rather be eaten alive than marry the devil that finally convinced him. No one should have to make that choice. He turned his head and dropped a light kiss onto her hand. "Well, at least you won't be facing them alone." Her brow wrinkled and her lips parted, ready to ask a question. "I'm coming with you."

"You don't have to do this."

"I really do."

* * *

When they returned to the house, it was mercifully quiet. Once in his room, Lorcan began to throw his belongings into his backpack. For someone who must do it regularly, he seemed to be particularly disorganized at packing.

Tanzi sat cross-legged on his bed, watching him. "Look, I dragged you into my problems because I didn't know where else to turn when I left the palace. That doesn't make you responsible for me."

He paused, looking directly at her. "You think I'm the sort of person who is going to abandon a friend just because things get tough?"

"Is that what we are? Friends?"

The word hung in the air between them. Then his smile, the one that made her want to clamber all over him like an overactive puppy, dawned. "I'd like to think so."

The moment—if it existed at all—was lost. And was that a bad thing? *Where exactly did you want this conversation to go as you set off on your journey to leave the world behind?* She tried a different approach. "You have commitments here."

"Not me. I never have commitments."

"Why is that?"

He shrugged. "Just the way I like it." He bent his head to fiddle with the zipper on his bag. The message was clear. It was another topic of conversation that wasn't going anywhere.

Tanzi ducked her head so that she could make eye contact with him. "Thank you." She wasn't sure what the wobble in her voice signified, but she did her best to disguise it by turning it into a cough. "So how do we do this? Valhalla can only be reached by boat. And all my belongings are in that—" she pointed to the bag he had retrieved from the imps "—which doesn't even contain an inflatable dinghy."

"I saw a map of the route to Asgard many years ago. It was fairly sketchy, and parts were uncharted, as it's not a way that's been taken very often. The truth is that the gods don't want anyone to know how to find them, so the exact geography is a closely guarded secret. And the route to Valhalla has been designed to withstand the onslaught of an army of giants. But that's a problem we'll deal with once we get there. Unless I'm mistaken, we're going to need something more substantial than a dinghy to navigate the Isles of the Aesir."

"The Aesir are gods, is that right?"

Lorcan nodded. "The Aesir are the gods of the sky and of consciousness and the Vanir are the gods of the earth and biological life. Odin is the patriarch of all the gods."

"Yet the Isles of the Aesir that lead to Valhalla are not inhabited by the gods themselves."

"No. The name comes from the fact that the islands are the approach to Asgard, not from their inhabitants. All that is really known about them is that they are notoriously difficult to navigate."

Tanzi swallowed the constriction in her throat. "Have you ever done any sailing?"

"A bit." His voice was cheerful. "A long time ago, when I was a lad, I used to lend a hand when the fishermen took their boats out." She wasn't entirely convinced they were the sort of credentials needed for the journey ahead of them. Grinning and hauling his backpack onto one shoulder, Lorcan held out a hand. "Ready?"

"Hold on a minute." Tanzi scrambled to her feet. Things seemed to be moving very fast. "Don't you have things to organize here?"

"Aydan will step up while I'm gone. They're well used

to me dropping in and out of this place. And we've not a minute to lose. Iago has been gone for a whole day. He could have reached Moncoya by now and yon bastard faerie feller—" He cast an apologetic grin her way. "Sorry, that's become my name for him. Your father will be plotting his next steps."

"So we go. Just like that." She shook her head. Reminding herself again that she had no choice, she picked up her bag. "Where will we start?"

"The place where all difficult journeys start… La Casa Oscura."

Tanzi ground to a halt again. "I can't go back there."

"I wasn't suggesting you stroll back in through the front door as though nothing had happened. You'll have to stay hidden. But we will have to get back to Otherworld to start our journey, and there's someone I need to talk to before we set off." He held the door open so that she could go through it before him. "I have to see a friend about getting us a boat."

Chapter 9

La Casa Oscura was an imposing mansion set high on the hillside above the city. Its rear aspect afforded spectacular views over the whole of Barcelona, but the other three sides were shrouded by trees. It was well-known as one of the most beautiful and quirky architectural features in the Catalan region. It was also the center of much recent press attention since its owner, billionaire electronics wizard Ezra Moncoya, had vanished without a trace a few months ago.

"I still don't understand why he wanted to be a celebrity in the mortal realm. Sure, wasn't being King of the Faeries enough for him?"

They had paused on the roadside a few hundred yards from the house. Half-hidden behind a laurel hedge, they could observe the entrance to the house without being seen. The afternoon sun was sinking behind the mountains and dusk was approaching, streaking the sky with

ribbons of violet and rose. One or two cars wound their
way slowly up the steep road, and Tanzi wondered what
the occupants would say if they knew the house they
had just passed was the portal to Otherworld. Enter its
doors and from there you could access the faerie king's
palace and the mystical realm that lay beyond. If you believed you could.

"I don't think anything would ever be enough for my
father. He will always want more than he has. To be more
than he is. And he wanted to find a way to attract the one
who would become the necromancer star. He had to don
a mortal disguise to do that."

"Luckily Stella saw through him. She fell in love with
Cal instead."

"My father will never forgive that." Tanzi felt obliged
to warn him.

"Hell hath no fury like a faerie scorned?" He saw her
wince at his use of the word *hell* and grimaced apologetically. "Sorry, I forgot. I think Cal and Stella know
Moncoya holds a grudge, but I don't picture them spending the rest of their lives looking over their shoulders."

"Is it Cal you need to talk to now?"

"Yes. I'm hoping the big feller will be able to help
out in the boat department. What's the point of having
Merlin as a friend if he can't conjure up a luxury yacht
when you need one?"

Tanzi looked across at La Casa Oscura. Only its terra-
cotta roof tiles were visible above the trees. A slight chill
sent a prickle of anticipation down her spine. "While you
confer with Cal, there is someone I must see."

"I've been thinking about that. It might be better if
we hide you away somewhere while I go inside. You'll
be recognized as soon as you enter the palace. I can get

everything ready for the journey and then we can enter Otherworld a different way."

Tanzi gave him a mischievous smile. "I won't be recognized if I'm in disguise."

Her smile was echoed in the blue velvet depths of his eyes. "Ah, yes. I was forgetting about your inner cat."

She cast him a sidelong glance. "I think you like my inner cat a little too much to completely forget her."

The smile reached his lips at that. "True. I've grown quite fond of her. Whom do you want to see?"

"My sister." She sighed, struggling slightly to find the words to explain the mystery that was her relationship with Vashti. "We have a strange connection. Often we are antagonistic, even combative—I have the scars to prove it—but she is the only person who understands me, and I her. She was badly injured in the battle. I want to make sure she continues to heal...and I want to warn her."

"Warn her?" Lorcan raised his brows.

"With me out of the way, my father may turn his ambitions for this pact with the devil to her."

"You mean he will force Vashti into marriage with the devil in your place?"

Tanzi's amusement was genuine. "No one forces Vashti to do anything. I would just like her to be prepared. She is very like my father."

Lorcan whistled. "So she's evil, too?"

"No!" Tanzi was shocked that he would think such a thing. Then she remembered that he had only ever seen Vashti's public face. The belligerent, swaggering, street-fighting facade she showed the world. "My sister is not a bad person. Impulsive and misguided, yes. Inflexible, arrogant, headstrong—" Tanzi broke off, realizing she was probably not doing a great job of convincing him of Vashti's good points. "She and my father are both so stubborn they will lock horns like a pair of mountain goats. And Vashti cannot waste time feuding with him. I need her to take my place on the council. She must be the faerie voice within the Alliance from now on."

"It matters to you, doesn't it? That the faeries get the representation they need."

She nodded. "I wish I could see that through. The least I can do is make sure there is someone I trust to take my place." Her throat tightened inexplicably. It must be the culmination of the day just gone. An overwhelming tiredness brought on by the physical exertion at the farmhouse and the lake, the discovery about Iago and the finality of her decision to join the Valkyrie. Lorcan's expression was sympathetic, and that somehow made the feeling worse. Hiding her confusion at the discomfort caused by the sensations, she became brisk, nodding toward the house. "How do we get in?"

"Well, we can't just march up to the front door. The one time I tried that, it got messy." His expression was reminiscent and, if they'd had time, she'd have asked him to tell her the story. "The house itself is a front. It's used by Moncoya Enterprises as its head office. Mortal employees come and go every day without knowing what it is, but it's also closely guarded. The cover story is that rival companies are always trying to steal Moncoya's secrets. And to be fair, that's true. Stella tells me the little shit's a genius when it comes to games design." He ran a hand through his hair, his expression rueful. "Ah, I'm so used to calling him names, I keep forgetting he's your father."

"Don't mind your tongue because of me. For what it's worth, I think he's a little shit, too."

He studied her expression thoughtfully. "And you have more reason than any of us. Okay, back to the breaking-

and-entering problem. We need to get to the rear of the house, to the terrace that overlooks the gardens. That's where the portal from this side into the palace is. And, in theory, it shouldn't be *too* difficult at this time of day because—" he glanced at his wristwatch "—at any minute now, those gates will open, the day shift will start leaving and the night shift will take over."

"Won't the employees have to show identification in order to get in?"

Reaching into his pocket, he gave her one of his impudent grins. "You mean like this?" Lorcan held up a white plastic card that bore his photograph alongside the Moncoya Enterprises logo. According to the heading on the card, his name was Rodrigo Martinez and he was a software engineer. "It's got me—or rather, it's got Rodrigo—in a few times. The thing that I was puzzling over was how we were going get you in, but you've solved the problem for me. As a cat, you can be over that wall or through the gate faster than I can say 'Here, kitty.'"

"It looks like the gates are opening." Tanzi pointed across at the great iron structure.

"No time to waste. See you on the terrace in five, my feline friend."

Entering Otherworld had never been a problem for Tanzi. *Because, until now, I have never really left it.* The only times she had ventured into the mortal realm in the past, she had been escorted there and back by her father's bodyguards and had given no thought to the transition between worlds. When she met Lorcan on the terrace at the rear of La Casa Oscura and looked out at the dusk-laden city of Barcelona, she thought, for the first time, of the legends surrounding entry into her homeland. Otherworld was hidden from mortal eyes by the strongest magic, woven by the gods in a time beyond memory. Mortal rules could not be applied to Otherworld. A year might go by there while at the same time in the real world centuries may have passed. Or the opposite might be true. Time could stand still in the place known to the ancient Celts as the "delightful plain." Those who dwelt in Otherworld did not age like mortals. Instead, they remained forever young.

Ancient scholars speculated about its location. Was Otherworld a vast underground palace? A series of enchanted, shimmering islands, visible only at dusk and dawn? Was it set in some distant planetary dimension beyond the stars? Was it underwater? Had Niniane, the sorceress known as the Lady of the Lake, created an illusion, disguising the entrance to Otherworld as an earthly lake? Did Otherworld move from one location to another according to the mood and whim of the gods?

The truth was simpler and yet more complex. Otherworld existed everywhere. It was right there, alongside the mortal realm, just out of sight but easily within reach. All that was needed was a knowledge of the location of the nearest portal, a belief in the existence of Otherworld and a desire to go there. The belief and desire had to be strong enough to overcome any doubts, fears or suspicion.

"Mortals don't have the ability to open their minds." That was what Rina had told Tanzi and Vashti many years ago. "That is why Otherworld remains closed to them."

"Ready, *Searc*?" Lorcan brought her back to the present by resting his hand lightly on her head as she sat on the terrace rail next to him. Unable to resist the temptation, she rubbed her face against his palm and he glanced down at her, his face registering surprise.

She hesitated for a moment. *What if I have become infected with mortal skepticism? I may never be able to go back.* It was time to find out. Closing her eyes, she conjured up an image of her home, so clear and sweet and sharp it stung the back of her eyelids. She needn't have worried. When she opened them, she was there. Barcelona had vanished. The sights, sounds and scents of the vast city had been replaced by tumbling turquoise waters crashing onto rocks far below her and cliffs rearing high above her head. She was home.

Tanzi had thought she could be content in the mortal realm. During her stay in the safe house—if anyone had asked her—she would have said that she would be able to stay there forever. Of course she would. Her warrior training meant she had been instructed in survival techniques. She could adjust to any environment, cope with any hardship. And because she was Moncoya's daughter—and she didn't do sensitivity—missing the palace where she had lived all her life, her awkward, irascible sister and the servants who had been like an extended family were beyond the scope of her feelings. Yet now, as she breathed the air of Otherworld again, she knew she had been fooling herself. She had missed this place without knowing. Longed for it without understanding the promptings of her own heart.

The sight of the elegant white marble palace set in jeweled gardens and flanked by soaring mountains made her heart quicken with something that, had she been capable of it, might have been called love. The crisp scent of pine, the sounds of distant waves and mournful gulls, these things were in her blood. She was a child of Otherworld. The thought brought with it a new sadness and a new awareness. *I must leave this place all over again. Forever. It's also about time I stopped fooling myself and accepted that I have failed my father in more ways than*

one. I have no immunity to emotion. It affects me just as
strongly as anyone else.

Lorcan, with that unique radar he had for the feelings
of others—*so different to me. He is attuned to others,*
while I don't even know myself—gave her a few minutes
alone to drink in the view. When they approached the
palace they did so together yet apart. Lorcan was in full
view while Tanzi slunk through the longer grass as she
had done so many times before in her cat guise. During
the battle, part of the palace had been damaged when the
Iberian sidhes planted a bomb in one of the four turrets.
There were signs that restoration work was now under
way. That and the presence of the peacekeeping force
led by the elves were the only indications of change. Everything else was exactly as it had been since she was a
child. *It will continue to look like this when I am gone.*
She didn't know whether to be comforted or alarmed by
the thought.

"Be careful, *Searc*." Lorcan's continued use of the
nickname had a soothing effect on her disordered senses.
"I'll meet you by the lake."

Tanzi knew from experience that the best way into the
castle in her cat form was through the grotto. Padding
across the grass to the side of the vast building, she made
her way stealthily along the wall until she reached the
place she was seeking. As a child this had always been
her favorite part of the palace. Moncoya's designers had
created a fantasy area, an artificial cave, with colored
lighting and a decorative waterfall. This could be entered from the gardens and Tanzi slid inside. The cave,
as she had anticipated, was empty. Counting on the fact
that the glass door leading from the grotto to the conservatory was usually open during the day, Tanzi made
her way through to the back of the grotto. Sure enough

the door was open and, pausing briefly to drink in the spectacular, uninterrupted views of the mountains from the full-length windows, she padded softly through the conservatory and beyond. She was in dangerous territory now, as the corridor leading to the east turret and Vashti's rooms was a busy thoroughfare used constantly by the servants.

After being forced to hide in the shadows on two occasions to avoid being seen, she managed to make her way up the wide, sweeping staircase and eventually found herself in the circular turret that housed Vashti's suite of rooms. Another pang of sadness swept through her, and she recognized it for what it was. Homesickness. The opposite wing on the west side of the palace was the one she had called her own.

Resolutely putting aside the thought, Tanzi cast a swift glance around. Reassured that there was no one else here, she cast off her shifter illusion, emerging in her true form to open the door to Vashti's chambers. Once inside, she paused, leaning against the door for a moment to catch her breath. The sitting room and bedroom were both empty. Beyond that was the bathroom, and her keen ears caught faint noise from that direction. Making her way into the bedroom, she smiled slightly as the sounds became clearer. The shower was running and Vashti's voice could be heard, lifted in song above the sound of the water. Tanzi tugged off her sneakers and climbed onto the vast, luxurious bed. With a soft sigh of satisfaction, she curled up among the cushions and awaited her sister. It seemed like seconds later that she was disturbed from slumber.

"Where the hell have you been?" The words, each one throbbing with suppressed fury, penetrated the fog of her consciousness.

Tanzi sat up abruptly, biting her lip. So much for being on high alert. "Fell asleep," she mumbled. As if it wasn't obvious.

"I can see that. My God, Tanzi, what are you *wearing*?" Clad in a pristine white robe, with her hands on her hips, Vashti was looking her up and down with an expression that was close to horror.

Fully awake now, Tanzi had time to take in every detail of her sister's appearance. Vashti's injuries during the battle had been severe and for the first few days there were real concerns that she might not live. She had sustained internal injuries as a result of a broken pelvis and fractured ribs. Tanzi had helped nurse her, and something in their volatile relationship had changed during that time. A different bond had been forged, even though neither of them had spoken of it.

"You look much better."

Vashti came and sat next to her on the bed. *The way we used to when we were little and Rina would read us a story.* Memories were determined to surface. "I am much better." She drew a deep breath. "Thank you."

Tanzi looked into the face that was so like—and yet so unlike—her own. Since the battle, Vashti had lost weight, so that the angles of her face were sharper. Her eyes, the same size and shape as Tanzi's, were lighter and icier, and the blond of her hair, which she wore cropped determinedly short, was a shade or two darker.

For a moment, a hug hung in the balance. It never materialized. They had never been a tactile family. *Perhaps if we'd had a different father things might have been easier between us.* Tanzi couldn't recall a single occasion upon which Moncoya had shown physical affection to either of his daughters. He could be lavish with purring praise when they followed his orders to maim or kill, but hugging had never been part of his parenting agenda.

"So where *have* you been?"

"Living in a resistance safe house in the mortal realm," Tanzi stated matter-of-factly, in answer to Vashti's question.

Her sister blinked once. "Was it nice?"

The unexpected question struck Tanzi as humorous and she began to laugh so hard that she found herself unable to stop. After regarding her in bewilderment for a moment or two, Vashti started to giggle as well, and before long they were both engulfed in helpless gales of laughter. It was sometime later before they were able to resume their conversation.

"So was it a bet? A dare? Some sort of bizarre self-punishment?" Vashti asked when they had finally recovered from their mild bout of mutual hysteria.

Her words had the effect of chasing away any final trace of frivolity from Tanzi's response. "Have you heard from our father since I left?"

"He managed to smuggle a few messages to me. That reminds me, he is very keen for you to get in touch with him. He wasn't convinced that I didn't know where you'd gone."

"Did he say why he wanted to see me?"

"No, but I'm not stupid. Even if I hadn't worked out that your disappearance was linked to him, the look on your face right now has convinced me of it. You may as well just tell me what's going on."

So, in a few short, blunt sentences, Tanzi did just that. "So if our dear father gets his way, you could be aunt to Satan's child."

Vashti's short, straight nose wrinkled. "He has always had the most grandiose schemes where we are concerned, but that one is unhinged. Even for our father. Mind you—" she cast a sidelong glance at Tanzi from under her sweeping lashes "—I wonder what sort of a lover the devil would be. Fast and fiery, I imagine. What do you think?"

Vashti delighted in making risqué comments, but Tanzi knew the truth. They were both equally inexperienced. Neither of them had ever dared consider defying their father regarding the question of their purity. She shrugged in response to Vashti's question. "You can find out if you really want to. I'm sure our father would accept you as a substitute. It's what I came to warn you about."

Vashti leaned back on the pillows, linking her hands behind her head. "I'll pass. I've no wish to get involved in a love triangle with you and the horny horned one." She held up a hand in a pacifying gesture at Tanzi's angry expression. "Okay, it wasn't funny. So you ran away to live in the mortal world. Why have you come back again?"

"Because our father will have learned of my hiding place by now." She took a deep breath. "I am going to Valhalla to join the Valkyrie."

"That's pretty final."

"So is relocating to hell."

Vashti gave this some thought. "True. Do you think *she* will be there?"

Tanzi interpreted the question to be about their mother. "Will I even know her if she is? She left us when we were babies, remember. Besides, we don't know for sure that she returned to Valhalla once she walked out on our father."

"The journey to Valhalla will be fraught with danger. You really shouldn't attempt it on your own."

Tanzi bent her head to fiddle with a frayed thread on the worn pair of jeans she was wearing. She hoped the curtain of her hair hid the blush that tinged her cheeks. "Can I get a shower?"

Vashti sat up with an enthusiastic bounce. "Hold on a minute. You *won't* be alone, will you?"

"What makes you think that?"

"We're twins, remember? Plus, your voice is doing that husky, embarrassed thing it always does when you try to hide something from me. Who is he?"

Tanzi sighed. "Lorcan Malone."

"The necromancer?" Squirming slightly, Tanzi nodded. "The Irish one?"

"Yes." She risked a glance at her sister's face. Vashti was grinning like a cat about to torture a mouse.

"The *hot* Irish necromancer?"

Tanzi squirmed some more, if that was possible. "That's enough. You've had your fun."

"I haven't even started yet."

Tanzi rose from the bed. "I don't have long. Shower first, then you can get me some food and interrogate me while I eat. Deal?"

Vashti nodded. "Even better. I'll burn those clothes and lend you some of mine."

Despite their upbringing, Tanzi did hug her sister then.

Chapter 10

Lorcan found Stella in the formal gardens at the rear of the palace. She was seated on a carved wooden bench, with her legs tucked beneath her. She wore headphones and was humming along with a song he didn't recognize while her fingers flew back and forth over the keys of her laptop. He paused a few feet away, watching her with a smile for a moment. Tiptoeing over up behind her, he removed her headphones.

"I'm not even going to ask how you've managed to get Wi-Fi here."

Stella started in surprise, swinging around to face him. Realizing who it was, she gave a squeal of delight before putting the laptop aside and leaping up from her seat to hug him. "I could explain it, if you want." When he gave her a baffled look, she continued. "The Wi-Fi thing, it's quite easy once you know how."

"I'm happy to let it remain a mystery known only to

you computer geeks." Lorcan held her at arm's length, smiling down at her. "Ah, but you're looking wonderful, me darlin' girl. Marriage obviously agrees with you."

Cal's voice interrupted them. "Is this what happens every time I'm gone for more than two minutes? You start cuddling good-for-nothing Irishmen?"

Lorcan turned to face the man who had been his friend for as long as he could remember. The man who had rescued him from the witch finder's flames and then gone on to save his life more times than he cared to count. The man whose name conjured up a thousand legends. Merlin Caledonius. Known the world over and throughout the mists of time as Merlin…a name the great man himself had always hated. He was Cal to his friends. Tall, muscular and strikingly handsome. Clad in torn and faded jeans and a black vest, the Cal of reality was as far from the white-haired, long-robed, bearded wizard of folklore as anyone could be.

"Where the fuck have you been, Malone?" A frown descended on Cal's brow as he covered the distance between them.

"Cal!" Stella's tone was shocked as she swung around toward her husband.

"Sure, isn't that his standard greeting for me?" Lorcan laughed. "It was what he said when I turned up a few minutes late when that whole sword-in-the-stone challenge was going on. Then he said it again the time King Arthur was in danger because Morgan le Fay and Mordred had arrived at Camelot and I wasn't there to help. And I clearly remember the same words being used on one occasion when he wanted my support with driving a rogue genie out of Palmyra. Sometimes he varies it and uses 'What the bloody hell kept you?'"

"It's a wonder I'm ever able to get a word in to say

anything." Cal rolled his eyes at Stella. "You know how there's a legend that the Irish kiss the Blarney Stone to give them the gift of eloquence? There's a postscript. It reads 'Lorcan Malone needn't bother.'"

"Ouch." Lorcan clasped a hand over his heart in mock hurt. "At least I've not been using a piece of flint to sharpen my tongue."

"If you two have finished insulting each other, can we go inside and get a drink like civilized people do?" Stella pleaded, linking an arm with each of them. "And then you can tell us why you're here, Lorcan."

"I'm glad you *are* here at last. There's something I need your help with." Cal spoke to Lorcan over Stella's head as they walked into the palace. "Something that makes Excalibur, the Djinn, even Morgan and Mordred look like a kid's play fight."

Lorcan was saved the immediate dilemma of answering as Stella added shyly, "And we want you here in five months for a very important job." She slid a protective hand over her stomach. "Our baby will need a sponsor."

"Ah, isn't that the grandest news ever?" Lorcan gave Stella another hug and shook Cal's hand. "You can count on me, big feller."

"I know it." The look in Cal's eyes conveyed much more than the words. Despite his gruff greeting, Lorcan knew that Cal had never once doubted his loyalty. They had been through too much together for it to be in question. *Shit. And now, just when he says he needs me more than ever, I'll have to tell him I can't stick around.*

Moncoya had designed the palace for elegance and aesthetic impact rather than comfort, but Stella had commandeered one of the smaller rooms on the ground floor and made it into a private sitting room for her and Cal. Collecting furnishings from around the palace that she liked and had selected for relaxation rather than grandeur, she had created a cozy haven where they could retreat when the demands of coordinating the new peacekeeping council became too great. While Stella went away to organize refreshments, Cal brought Lorcan up to date with the latest news about the Alliance. It was obvious that Cal still viewed his status as the head of the Alliance of Otherworld dynasties as temporary, even though the other leaders were calling for it to become a permanent presidency. It was also apparent that it was a troublesome and taxing role.

"It's like living in a hotel where the other guests all have their own agenda and think nothing of knocking on our door at three in the morning to lobby us with their latest idea," Cal was saying when Stella returned, carrying a tray of coffee, sandwiches and cake. "This palace has become the political hub of Otherworld, and that's a good thing because it brings all the leaders together in one place and keeps them talking. But it sure as hell is not how I want to spend the rest of my life. Besides, it was never in the prophecy that *I* would be the one to lead Otherworld."

"Remind me of the exact wording of the prophecy again." Lorcan accepted a mug of coffee from Stella with a grateful smile.

"When the three-tailed comet returns to Iberia's skies and the brightest star has seen five and twenty harvests, then he who claims the heart of the necromancer star will unite the delightful plain." Cal was word perfect. He should be. After all, it was his prophecy. He was the one who had foreseen what would happen.

"Okay, so that was what you predicted…when was it? A thousand years ago?"

"Longer. Probably about fifteen hundred years. But

you know I never see the detail of my prophecies. I only get a general feel for what will happen." Cal's voice was frustrated.

"Yet, in all that time, you've never been wrong. And, vague or not, I know how important the wording is. Ever since you made that prediction, the world—including every ambitious, bloodthirsty leader in Otherworld—was on the lookout for the necromancer star so that they could claim his or her heart and, with it, Otherworld itself." He grinned at Stella. "Yet you, me darlin' girl—the necromancer star of the prophecy, the one we were all waiting for—chose *him*."

"I know." She shook her head teasingly at Cal. "What was I thinking? I had my choice of them all. Moncoya, Prince Tibor, Nevan the Wolf—" She broke off laughing as Cal pulled her down onto the sofa. She curled up next to him, content to listen to the conversation between the two men.

Lorcan continued. "You are the one who has won Stella's heart, Cal. You fulfilled your own prophecy. End of story."

Cal was adamant. "The words of the prophecy are clear. My job is to unite Otherworld, *not* to rule it."

"Sure, isn't that just down to a minor interpretation of meaning? You can do both. The other leaders want it. There's no one who could do a better job of it."

"No. I've discussed it with the angel of the Dominion—"

Lorcan interrupted with an expression of distaste. "You had to go and spoil my day by bringing angels into the conversation."

"Hear me out. He agrees with me. Moncoya is still a danger. Although the battle eliminated him as an immediate threat, it allowed him to escape and remain as King of the Faeries. He is a king in exile. Perhaps even more dangerous now that he is hidden from view."

"You're no closer to discovering where he is?" Lorcan didn't really hold out much hope. If Moncoya had been captured, it would have been big news across Otherworld and reached the ears of the resistance in the mortal realm. Nevertheless, it was worth clinging to a thread of optimism. With Moncoya behind bars, Tanzi would be safe. The journey to Valhalla would not be needed. She would have a future. One over which she had control... Determinedly, he forced his mind back onto what Cal was saying.

"Wherever he is, his followers have him well guarded and well hidden. He knows many of the sidhes remain loyal to him. They have known nothing but his rule for centuries, and Moncoya is good at propaganda. The faeries are frightened. They don't know what the future holds. You've heard about the recent terrorist attacks?"

"A little, but I don't know all the details. I take it those responsible are Moncoya loyalists?"

Cal nodded, his face grim. "He's been winding them up, playing on their fears. How will they feel if Prince Tibor, the vampire ruler, becomes King of Otherworld? Worse still, what if the faeries must swear allegiance to the wolves? That could happen, he says, if his people have no strong leader. If they give up their rights. He has made the Alliance the target of his venom, pouring scorn on our efforts to bring the dynasties together. It is a sham, a guise behind which I am plotting to strip the faeries of any power and hand them over to their enemies."

"Every time I think that evil little bastard can't get any worse, he pulls another stunt to prove he can." Lorcan shook his head. "Does he give any clues about your supposed motives?"

Cal laughed. "Of course he does. It's all a personal attack on him. I hate him because he's my handsome, successful, *legitimate* brother."

Lorcan nearly choked on the sandwich he was eating. "You can't let him get away with this."

"I don't intend to. But in order to stop him, there is someone I must find. Someone I have never met, know nothing about and have no idea how to track down. That's where I need your help."

"I get all the easy jobs," Lorcan said in a long-suffering voice. "Who is this mysterious person?"

"The rightful King of the Faeries."

"I've been thinking about what I can do to help you." Vashti was dragging items of clothing out of her wardrobe and either discarding them or folding them into a large gym bag.

"You've done everything I needed you to. You've let me use your shower, fed me and—" Tanzi pointed to the gym bag "—lent or—since I've no way of getting them back to you—*given* me some of your clothes."

"I might be able to do even more. While you were gone, I did some serious thinking. You can't move around much with a healing pelvis. Reading and pondering are among the few activities available. Do you remember when we were children and Rina would talk to us of the unique connection between faerie twins? She said we should have the most powerful telepathic bond two beings would ever feel."

"We were a disappointment to her." Tanzi shook her head in mock sadness. "We never felt it."

"That was because we didn't really try," Vashti reminded her. "We were always too busy competing with each other to work together. What if we have the bond and have just never used it?"

"You mean we suppressed it because we've always believed we didn't really like each other?"

Vashti grinned. "Something like that."

"How would we know? I wouldn't have a clue where to begin."

"I did a bit more than just think about it," Vashti confessed. "I asked Rina."

"You've seen Rina?" Tanzi sat up straighter. "When did that happen? And where?"

"She came to visit me when she heard I had been hurt."

Tanzi thought of the woman who had brought them up. The only person to show them any care or affection throughout their formative years. It was to Rina they would go when they were injured or troubled. Rina would answer their many questions about what life should be like as a faerie princess. Moncoya had sent her away when they were twelve because he suspected his daughters might be too close to their nurse. Her throat tightened painfully at the memory. The sensation prompted her to ask Vashti a question.

"Have you ever thought that our father was wrong when he told us we were above experiencing emotion?"

Vashti regarded her in surprise. "What do you mean?"

"Lately I have begun to suspect that I can feel. More than that… I *do* feel. It is just that for so long I was conditioned to believe that fervor, passion—call it what you will—were beneath me. Our lives here in the palace did not expose us to situations where we encountered strong feelings. Or perhaps our father taught us so well that our instinct has always been to crush our emotions at the first sign. But what if we can feel love, hate, despair, joy and sadness in the same manner and depth as everyone else?"

"It would not be the royal way." Although Vashti held her head high, for the first time in her life, Tanzi saw a glimmer of doubt in her sister's face.

"What if the royal way—or rather, our father's way—is not the right way, after all? We have been the fairy-tale princesses in the tower. Shut away from the world until our prince comes to claim us. Only it wasn't a fairy tale. It was part of a bigger plan. We were being conditioned to accept our prince no matter who he was. I was supposed to go through with marriage to Satan without protest. If I really was above feeling emotion, perhaps I could have done that." She watched Vashti's face carefully as she made her next suggestion. "If our father comes to you now with the same proposition, will you be the dutiful daughter and marry the devil?"

"No!" The word was filled with revulsion.

Tanzi allowed herself a brief, triumphant smile. She was right. Now she just had to learn to control all these newly discovered emotions. Particularly when she was around a certain Irishman. She steered the conversation back to the subject Vashti had raised. "Maybe that is why we didn't feel the bond. We thought we couldn't *feel* anything. Tell me what Rina said."

"She reminded me of what she told us when we were children. That twins of all species share a special bond that manifests itself in shared thoughts. An example is when one twin is in danger, the other will feel it. With faeries, the connection should be even stronger."

"Why?" Tanzi wished Rina was here to explain it in her unique, storytelling way.

"She said it goes back to the ancient times when the distinction between faeries and witches was less clear. Both had the same power to bless and curse. Mortals once believed that a witch was the child of a mortal woman who had spent seven years in Otherworld with a faerie lover learning the art of love and magic. If the woman bore twins, the babies must be returned to the faeries because their telepathy would be too strong for the mortals to behold. Since then, all faerie twins have been bequeathed the same power." Vashti finished her perusal of her wardrobe as she was talking and closed the zipper on the gym bag. "According to Rina, you and I should not only have a psychic bond, we should be able to hold a telepathic conversation no matter how far apart we may be."

"Our mother was not a faerie, we are only half sidhe. Perhaps that explains our lack of ability." Tanzi groped around, trying to find an explanation for why they had failed to do what should come naturally.

"I thought of that. It turns out we have been wrong all these years. Our mother *was* a faerie. Like us, she was a sidhe who trained with the Valkyrie. She even fought with them as you intend to do, but she was not one of Odin's daughters. Rina told me that. Our faerie blood is pure, Tanzi. Which means the bond must be there. Don't you see what this means? If we can find it and use it, you can send me a message whenever you need me. No matter where you are, I will get help to you."

Tanzi felt tears prickle the back of her eyelids and, to her surprise, saw a shimmering reflection of them in Vashti's eyes. All those wasted years. Years barren of feelings for a sister who was close by and yet so far away. "Then all we need to do is find how to use it. I don't suppose Rina told you that?"

Vashti smiled, blinking away her own tears. "As a matter of fact, she did."

Lorcan glanced at the darkening landscape beyond the windows and hoped that Tanzi wasn't already waiting for him down at the lake. He hadn't anticipated his conversation with Cal would take this long. *What did you expect to say to the friend you haven't seen since you were both embroiled in a cataclysmic battle? Nice to see you again and, by the way, is there any chance you could lend me a boat?*

"So how are things with the resistance?" Stella had gone to deal with an issue over a contingent of Fauns who were unhappy with their room allocation. Since Cal hadn't yet told Lorcan how he planned to find the true King of the Faeries, the man who could challenge Moncoya for his crown, the abrupt change of subject caught him off guard.

"Not good." Omitting any information about Tanzi for the time being, Lorcan filled him in on recent events. "Have you heard of a necromancer named Iago?"

Cal frowned. "No. And yet…" He shook his head as though to clear it. "There *is* something vaguely familiar about that name. Sorry. I can't think what it is. Maybe it will come to me. In the meantime, you can tell me what's bothering you."

"Ah, now, what makes you think there's anything bothering me?"

"Don't try to bullshit me, Lorcan. I know you too well."

Lorcan held up a hand in a gesture acknowledging defeat. "Okay, you're right. And I thought I was meant to be the perceptive one. What's bothering me is I feel like a failure. I came back to tell you I have to go on journey, and here you are telling me my help is needed right here."

Cal folded his arms across his chest, stretching his long legs in front of him. "How about you tell me the details of this journey and why you have to go on it before we decide if you're a failure or not?"

"It concerns Moncoya." Lorcan risked a glance at Cal's

face. It remained impassive. "And the reason why Tanzi disappeared." Still nothing. "He was trying to force her into a marriage with the devil."

Lorcan had heard Cal swear countless times before but never for so long or so fluently as he did then. When he'd finished using every possible curse he could think of to describe Moncoya, Cal drew a breath. "He wants to replicate the plan our father had for me, doesn't he? To give Satan a child that he can raise to become ruler of the mortal realm."

"That seems to be a pretty good summary."

"Why didn't Tanzi come to me? She must have known I'd help her." Cal was so angry he rose from his seat and began pacing the room.

"She probably didn't know whom she could trust. And I don't suppose you think straight when you get told to start planning your wedding to the devil. At least she escaped. For once in her life, she didn't obey Moncoya's orders and rush out to buy herself a black dress and a wreath of lilies."

Cal's eyes narrowed. "No, she came to you. Why was that?"

Trust Cal not to miss anything. Lorcan kept his voice casual. "I helped her when she got hurt during the battle. She remembered and thought I might do the same thing again."

"Where is she now?"

"You're going to use up your twenty questions pretty fast at this rate." His attempt at humor failed miserably, and the frown darkened Cal's silver eyes to thundercloud gray. "She's here. Saying goodbye to Vashti. But we're leaving as soon as we can. That's the journey I mentioned. She wants to go to Valhalla and I said I'd take her."

"Have you lost your mind?"

"Probably." Lorcan waved a hand at the seat Cal had just vacated. "Look, it's tiring me out watching you pace." After a pause during which the outcome was in doubt, Cal flung himself back down onto the sofa. "Don't imagine I've given this no thought. Ever since Tanzi suggested the idea, I've tried to come up with an alternative. But think about it, Cal. Until Moncoya is captured, nowhere is safe for her. And let's be realistic. Moncoya is such a slippery little snake he may never be captured. What you've told me today about his influence over the sidhes has only reinforced the danger Tanzi is in."

"But Valhalla? You are proposing to traverse the Isles of the Aesir? Do you know how many times that's been done?"

"Not many, I imagine." Lorcan's grin was rueful.

"And all to help a girl you hardly know?"

"Ah, come on, now. Are you telling me you wouldn't do the same? Have you forgotten the time the trolls were terrorizing Old Kettleby?"

Cal looked slightly embarrassed. "That was different."

"Was it, now? We were supposed to be in Breton, but, if I remember rightly, we stayed and dealt with the troll problem because a girl *you hardly knew* begged you to help."

Cal's sigh came from the heart. "Okay. I can't believe I'm saying this, but how can I help?"

"A boat and a map would be a good start." Ignoring his friend's disbelieving laughter, Lorcan asked the question that had been intriguing him. "Who is the true King of the Faeries?"

"A descendant of King Ivo, the just and benevolent sovereign who ruled before Moncoya. The heir we are seeking was a baby when Moncoya had the king and all of his family slaughtered. There has always been a rumor that he was smuggled out of the palace during the massacre. The angel of the Dominion confirmed it is true. The problem is, his identity has been so well concealed that he himself is unaware he is actually the king."

"How were you proposing I should help you find him?"

"Funnily enough, I was going to ask you to go on a journey." In answer to Lorcan's raised brows, Cal elaborated. "I can't leave here and go around asking questions. You, on the other hand are known to be a wanderer. No one will think twice if you turn up in different places and, at the same time, try to discover where this long-lost descendant of King Ivo may be. In fact—" Cal's face became thoughtful "—perhaps the journey you are going on could have a dual purpose? You could escort Tanzi to Valhalla and also find out what you can about the true King of the Faeries on your way there and back."

Lorcan felt his jaw muscles clench. "I will not work for the Dominion."

"In all the years we have known each other, I have never asked you to explain the reason why you hate the angels."

Lorcan hunched a shoulder, turning his face away from the man who throughout the centuries had been his only true friend. "Does it matter?"

There was sympathy in Cal's voice as he responded. "I think it must matter a great deal to you if it brings you such pain that you cannot speak of it even to me."

Lorcan let go of the breath he had been holding. There was no hiding anything from Cal. "Let's just say the Dominion let me down when I needed them."

He felt Cal's eyes probing his profile. "If you won't do this for them, will you do it for me?"

"Ah, fight fair, Cal. You know I'd do anything for you."

"In return, you know I wouldn't ask if it wasn't important." Cal waited and, after a long moment of hesitation, Lorcan nodded. "Thank you. It's the longest of long shots, but you may just discover something that will help."

"Why does it matter so much? If so many of the faeries are loyal to Moncoya, will this challenger be able to sway them against him?"

"One of the first principles of the Alliance is democracy. Each dynasty is to be given a vote to choose its own leader." Cal's voice was somber.

Lorcan caught on fast. "And if the faeries vote for Moncoya, that's the end of the Alliance?"

"None of the other leaders will sit at a table that includes the man who has for centuries tried to systematically destroy them by invading their territories. I have to find this challenger and at least offer the faeries an alternative to Moncoya. King Ivo was loved and is still remembered."

Lorcan nodded. "No promises, but I'll try." Even as he said the words, his thoughts went to Tanzi. What would she make of this new turn of events?

Cal's unusual light silver eyes scanned Lorcan's face again, as if reading his thoughts. "Take care on this mission, my friend. Princess Tanzi is not just any girl."

The somber mood dispersed with Lorcan's laughter. "Don't I already know it?"

Chapter 11

"The oak tree is the guardian of both worlds. Rina told me that in ancient times, mortals believed its roots anchored it in the mortal realm while its branches reached into Otherworld. That gave it a unique role, spanning both psychic vision and soulful thought."

They were standing in the garden at the rear of the palace. Darkness was looming and the first silence of night was descending. Inside the palace everyone was preparing for dinner, and Vashti had assured her that they would be the only ones around.

Tanzi regarded the huge tree thoughtfully, then turned to her sister with a shrug of her shoulders. "I'm getting nothing. You?"

"Have a little patience." Vashti spoke to her in the tones of a parent chiding a disobedient toddler. Reaching up to the lower branches, she pulled two acorns from the tree and held her palm up so that Tanzi could see them by the light of the flashlight she carried.

"The acorn is a psychic talisman. Rina said if we exchange acorns, it will help to strengthen our bond."

"The bond we don't have, you mean?" Tanzi asked gloomily.

"Look, I'm not the one heading off into uncharted waters with a man I barely know so that I can join the Valkyrie and spend the rest of my life lurching from one bloody battle to the next. Now, do you want to do this or not?"

"Sorry. Let's do it." She took an acorn from her sister's hand and closed her fingers around it. Was it her imagination or did she feel something? The faintest tingle, a slight heat against her skin? "What now?"

"Now we swap acorns." Vashti's voice was solemn.

"Don't we have to say anything? Isn't there an incantation that goes with it—?"

"I love you, Tanzi." Hearing those words from her sister for the first time shocked her into silence.

"Oh." She opened her palm. Vashti took the acorn from it and replaced it with her own. "I love you, too."

"Say it again, but not out loud this time."

They faced each other in the sweet, pine-scented darkness of an Otherworld nightfall, each clutching the other's acorn in her hand. Tanzi closed her eyes and felt it immediately. It was a surge of emotion so powerful, so all consuming, it almost knocked her off her feet.

The acorn isn't a magic charm. Our love for each other is the talisman. That was what we were missing all those years ago.

The thought was answered instantly by Vashti's voice inside her mind. *We always had it, we just never knew it was there.*

Tanzi opened her eyes and smiled. *You think we can do this no matter how far apart we are?*

I think we can do anything.

"I'm glad you said that," Tanzi spoke aloud again. "Because there is something else I need you to do for me."

"I've already said I'm not going to marry the devil in your place."

"Just keep repeating those words each time our father asks and you'll be fine. No, this task is easier...but not much. You must take my place as the faerie representative on the Alliance."

Vashti shook her head decisively. "I wouldn't know what to do. And I will not betray our father by being part of an organization that seeks to destroy him."

Tanzi tried to recall a time in the past when she had managed to convince her sister to change her mind. It must have happened at least once, surely? No, she couldn't remember a single occasion when she had succeeded in getting Vashti to consider a different point of view. Vashti was as stubborn as their father. One thing was for sure, arguing with her was time-consuming, and time was something Tanzi didn't have. She wondered if Lorcan might, even now, be down at the lakeside wondering what the hell was keeping her. "Very well, I will ask Cal to find someone else."

"Who?"

"Does it matter? I *can't* do it, you *won't* do it. The faeries must be represented. I'm sure Cal will choose someone suitable." She picked up the gym bag. "I have to go."

"Wait a minute. When did *suitable* become good enough for our people? When did Merlin Caledonius become the right person to make faerie decisions?"

Tanzi paused. This was the moment at which she would normally wade in with an angry riposte about her sister's contrariness, the conversation would deteriorate into an argument and one of them—usually Vashti—

would storm off. A few days of sulky silence would generally ensue. Some newfound perception, aligned perhaps to her recent discovery about her ability to experience emotion, made Tanzi decide to try a new approach. "You're right."

"What?" Vashti regarded her with suspicion.

"Cal is only half faerie. So is Stella. What do they know? Whom do *you* think should do it?"

"How am I supposed to know?" The yellow glow from the flashlight made Vashti's expression appear belligerent. Scratch that. Made it appear more belligerent than usual.

"How about General Thomasin? He is well respected."

Vashti snorted. "That old toad? He would roll over and show his belly at the first sight of a wolf."

Tanzi bit the inside of her lip to hide a smile and searched around for another, equally unsuitable name. "Lord Cornelius?"

"Have you taken leave of your senses? It's well-known he's been in league with Prince Tibor for years. We'd be ruled by the vampires the day after tomorrow." Vashti heaved a sigh of resignation. "Very well, if those are our only choices, I will have to be the one to do it."

"Your sacrifice for our people does you great credit." Tanzi hoped the note of amusement in her voice wasn't obvious. "Now I really must go down to the lake to meet Lorcan."

"Did you just manipulate me?"

"I don't think so. I'm not sure I would know how. Do you feel manipulated?"

"All I know is I just agreed to something I didn't want to do and I'm not sure how it happened." Vashti fell into step next to her. "Has your necromancer friend been teaching you the skill of finagling while you've been in the mortal realm? Or is it something you've acquired through your familiarity with the earth-born?"

"If I have, I was unaware of it. But—who knows?— maybe the ability to get people to do what I want might come in handy on the journey ahead."

A shiver of anticipation ran through her. Getting Lorcan to do what she wanted was a very interesting proposition, particularly as they were going to be alone together for some time to come. The searing heat between them just before Lisbet and Aydan had interrupted them burned its way into her memory. Every fiber of her being was crying out to explore it further. Whom was she kidding? She didn't just want to explore it…she wanted to increase that heat to molten-lava intensity, let it scorch her to the point of spontaneous combustion, quench it and then repeat the cycle. Over and over. Would she give in to that impulse or spend her time fighting it? Either way, this was going to be an interesting journey. She choked back a laugh, so that it came out as a sound somewhere between a cough and a gasp.

"Are you okay?" Vashti regarded her in surprise.

"You know what? I really am."

"Necromancer!"

At the sound of the woman's voice, Lorcan turned away from the ornate lake. A figure approached him out of the darkness. Whoever it was held a flashlight in front of her face, and he was momentarily blinded by its light. An object was thrust at his chest and he grasped it instinctively. It was a large bag.

"Take care of her or I will hunt you down and make you pay." Although the voice was gruff, he recognized it as Vashti's.

"She insisted on coming with me so she could say that

to you." Tanzi spoke from the gloom somewhere behind Vashti. "Have you met my sister?"

"We've not been formally introduced. The last time I saw her this close, she had Cal pinned to the floor with a sword pressed between his shoulder blades."

"And if my father had allowed me to kill him then, how different things would be now."

Lorcan laughed. "Has anyone ever told you you're the living image of your father? Even if you'd succeeded in killing Cal before the battle—and the fact that you didn't had nothing to do with Moncoya and everything to do with the great man himself—I expect the deal with the devil would still have been struck, don't you?"

Vashti turned to Tanzi. "You know all those women who say that Lorcan Malone is a charmer?" She turned the flashlight on Lorcan again. "Misguided fools."

"Well, nice as it's been meeting you and spending time chatting like this, we'd better get going." Lorcan moved to Tanzi's side. "All of a sudden, I can see why you chose Valhalla."

Vashti ignored him. "Keep my talisman with you at all times and I will keep yours. Remember what to do if you should need me." She gave Tanzi a quick, awkward hug, handed her the flashlight and disappeared into the darkness.

Tanzi had obviously decided there was no need to shift into her cat form since the all-consuming cloak of an Otherworld night was doing its own job of concealing her identity. There were no streetlights or passersby here. When she spoke again now that they were alone, her voice was strangely quiet and shy. Almost as if they had become strangers again. "Did Cal manage to get us a boat?"

"Never doubt the big feller. He said there'll be a boat

waiting for us down in the cove. It'll be newly fitted out, have the provisions we need for the journey on board and there'll be the most up-to-date maps and charts for the journey we're to take." He hoisted his backpack farther onto his shoulder and lifted her bag. "Shall we go?"

Holding the flashlight in front of her, Tanzi walked alongside him. "How can he do something like that on such short notice?"

"He's Merlin. The impossible is what he does best."

"Will he also have left detailed instructions on how to sail this boat?"

Lorcan laughed. "Luckily we won't need them. Never doubt me either. I told you, I used to go out with the men on the fishing boats when I was a lad. And, over the years, Cal and I have had one or two adventures that have taken us onto the high seas. I might be a bit rusty, but I can handle a boat."

"How long have you known Cal?" The probing way she asked the question was the giveaway. She was on to him. And he'd always believed he was good at keeping secrets.

"Most of my life." Perhaps if he kept the response deliberately vague she'd leave it alone.

No such luck. "How many years is that?"

They came to the edge of the cliff and Lorcan paused, allowing the breeze to cool his face. Why did it matter? After all this time, why was he still guarding his privacy? And from whom? He'd called Tanzi his friend. In return she'd placed her absolute trust in him. Surely he could give a tiny bit of himself in return?

"A lot," he said at last. Aware of her eyes on his face in the darkness, he raised his hand. Instantly, a glow, brighter than that of the flashlight, illuminated the scene around them. "I gave up counting after the first few centuries."

"I don't understand. I thought all necromancers were mortal." Her eyes were twin pools of midnight blue, the ring of fire barely visible.

"Sure, a pure-blood necromancer is born mortal. But we're a rare bunch and we don't like to share too much of our history. What most people don't know is that there are also hybrid necromancers. Cal and Stella are the most powerful necromancers around, yet they are both half faerie. Although necromancy is unusual, it is not confined to one species. Over the years, I have met satyrs, elves, witches, even demons who had the power in differing degrees. One thing we all have in common is that our gift—the fact that we are necromancers—confers immortality upon us…if we choose to accept it."

"So that is why you have lived for so long? You are a pure-blood necromancer who has been granted immortality?"

Lorcan shook his head. "No, I wasn't born mortal. I'm one of the hybrids." Deciding he'd had enough of confidences for one night—hell, he hadn't confided this much to anyone else throughout the past millennium—he gestured out into the dark space beyond the cliff edge, silencing her before she could question him further. "Shall we go and check out this craft Cal has organized for us? For all we know he could be playing a trick on us. We could find ourselves setting off for Valhalla on a raft with two paddles."

Although there appeared to be a sheer drop down to the tiny bay below the cliffs, there was a series of steep steps cut into the rock. Tricky enough to navigate in daytime, it could be treacherous at night. Lorcan went first, lighting the way for Tanzi, who, sure-footed as her inner cat, followed him easily. So much for chivalry. He suspected she was unaware of his attempt at courtesy. It was another reminder, if he needed one, of her unconventional upbringing.

Minutes later, their feet crunched onto the sandy beach and, sure enough, Cal had been true to his word. A dinghy was pulled up onto the sand and, as Lorcan raised his hand higher so that a wider area could be illuminated, he saw a larger vessel bobbing on the waves in the deeper water. It looked bigger than anything he had handled before, but he decided not to mention that fact to Tanzi. *I'm a fast learner. How hard can it be?*

Tossing their bags into the dinghy, he tugged off his boots and rolled up his jeans. "Get in and I'll pull it into the water before starting the motor."

Tanzi paused, looking from the dinghy to the sailboat with a bemused expression. "Are we really going to do this?"

Lorcan started to laugh. "Second thoughts?"

She seemed to give herself a shake. She definitely gave him a reproachful look. "Of course not." Tanzi was the only person he knew who could clamber into a dinghy and make it look graceful, Lorcan decided.

His experience of dinghies had, in the past, not always been positive. He found they tended not to be the most reliable form of transport. *Speed, maneuverability* and *reliability* were not the first words he associated with a dinghy. There had been one or two close calls when, if he hadn't been with Cal—whose magical powers had enabled him to supercharge their vessel—a dinghy would have landed Lorcan in a lot of trouble. This one appeared determined to make amends for its fellows and prove him wrong. It started like a dream and skimmed lightly over the waves, reaching the boat in no time.

"It's not what I expected." Tanzi looked up at the sailboat as the dinghy bumped against its side.

"What did you expect?" Lorcan busied himself securing the dinghy to the rear of the boat.

"I don't know. Something rough and ready. But this looks—" she made a helpless gesture "—slick, even luxurious. As though we were going on a vacation."

"Tanzi, rid yourself of that notion right now." Lorcan threw their bags onto the deck and then sprang from the dinghy to the boat. Reaching out a hand, he helped Tanzi do the same. "Whatever may be in store for us in the near future, it won't be anything like a vacation."

Although, as they explored the accommodation together, Lorcan was forced to admit that Tanzi was right. The boat really was more upmarket than he had expected. Although compact, it was comfortable and stocked with every provision they would need for the journey. The saloon had a cushioned bench settee and a central chart table that could be used for both dining and map reading. Beyond it there was a spacious aft cabin with a double berth, storage and en suite shower and heads. The whole living area was paneled in light oak wood and the upholstery was new and expensive.

Tanzi's eyes were wider than ever. "Could we be on the wrong boat?"

"It crossed my mind." Lorcan went to the table and picked up the single sheet of paper that lay on it. Three words were scrawled across it in a familiar hand. *Don't fuck up.* It was typical of Cal and strangely reassuring. "But, no, this is definitely ours. This note and the boat's name say it all."

"I didn't notice the name."

"Welcome aboard the *Igraine*."

"*Igraine?*" Tanzi wrinkled her nose in confusion.

"The name of King Arthur's mother. It's a message from Cal."

"Oh." Tanzi took a moment to digest that information. "There is only one cabin."

"So there is." He kept his eyes steady on hers. *Ah, shit.* It was no good. He wasn't cut out to be a seducer. "You take the cabin. I'll sleep out here."

Her lashes swept down, hiding her eyes. "Maybe, before we even consider the sleeping arrangements, we should plan on getting away from here before daylight."

"Good thinking. I knew there was a reason why I brought you along, *Searc.* You can be my first mate."

At what point was he going to tell her about his deal with Cal to find the challenger for Moncoya's crown? How was he going to drop that one into the conversation? *By the way, you know how centuries ago your father stole the faerie throne by massacring the rightful king and all his family? Well, it turns out there was a direct descendant, a baby, who escaped the bloody coup. Yeah, his nurse stole away into the night with him. Turns out he's safe and well somewhere and has no idea who he is. Anyway, while we're on our travels, I've promised to keep my eyes and ears open and see if I can discover his whereabouts. Why? Oh, so he can be brought back to the palace and challenge your father for the crown. That's right. So he can strip you and your sister of your birthright...your royal titles and status. Your whole identity. So you'll spend the rest of your lives as objects of scandal and scrutiny. And, of course, the faerie people will be thrown into chaos as your father and the true king slug it out for who will reign.*

Right. That was the sort of thing you just blurted out at the first opportunity. Unless, like Lorcan, you were cursed with extraordinary empathy. And a perception so strong you knew that, even though this un-fey, fae girl claimed not to feel emotion, you would devastate her if you told her you planned to strip her of her everything she and her people knew and believed in.

Lorcan became brisk and businesslike, peppering his conversation with all things nautical, including engine power, diesel and cruising speed. It was like a foreign and alarmingly masculine language. Almost as though he wanted to divert her attention. From what, Tanzi had no idea.

"I thought it was a sailboat." Tanzi revealed her confusion when he paused for breath.

His response was the pitying glance of a master to a novice. "We're not doing this for fun or sport, Tanzi. We need an engine to take us round in a tight circle, through a narrow channel or around tricky rocks. I'm good, but not good enough to get *Igraine* into a shallow bay under sail. Safety comes first."

Chastened, she begged his pardon and went away to make coffee. Minutes later, the engines chugged into life and she staggered slightly as the boat broached the first waves. When she emerged onto the deck, carefully carrying two mugs of coffee, Lorcan looked very much at home. He was surrounded by his own necromancer glow, which made the waters beyond the boat appear darker and somehow mysterious.

"We seem to be going very fast." They were skimming over the waves so quickly the impression was that they were almost flying.

"This is the big feller's work. I've seen Cal do this before with other vehicles. I'm not sure how he does it, or even if he's done anything to the boat itself. Maybe he's managing to make us go faster by using mind control from a distance. He does have that sort of power. But this boat is somehow attuned to me, as if it's doing what I want it to. You're right, though. It shouldn't be possible for a boat with an engine this size to shift at this speed."

"At least this pace will make it difficult for my father to find us or have us followed."

"I expect Cal has that covered, as well. The cave where he lived in Wales was surrounded by so many warding spells it was impossible to get near it unless he wanted you to. I wouldn't be surprised if this boat had a similar barrier around it."

"Then he's earned my gratitude. I was afraid my father would get to us before we'd even begun this journey. Cal certainly does seem to have thought of everything. There's enough food down there to feed a small army for a month." Tanzi curled up on one of the padded seats that formed a U shape around the deck, content to watch him as he stopped to check the instruments. Lorcan's intervention didn't appear to be necessary. *Igraine* was literally propelling herself through the water.

Lorcan glanced up with one of his heartbreaking smiles. Tanzi wished he'd give some sort of warning when he was about to do that. Just so she wasn't left feeling at such a giddy disadvantage. "I thought you didn't do domestication."

"I don't, but even I can open a can." She grinned over the top of her cup. "Maria showed me how."

He quirked a brow at her. "You might just be every man's dream. Not only can you look good while kicking the shit out of a crowd of zombies, you can heat up a can of soup for afterward."

"Only one of those skills is going to come in useful to me as a Valkyrie.

Was it her imagination, or did his face harden slightly

at the reminder? Although she watched him carefully, the expression was so fleeting she couldn't tell if it was real. "True. I imagine Odin has enough people to do his cooking already." He gestured to the bench below her seat. "The life jackets are stored there. It's best to wear one while we're moving."

The advice struck Tanzi as so funny that she went off into a peal of laughter so intense that it was some minutes before she could speak. Lorcan seemed happy to watch her, a slightly bemused expression on his face. "It's just that this preoccupation with safety is misplaced," she explained, wiping the tears from her eyes. "Given our destination."

Lorcan held up his hands in a conciliatory gesture. "Okay, I'll ease up on the overprotective mode." They finished their coffee in silence. "Why don't you go down below and get some sleep?"

"What will you do?"

"Get us far enough down the coast so that no one will see us and be suspicious. I reckon a couple of hours at this speed should be enough. In the morning we can study the charts and plot a course to the Isles of the Aesir."

Tanzi picked up the coffee mugs. Feeling suddenly awkward, she hesitated. "Lorcan?"

"Yes?" He had half turned away to fiddle with the boat's instruments, but he swung back to face her.

"Thank you. And—" she took a deep breath. *Do it now before he looks away again.* "—we can share the cabin."

Even in the faint light she saw something darken in the depths of his eyes. Something that made her pulse race madly and her throat tighten. He gave a single nod and, clutching the coffee cups against her chest, Tanzi made her way down into the living quarters.

Okay, so you are all alone on a boat with a notorious

womanizer, and I think you have just agreed to have sex with him. Laughter bubbled up inside her. *Agreed? You* offered *to have sex with him.* The laughter was replaced by panic as she tipped the gym bag containing Vashti's clothing out onto the bed. True to form, there was nothing remotely feminine in there. Her sister had packed for practicality, not seduction. *And let's face it, Tanzi, even if you had the right outfit, you know nothing about technique anyway.*

In the end, having stored her clothing away, she washed and brushed her teeth before slipping one of Vashti's serviceable nightshirts over her underwear. The bed was surprisingly comfortable and the sound of the engines, together with the sway of the boat, lulled her. Before long she forgot the anticipation of what would happen when Lorcan joined her and allowed her eyes to drift closed.

Chapter 12

W_{hy} was he lingering here on deck, when the most desirable woman he had ever known—scratch that, ever dreamed of knowing—was just a few feet away? Lorcan's body insisted on asking his mind the question. Precisely that reason, his rational self responded. He wanted Tanzi with a fierceness that hurt. So much that he could actually taste his longing for her, feel it in every pore and nerve ending. It was exhilarating and dangerous at the same time.

It didn't fit with the whole can't-tie-me-down, roguish persona he worked so hard to maintain. And you couldn't exactly have a one-night stand on a boat this size. In any case he had a feeling he would want more from Tanzi than one night. It was an option he had never considered before. What if he found out he wanted forever? From a girl who had no future? In the end it came down to one simple thing. He could stay up here on deck until dawn and keep overthinking this or he could do what his body cried out for and go to her. Which was why he dropped *Igraine*'s anchor off a small island many miles from Moncoya's palace and made his way down to the cabin.

A smile touched his lips as he looked down at the figure on the bed. Tanzi lay on her stomach, sprawled like a starfish across the center of the mattress. She must have fallen asleep as soon as her head hit the pillow. In fairness, it had been quite a day. The bed was large enough for two, but there was no way he could join Tanzi in it without disturbing her. She looked so peaceful and, as he pulled the quilt she had kicked aside back over her, Lorcan decided not rousing her was for the best. It meant he could shelve his doubts. Listen to his head, not his heart—or other, decidedly less well-intentioned parts of his body. Get back to the important business of plotting a route through dangerous, uncharted territory without distraction.

Keep telling yourself that, Malone. He closed the cabin door behind him and eyed the bench seat next to the chart table dubiously. *If you say it often enough, you might even start to believe it.*

He found blankets and pillows in the overhead storage and settled his long frame onto the cushioned bench. Preparing to face an uncomfortable night, he was pleasantly surprised to almost immediately feel slumber tugging at the edge of his consciousness.

The smell of toast and coffee woke him. It seemed like mere minutes since he had fallen asleep, but bright sunlight streamed through the open hatch and Tanzi's wet hair and clean clothes signaled that she had already showered. Although breakfast was a pleasant sight, she was even more welcome. Feasting his eyes on her bright beauty, he sat up, stretching and kicking aside his blankets.

He sensed something troubling her as she passed him a plate of toast and a steaming mug of coffee. Sometimes intuition was a curse. "It was late when I dropped anchor last night. I didn't want to disturb you."

"Oh." Her brow cleared and a shy smile dawned. "I wondered why you slept out here."

She came to sit close to him on the bench, and the fresh, clean scent of her invaded his senses, knocking his thoughts off-kilter. Many things had happened in his life that could be considered unfair, but for the first time, as he looked into those endless eyes, Lorcan asked the age-old question. *Why me? Why let me find her, offer me a glimpse of what might be, only to snatch her away again?* The answer came back loud, clear and instantaneous. *Because life isn't fair. You already knew that. Deal with it the way you have learned how.*

He rose abruptly to his feet, draining his cup. "I need to shower." Ignoring Tanzi's blink of surprise at his brusque tone, he stalked away into the cabin.

The charts Cal had provided were like an incomplete jigsaw puzzle. The missing pieces were the most important ones. They had been sitting side by side, poring over them for close to an hour, and Lorcan had figured out how their journey should start. The middle remained a vague idea, and he had no clue how it would end.

He tapped the chart with one finger. "The first waters we need to travel through are vampire territory. We need to ask Prince Tibor's permission to enter them."

Tanzi looked up from the map with a frown. "Can't we sail around Tibor's islands instead?"

Lorcan shook his head. "That would take us too far off course, and the waters beyond are dangerous for a small craft like *Igraine*."

"Do we really need permission? Surely you can necromance us past a few vampires?" Tanzi's voice was light, but he sensed tension behind the words.

"Prince Tibor is not a great fan of the ancient dark art of necromancing. And who can blame him when a single necromancer can control a hundred vampires with just one word? The prince goes so far as to view sorcerers like me as a direct challenge to his authority. In fact, he dislikes necromancing so much that he has passed a law forbidding any sign of it anywhere within his territories. An attempt on my part to exert my influence over his subjects could earn me the death penalty. No. There's nothing else for it. We'll have to go and grovel to the prince of the bloodsuckers." He studied Tanzi's expression with sudden interest. "Is that a problem?"

Tanzi bit her lip. "It might be." A blush tinged her cheeks.

Something sharp and dark heated Lorcan's insides. Something he told himself he had no right to feel. "Is there history between the two of you?"

Tanzi's nod did nothing to dispel his unease. "When Tibor and my father were allies, there was some talk of a match between us. The prince was—" she bent her head and fiddled with her thumbnail "—very attentive toward me."

How attentive? For some reason it mattered. Had Tibor's attentions taken the vampire form of flowers and chocolates? A few stolen kisses? More? Lorcan discovered that his hands were clenched into fists, his jaw muscles tight with tension. He willed himself to relax. "That was in the past. Why should it be a problem now?"

Tanzi squirmed slightly, still not meeting his eyes. "Tibor is a very attractive man." She said it as though that simple statement explained everything.

"So you were willing to be his wife." Lorcan kept his voice deliberately neutral, making it a statement instead of the accusation he wanted it to be.

She looked up at him again, her eyes bright on his face as though pleading for his understanding. "I was not unwilling. It is our way, Lorcan. Ever since I was a child, I have known that my fate would be to further the greatness of the faerie dynasty through the right marriage." She gave a hollow laugh. "And my father's recent antics have proved that there are worse partners than Tibor."

"Do you love him?"

She was silent for long moments as she gazed up at him, her midnight blue eyes darkening to a point where they were almost black. "I am a faerie princess. Love is a mortal emotion and not one I am able to experience." The words were mechanical, spoken like a chant she had learned as a child. The way he had memorized songs and nursery rhymes. She turned away to look out through a porthole and across the water. The motion allowed Lorcan to see the pulse that beat wildly in her throat.

"Then you should be able to meet Prince Tibor without any problem."

She nodded, a slight smile touching her lips. "He might not feel the same way."

Lorcan groaned. "So what you are really trying to tell me is that the Prince of the Vampires is desperately in love with you?"

"Something like that." The smile deepened and became mischievous. "The last time I saw him was at an Alliance meeting before I left and came to find you at the safe house. A lot has happened for me since then. Who knows what's been going on in Tibor's life? His feelings might have changed. Maybe he's forgotten about me and found someone new."

"Don't get your hopes up. You're pretty unforgettable."

He caught the sound of her indrawn breath, and the blush deepened in her cheeks. When she spoke again, her voice was studiously casual. "How long will it take us to get there?"

"It should take a few days, but whatever Cal has done to supercharge this boat means we can cover most distances in less than half the time. We are probably only a day and a half from Tibor's boundary. The vampire archipelago is the closest territory to that of the faerie isles, which is why, I suppose, your father and Tibor have always been such close allies."

"Either that or they were drawn together because they are both evil." She turned her head away to study the turquoise waters once more. Somehow the perfection of the scene mocked the mission they were about to embark upon. Lorcan reviewed all the reasons he already had to loathe Moncoya. All the ruined lives he had seen through his work in the resistance. All the centuries during which Moncoya had sought to destroy Cal, his own half brother. All the atrocities the faerie king had committed against those of his own people who dared to oppose him. All faded into insignificance compared with what he felt when he thought about what Moncoya had done to his own daughter.

"Right, that's enough sitting round here reminiscing about your old boyfriends. We'd better make a start. I've got a feeling sailing into vampire waters will be mild compared with what's to come once we reach the Isles of the Aesir."

"You and your feelings." Tanzi gave him a teasing glance.

"You and your lack of feelings." He returned the look. *Careful, Malone.* This was starting to feel a lot like flirtation. He'd seen Tibor rip a grown man apart with his bare hands on more than one occasion. Did he really want to risk inciting the vampire prince to jealousy?

"I've been discovering lately that I might be able to feel more than I believed I could." Her sidelong glance was a combination of invitation and confusion.

To hell with Tibor and to hell with caution. Lorcan never did work out which of them was the most surprised when he pulled Tanzi into his arms. All he knew was the action was long overdue. At first he was content to just hold her, resting his cheek against hers while his hands caressed her shoulders and upper arms. Raising his head, he saw his own need reflected in Tanzi's eyes and he brushed his lips lightly over her mouth. Her shudder vibrated through them both and he drew her closer still. Forcing himself to take things slowly, he kissed her forehead, then her nose before pressing a trail of tiny kisses along her lower lip. When Tanzi's lips parted in surrender, he claimed her mouth with his own. The movement ignited an inferno. As their tongues entwined and moved sensuously against each other, Lorcan controlled and varied the tempo of their movements. Soft and languid one moment became fast and furious the next, until, when they broke apart, they were both breathing hard.

"We really should go." He rested his forehead against Tanzi's.

"Oh. Okay." She rose to her feet and moved, slightly unsteadily, toward the hatch.

"That's not what I meant." Rising to his feet, he caught hold of her hand and drew her with him into the cabin.

It was darker and cooler inside the cabin. Lorcan lay on his back on the bed while Tanzi raised herself on one elbow beside him. With a featherlight touch, she traced his naked upper body, enjoying the way his breath hitched beneath her fingertips. She moved from his chest to his shoulders, down over his well-defined biceps and back over the outline of his pectoral muscles. Running her fingers up his neck, she tangled them in his hair, finding it softer than she'd imagined. Moving lower to trail along his eyebrows, then his closed eyelids, the straight length of his nose, the contrasting stubble of his jaw, she lingered longest on the soft cushion of his lower lip.

She sensed it was taking an almost superhuman effort of willpower on his part to stop himself from touching her in return. This man who lay beside her—his need for her obvious in the thick ridge that strained the zipper of his jeans and the tension that quivered through his frame— was powerful, with a coiled strength that could crush her to him with one hand if he chose. Yet she knew he was determined to be gentle and patient while she learned more about his body.

It was a body that was perfect. Lorcan was beautiful. And, right at this moment, he belonged to her.

She pressed her lips to his chest, moving lower to trace the hard ridges of his abdominal muscles with her tongue. This was what she'd dreamed of doing for so long. She wanted this...whatever *this* was. More than that. She needed it. Needed Lorcan. Craved him. Ached for him.

Sensing the change in her mood from scrutiny to readiness, Lorcan cupped the nape of her neck, the warmth of his hand searing her flesh. His touch thrilled through her. Insistently, he increased the pressure, urging her toward him. Anticipation mounted. Tension spiraled. Time melted away. Tanzi lay across his chest as he tasted her, nibbling and teasing before demanding more. Her lips parted beneath his. As his tongue plunged into her mouth, her mind whirled with the reality of what was to come.

"Are you sure this is what you want?" Lorcan's voice was husky.

"So much." She was trembling with need. With raw, unbridled wanting.

He fumbled with his jeans, his fingers shaking as he shoved the denim down over his hips. His briefs followed. Seconds later, he was naked, his cock rigid and straining upward. Heat seared through Tanzi's body, robbing her of her remaining breath and leaving her scorched. All those lessons and diagrams, but nothing had prepared her for such an imposing, throbbing display of Lorcan's desire for her. *Magnificent.* That was the word. Huge, impressive, arrogant maleness that invited her touch. She continued her exploration, brushing the tip of one finger over the head, enjoying the silken feel of his flesh. Lorcan's groan reverberated around the cabin.

Tanzi felt a surge of triumph. "I might not know much about these things, but I can see that this is what you want." Lightly, she stroked his shaft. Raw heat throbbed beneath her hand.

His response was ground out between clenched teeth. "One of us is way overdressed for this conversation." Reaching up, he tugged her vest over her head. His gaze locked on her breasts. Tanzi's heart pounded wildly against her rib cage, her entire body reacting to the expression in his eyes. "God, Tanzi, you're gorgeous."

Her nipples tightened until shards of exquisite pain ripped through her. If he could do that to her with a look, what would his touch do? She didn't have long to wait before she found out. Lorcan raised himself on his elbow, mirroring Tanzi's position. His mouth was hot and demanding as it closed over her nipple. Tanzi writhed against him, her hand reaching around the back of his head to hold him to her. He flicked her nipple with his tongue and she arched toward him, overwhelmed by the storm of passion blazing through her.

"Now these." Lorcan's hands moved lower to unbutton her shorts and tug them and her underwear down over her hips and thighs so that Tanzi could kick them off. Slowly, he moved his hand up her inner thigh. Tanzi fell back, closing her eyes and basking in the infinite lightness of his caresses. His touch felt as if it was imprinted on her skin. So gentle and at the same time purposeful. Shifting position abruptly, Lorcan dipped his head between her thighs, his lips replacing his fingers. Feathery kisses continued until his mouth reached the apex at the top of her legs.

Using his thumbs to hold her outer lips apart, Lorcan continued to probe with his lips. The unexpected glide of his tongue felt so shockingly good that she jerked violently upward. Lorcan gripped her hips, holding her down. His tongue probed her entrance before tracing an upward line to toy with her clitoris. He licked the sensitive nub, then captured it between his lips and sucked hard. Tanzi's fingers tightened in Lorcan's hair. When he pushed his tongue right inside her, she cried out and rocked her hips in time with his thrusts. Her every muscle was taut, strained to the point of pain, and crying out for release. Each breath was torn from her chest in a great fiery gasp.

The pleasure continued to soar until her body reached a crescendo and exploded. Lorcan continued to lick and tease as Tanzi's whole body rippled with waves of ecstasy. Pulling her against him as the aftershocks finally subsided, he kissed her hair, stroking a hand down her back as she shuddered into stillness.

After a few minutes, he reached for his jeans, withdrawing a foil square from the pocket. "Condom. We don't need any more complications."

Once his cock was sheathed in rubber, he moved between her legs, spreading them wider so she could grip him with her knees. His mouth found hers in a searing kiss as the tip of his cock entered her. Tanzi lifted her hips, assisting him and welcoming him into her body. He murmured appreciatively as she offered herself to him, then, in one quick thrust, he pushed all the way inside her. Tanzi gasped at the sensation of him filling her completely.

"Did I hurt you?" Lorcan brushed her hair back from her brow.

She shook her head, unable to speak. How could she explain that nothing she had ever experienced in her whole life came close to feeling as wonderful as having him inside her? Instead, she arched her back, urging him to continue. Lorcan rocked his hips slowly against hers and Tanzi was instantly lost. He kissed her, drawing her tongue into his mouth. Tanzi moaned and pressed closer, craving the feel of his skin on hers, wanting to draw him deeper into her. Lorcan increased the tempo and began to pump harder, leaving her wanting more without knowing what more there could be. How could anything possibly match the heights he had already taken her to? She met his thrusts, her hips slamming against his in a rhythmic, unending motion. Sweat coated their skin. Lorcan eased away slightly, lifting her legs higher so that she could press even more closely against him. Tanzi clawed wildly at his back as he plunged deeper still.

A moment later her world splintered into a million tiny pieces. She clenched her muscles tightly around his cock, everything else but Lorcan and her release fading out of existence. A cry escaped her and she closed her eyes, concentrating on the waves of ecstasy. A growl from Lorcan made her flick her eyelids open again. She wanted to see how it felt for him. One hand crushed her hair as he threw his head back and his movements stilled. He swelled inside her and instinct made her squeeze her muscles around him, gripping him tighter as his cock pumped out its release. When he withdrew his body from hers, and pulled her into his arms, the kiss he gave her was a sweet infinity.

For a long time, Tanzi lay still. But stillness was the last thing she felt inside. Her thoughts were racing. It was as if Lorcan had flicked on a light switch inside her. *So this is who I am. I am supposed to be a vibrant, loving person. I was never meant to be a cold-blooded killing machine.* She turned her head to look at Lorcan's face. His eyes were closed. He might almost have been asleep, but she knew he wasn't. She suspected his supercharged instincts were at work and he was allowing her time to assimilate what had just happened. "Thank you."

He opened one eye, his expression startled. "Pardon?"

"For showing me how to feel all those things. I would never have known emotion like that existed if it wasn't for you." Lorcan started to laugh. "What's so funny?"

"Only that it's not every day a guy has mind-blowing sex with the most beautiful girl he's ever met and, on top of all that, she thanks him for it. I wasn't expecting that." He pulled her closer against him. "What can I say? I'll start with 'you're welcome' and 'anytime.'"

"*Any*time?" Tanzi ran a finger down his chest. "Really?" The finger continued lower. "Because, if you've got nothing else planned…"

Chapter 13

Could a day spent having sex with Tanzi and swimming naked with her in the glorious turquoise waters around *Igraine* be classified as wasted? Lorcan dismissed the question as soon as it entered his mind. Because it was the stupidest thing he had ever asked himself. Had the most amazing twenty-four hours of his life just been squandered? If they had, he would love the opportunity to misuse every day in the same way. Nevertheless, they hadn't moved an inch on their journey the previous day, meaning they now had some serious ground-making to do. Even with Cal's powerful spells guarding them against discovery, they had a difficult journey ahead of them. With that in mind, he had risen early. Reluctantly, he had eased Tanzi's naked, slumbering form out of his arms, donned a pair of shorts, gone up on deck and started *Igraine*'s engines.

The early-morning breeze ruffled his hair and he tried to let it clear his mind, but his thoughts remained stubbornly fixed on one thing. Tanzi. *You stupid bastard.* But it was no good. Even as he tried to berate himself, the thought of her brought a smile to his lips. He needed to go a bit easier on himself. *Because I didn't suddenly fall in love with her when I was inside her yesterday. It wasn't even back in the safe house when I started to get a glimpse of who she really was. She had me the very first time I held her in my arms after the battle. The first time she snarled at me and called me "necromancer" in that I'm-a-princess-and-you-are-not-fit-to-kiss-the-hem-of-my-designer-gown voice she uses, I was hers to command.* The thought brought a fresh realization in its wake. The heart he believed he'd encased in steel had broken free of its restraints after all these years. What a pity he couldn't give in to its promptings and let Tanzi know how he felt. Not only because of who she was, but also because of who he was. *Ah, well. What we had yesterday was pretty spectacular. It will have to suffice. We both knew there'd be no tomorrows for us.* He didn't care to dwell on whether his heart—his big, sensitive, *fragile* heart—already so badly damaged by his past, could be mended again once he'd said goodbye to her.

"Why didn't you wake me?" The object of his thoughts appeared on deck, looking tousled and unbearably desirable in one of his shirts.

"It was early and you were sound asleep." He held out a hand and she came to stand beside him, nestling into his side and rubbing her cheek, catlike, along the muscles of his chest. His heart gave a thud so loud he was surprised she didn't recoil in surprise.

"Have you ever wished you could freeze time? Just stop it and remain in one place forever?" Tanzi raised her eyes to his, and the fiery ring around her irises blazed brighter than ever.

"Not until now." The conversation was straying across the border into dangerous territory. It was starting to resemble something it shouldn't. His head told him to get it back on track. His newly awakened heart told him it was okay to explore this theme. He went with his heart. "Until you."

Tanzi's lips parted, but he never discovered what she was about to say. Without warning, she clutched the sides of her head, recoiling from him. Her face spasmed as though she had been struck by an intense pain. As she dropped to her knees on the deck, he could have sworn he heard her say, "Stop yelling at me, Vashti."

Lorcan cut the engines and came to her side. By the time he reached her, Tanzi seemed to have recovered some of her composure. Sitting on the deck, with her back against the bench seat, she had her hands around her knees, hugging them tight up against her chest. She was breathing hard and her head was tilted on one side, almost as if she was listening to an invisible voice.

"Tanzi…" She held up a hand, silencing him. Instead of speaking, Lorcan slid an arm about her shoulders and she leaned gratefully against him.

After a few minutes, she spoke. "My father knows everything."

"You're going to have to rewind a bit and explain how you've just found that out. You scared the hell out of me."

"Vashti told me."

He shook his head. "Still not making sense."

"While I was at the palace preparing for this journey, we discovered, for the first time, that we have a psychic bond so strong we can converse telepathically no matter how far apart we are. She got a bit carried away just now and was shouting at me. It hurt." She smiled reassuringly. "Once she calmed down, I was fine."

"How can Vashti possibly know what information your father has?"

Tanzi bit her lip. "The same way I knew he wanted me to marry Satan. We have kept in touch with him during his exile. She has been to visit him." Her eyes pleaded for his understanding. "He is our father."

"Let me get this straight…you still feel a sense of loyalty to him?" Lorcan tried to keep the incredulity out of his voice, but he knew as he spoke the words he was failing miserably.

The single shake of her head was emphatic. "I don't. Not any more. Vashti? I think the sense of obedience he drummed into us is still too ingrained in her. And, after all, he hasn't tried to sell *her* to the devil. Not yet, anyway." Her eyes continued to scan his face, seeking comfort there. When his expression relaxed, she continued. "My father knows I was with you at the safe house. He sent Iago to spy on me and set a trap for you with the zombies. He knows we left Barcelona together and that we have embarked on a journey."

"How could he know that? Unless Vashti betrayed you?"

"I know you have no reason to like my sister, Lorcan, but you are wrong about her. She wouldn't harm me, and she would never break her word."

Lorcan ran a hand through his hair in a frustrated motion. "I'm sorry. I just don't understand how Moncoya can know we are together. Apart from the two of us, the only other people who know where we've gone are Cal, Stella and Vashti."

"And none of them would betray us. Someone must have spied on us at the palace. I did not stay in my cat guise when we left. There are many sidhes who are still loyal to my father. And many more who need money."

Lorcan stored up the interesting little snippet of information she had inadvertently let slip for another time. They had left the faerie palace less than two days ago. Which meant Moncoya's hideaway was close enough for his informant to get that information to him within a day. Once Tanzi was safe inside Valhalla, Cal would be able to make good use of that interesting piece of intelligence.

"Does Moncoya know where we are going?"

"Vashti said he does not. He tried to coax—and then threaten—her into telling him. He wouldn't waste time on that if he already knew. Nevertheless, he knows we are on a boat and she said he is using every means at his disposal to discover where we are. Including Iago."

Lorcan felt his expression harden. "I don't suppose Vashti was able to discover who your father's new best pal Iago might be?"

"Not exactly, but she did discover more about Iago's motive." Lorcan waited, his heart sinking as Tanzi's voice faltered. "My father told Vashti that Iago will not rest until you, Cal, Stella and Jethro are all dead. Only then will he feel the death of Niniane has been avenged. He blames the four of you for the fact that she was killed during the battle."

"Great. Vengeance. I hoped Iago was out to get me for money, but it's personal, after all. I didn't think Niniane, the Lady of the Lake, was capable of inspiring loyalty. Seems I was wrong about the coldhearted witch. Well, that settles it. We'd better get *Igraine* moving again."

The black outline of the Vampire Archipelago was thrown into stark relief against dusky pink skies and royal purple seas. Soaring cliffs and spiky basalt outcrops made an uneven outline along the length of the horizon.

"Although there are many small islands, they are divided into three main groups, and Tibor is the undisputed ruler of them all. Which is quite a feat, given the different beliefs of the main factions within the vampire dynasty." Lorcan had dropped anchor and they were looking across the channel that lay between them and the vampire territory while they ate a late dinner on *Igraine*'s deck.

"I must confess, I know a little of vampire politics, but not as much as I should." Tanzi looked at the unwelcoming, jagged shape of the rocks and shivered slightly. Had she seriously once believed she might be princess of these lands? How long ago that seemed. It was as if she was reflecting on the life of another person. Someone she knew well, but who had very different desires and goals.

"The islands on our left are inhabited mostly by those who subscribe to the legend of Ambrogio, the first vampire." Tanzi raised an inquiring eyebrow. "You don't know the story?" She shook her head. "According to Greek mythology, Ambrogio made the mistake of falling in love with Selene, one of the handmaidens of Apollo, the sun god. Enraged, Apollo cursed Ambrogio so that a mere touch of sunlight would burn his skin. With no way to contact Selene and tell her of his plight, Ambrogio killed a swan each night and used its blood to write Selene a message. After draining the blood and taking a single feather with which to write, he offered the body of the swan as a tribute to Artemis, the goddess of the moon. He repeated this action for forty-four days. What is it?"

Tanzi winced. "My mother was a Valkyrie."

Lorcan's grin was apologetic. "Sorry, I should have warned you the story contained cruelty to swans. To continue…on the forty-fifth night, Ambrogio had only one arrow left. He shot it at a swan and missed. He begged Artemis to let him borrow her bow and an arrow so he could kill one last bird and leave a final note for Selene.

Artemis took pity on him and agreed. He took her silver bow, and in desperation, ran to the cave that led to hell, determined to end his own life. When Artemis realized what was happening, she also cursed Ambrogio. The new curse caused silver to burn his skin. He fell to his knees, writhing in agony. Artemis then offered him one last chance. She would make him a great hunter, with the speed and strength of a god and fangs with which to drain the blood of the beasts to write beautiful poems to his beloved. In exchange for immortality, Ambrogio and Selene must worship only Artemis, the virgin goddess. There was one catch—all followers of Artemis must remain chaste, so Ambrogio and Selene could never kiss, never touch, never make love, never have children."

"They did not agree to that surely?"

"What other choice did they have? At least they could be together at last. They lived happily for many years, until, inevitably, Selene began to age and fell ill. Ambrogio, who had remained young, was distraught and begged Artemis to make Selene immortal, too. Artemis offered him one last deal. He could touch Selene just once…to drink her blood. Doing so would kill her mortal body, but from then on, Selene's blood mixed with his would give eternal life to any who drank of it. Desperate to save her, Ambrogio sank his fangs into Selene's neck and drank her blood. As he set her limp body down, Selene radiated with light, and rose up into the sky. Selene became the goddess of moonlight, and every night she reached down to the earth to touch her beloved Ambrogio as well as their children."

Tanzi's brow wrinkled in confusion. "I thought they couldn't have children?"

"Their children are the vampires who carry the mingled blood of Ambrogio and Selene. Their followers worship Artemis and the moon, shun the daylight—even though Tibor has proved that, with protection, there are ways that vampires can risk the sun's rays—and sacrifice swans."

"Ugh. Can we stay away from them, please?"

Lorcan's shoulders shook with laughter. "As you wish." He turned back to the view of the islands. "So, while on the left, we have the islands of the Ambrogio, on the right, we have the lands occupied by the Tepes."

"What are their beliefs?"

"You have heard the mortal story, no doubt, of Count Dracula? A work of fiction, but based on a real character. An Otherworld prince who lived as a mortal, ruling a Romanian province in medieval times. He was known as Vlad Dracul or Vlad Tepes, meaning 'Vlad the Impaler.' This was apparently a reference to his fondness for impaling his enemies on long wooden stakes. This real-life Dracula had a reputation for unfathomable brutality. And, of course, he was an aristocrat. It was his right to behave the way he did. His actions should not be questioned. That is what the Tepes, those vampires who follow the ways of Vlad, believe. That they have an absolute right to pursue their lusts without being answerable to anyone else. And they should be able to move among mortals, claiming them for their own. They are the ones who give rise to the vampire stories and legends that abound in the mortal realm."

"They must give Tibor a headache."

"They do, but Tibor has the advantage of being a direct descendant of Vlad Tepes. It means he is able to exert some authority over them. Heaven help the vampire dynasty—and the rest of us—if anything should happen to Tibor."

Tanzi shivered. "I get the feeling it may be too late for heaven to intervene. What about the middle islands?"

Lorcan's smile lifted the mood. "Pure Tibor. Escapist fantasy. He's a modernizer, your bloodthirsty admirer. His goal is to unite the whole vampire dynasty so that the divide between the Ambrogio and the Tepes is a thing of the past. You have to give him credit, it's a staggering ambition and he works bloody hard to achieve it. Generally, he tries to do it by showing them there is a third way. The new order. The modern vampire can interact in the mortal realm, can control his or her bloodlust, can even brave the light of day."

"Why would a vampire want all of those things? Surely all a vampire really wants is blood?"

"Don't let Tibor hear you say that. Vampires *need* blood to survive. Blood is their sustenance, but Tibor's approach is to show them that, if they can control their bloodlust, they can have all the things they *want*, as well. And what they want is what any of us want. Acceptance, friendship, love." The last word hung in the air for a moment as though challenging—or perhaps mocking—him. "All they have to do is follow Tibor's rules."

"I've never met a vampire yet who wanted to conform." Tanzi pushed aside the sandwich she had been eating and reached instead for her glass of soda.

"No one said Tibor's job was an easy one." Lorcan looked out at the islands. They were vanishing now as night draped a cloak of darkness over them. "I've never seen Tibor's castle, but I've heard about it. If it lives up to its reputation, this should be an interesting visit."

"Can we talk about something other than Tibor and vampires?"

"What did you have in mind?"

"I need a shower." Mischief lit her expression. "Will you join me?"

"It's a bit cramped in there for two." What was *wrong* with him? His cock had stiffened to the point where it resembled an iron girder at the very thought, yet here he was offering suggestions about why it was a bad idea.

"I thought that might make it interesting. But if you'd rather not...oh!" Tanzi let out a little squeal as, in one fluid series of movements, Lorcan rose to his feet, swept her up in his arms and carried her down into the cabin.

Lorcan was right. They had to stand pressed very close together under the warm spray of water. Not that Tanzi was finding it a hardship. And, judging by the look in his eye and the enormous erection throbbing against her stomach, Lorcan appeared to be enjoying himself, as well.

"Let me do that," he said, as she reached for the soap. Taking the scented bar, he rubbed it across the flat plain of her stomach, before moving it up to linger on her breasts. Her flesh ached with pleasure when he skimmed the soap around her nipples and then used his other hand to massage her slippery skin. Just when she was beginning to have difficulty staying upright, he moved his hand around to her back and she gasped as his soapy fingers probed between her buttocks. "Open your legs." His voice was a rasp above the sound of the water.

Tanzi obeyed and Lorcan moved the soap down between her legs, gliding it back and forth so that it brushed her clitoris. She trembled and clung to his shoulders. With a muttered curse, he cast the soap aside and lifted her against the shower wall.

"I can't go slow. Not when you drive me mad as soon as I touch you."

Tanzi wrapped her legs around his waist, pressing herself closer until she could feel the head of his cock right at her entrance. He felt huge and hot as he started to push into her. She writhed against him. "Now, please."

Lorcan paused, his breath coming fast and ragged. "What the hell am I doing?" With one hand, he fumbled for the condom he'd placed on the soap tray. "Help me out here, *Searc.*"

Between them they got the condom on, and Tanzi glanced up to encounter a look that almost scorched the skin from her face. Without any further warning, Lorcan drove the full length of his cock into her, impaling her against the tiled wall. Her head fell back and a helpless gurgle left her lips. Holding Tanzi in position, Lorcan pulled back before ramming into her again. Over and over. His thrusts were wild, masterful and completely without mercy. That connection, the friction at just the right spot, felt like nothing she had ever known. She loved the feeling of him buried hilt-deep inside her. She loved the feeling of him brushing her clitoris as he withdrew. It was maddening and wonderful at the same time. Tanzi's orgasm built and spiraled inside her until she screamed Lorcan's name as she came. As soon as her muscles clenched around him, Lorcan quickened his pace and continued to pump in and out of her. Tanzi's hands clawed his back as she felt another burst grow within her until she exploded into a second series of spasms. Lorcan's own release soon followed and they both sagged, panting, against the shower wall.

"You do have the best ideas, *Searc.*"

After letting the water play over them for a few more minutes, Lorcan wrapped Tanzi in a fluffy towel and carried her through to the bed. Placing another towel on top of the quilt, he lay down next to her and drew her into his arms, pressing a soft kiss onto her lips. She loved his tenderness after they'd made love. She loved *him*. She tried to wish the thought away, but it persisted. *This is because you have just discovered how to feel. This is your subconscious trying to make sense of this heady cocktail of emotions swirling around inside you. This is just sex. You don't know what love feels like.* It was no good. She could try to talk herself out of it, but it was a waste of time. She loved Lorcan with a strength and certainty that couldn't—wouldn't—be denied. Talk about a double-edged emotion. Fierce happiness tore through her. *I love him, and he's here in my arms.* At the same time, crippling sorrow made her want to curl up in pain. *Because I have to leave him.*

"What is it?" She should have known that Lorcan, with that acute extra sense he possessed, would pick up on her feelings. "Was I too rough? Tell me I didn't hurt you."

"No." She smiled shyly at him. "I loved it."

He groaned. "Ah, will you catch yourself on with that sort of talk? You'll have me dragging you off to the shower to do it all over again." His face became serious. "Although I was so crazed with wanting you, I almost forgot to use protection. I've never been so careless. We can't introduce a baby into this madness."

Tanzi's heart gave a dull thud. She'd never thought of herself as maternal, even though Moncoya had always made it clear she would be sold to a husband for her childbearing properties. When she took the decision to join the Valkyrie, the fact that she would never have a child had not even crossed her mind. Now she realized that there was nothing she wanted more than a life with Lorcan. A real life, in which she would bear his children. Children like him, blond, blue-eyed, laughing… Bright tears burned her eyelids, and she closed her eyes quickly before he saw them.

"How can you be sure Tibor will see you?" She sought wildly for a change of subject and, opening her eyes, saw Lorcan's surprise reflected in the cornflower depths of his eyes as she blurted the words out. She couldn't blame him. As mood killers went, bringing up the vampire prince who had a steaming crush on you was fairly effective.

"Oh, he'll see me. I'm his worst nightmare." His smile held no humor, and she was reminded of the darker side of his powers. "Even more than sunlight, crucifixes, daylight and garlic. Perhaps marginally less than a stake through the heart. In general, vampires are not afraid of other beings. There is bad blood between them and the wolves, of course. But that is born of centuries of conflict, not of fear. The vampires do, however, have a healthy respect for necromancers. Tibor knows I can make him and his followers dance to my tune, if I choose. Literally. He can pass all the laws he wants outlawing my powers, but it's my unpredictability that causes him the most alarm." He drew her closer into the circle of his arms. "I'll take the dinghy over and seek an audience with him first thing in the morning. In the meantime, I've one or two ideas of my own I'd like to discuss with you."

Chapter 14

There were two ways in which Lorcan could reach Prince Tibor's castle. One option was to traverse the largest island of the archipelago, having first moored the dinghy in the main port. He discarded this choice for two reasons. Firstly, he would draw too much attention to himself. Secondly, it would take a good two hours to get across the island, and much of the territory was dangerous. The only other alternative was to access the castle from the sea. As he approached the soaring edifice, set high on a cliff overlooking a narrow channel, he offered up thanks for good weather and a calm sea. Any hint of rough waves and his fragile craft would have been dashed onto the treacherous rocks.

Steps—he counted ninety-nine of them as he ascended—led up the vertical cliff from the sea to the castle terrace, and Lorcan knew as he climbed them that a dozen pairs of hidden eyes observed his progress. He hoped that Tibor would recognize that, by entering vampire territory alone, Lorcan was placing his trust in the vampire prince and had no aggressive intentions.

When he reached the top of the steps, Lorcan paused. He had expected to be greeted by Tibor's bodyguards, but the terrace was empty. The castle, a beautiful, pink-and-gold dream in the Renaissance style, loomed above him. In front of him, the view took his breath away. The island looped around almost in a circle, enclosing a small flotilla of sailing boats between golden sands and azure waters. White buildings with rooftops tiled in bright colors clustered below the castle walls like children around their mother's skirts. Majestic pines and exotic cacti provided splashes of brilliant green, their rich scents reminding Lorcan of Mediterranean islands slumbering in the sunshine.

"This is an unexpected surprise." Tibor's upper-class voice made him turn sharply. *Never let a vampire sneak up on you from behind.* He could almost hear Cal's voice saying the words. The prince was dressed casually in linen trousers and an open-necked shirt. As always, his cool, Nordic looks made him look un-vampire-like and nonthreatening. Appearances could be deceptive.

"Highness." Lorcan lowered his head in a deferential gesture. There was a time when he would have refused to show anything resembling homage to a vampire. Centuries of experience and Cal's guiding hand had taught him well. He had learned over the years that such acts meant a great deal to the rulers of Otherworld's dynasties. When he looked into Tibor's unusual, light turquoise eyes, he knew the prince wasn't fooled. They would both play the game. Lorcan would bow his head and Tibor wouldn't attempt any mind control tricks. Not that he was stupid enough to try them on a necromancer. "Forgive the intrusion. I have come to request a favor."

Tibor's lips curved into a smile that was almost sweet. "And here was I believing you came to admire my resort." His sweeping hand gesture indicated the castle and the vista beyond.

Resort? Was this some sort of vampire hotel? A holiday haven for the undead? The thought was amusing… and surreal at the same time. "Sure, it's quite a place you have here."

Sarcasm, even the faintest trace, appeared lost on the vampire prince. Tibor bowed his head in acknowledgment of what he clearly took to be a compliment. "Shall I confess to you my greatest ambition? Risk your laughter at my foolishness?"

"I think you underestimate your own authority, Highness." Lorcan spoke with feeling. The vampire leader had little to fear from any other being.

Tibor leaned on the ornate wrought-iron railing that bordered the terrace, looking out at the sweeping bay. "Very well. I would like, one day, to replicate this venture in the mortal realm."

Lorcan bit back the four-letter expletive that threatened to burst from him. Instead he raised his brows. "That is certainly ambitious."

"You think it cannot be done?" Those glittering eyes were watchful.

"It depends on what you are saying." Lorcan kept his tone studiously neutral. "A luxury hotel is one thing. But if you are suggesting that you want to go mainstream, that you want a luxury hotel in the mortal realm run by vampires, then I'd say you have your work cut out." He stopped short of saying what he really thought. It wouldn't do to tell the Prince of the Vampires you thought he was insane. Not unless you wanted your throat ripped out. He had seen Tibor in action. That courtly veneer disguised the fact that the most powerful vampire in Otherworld could move faster than Lorcan could blink. Those aristocratic manners hid the heart of a ruthless killer. If Tibor had a heart. It was an interesting point. He must have something if he'd fallen in love with Tanzi. And the guy had good taste, Lorcan had to give him that. Even though the thought of those full lips anywhere near Tanzi made him feel slightly queasy.

Tibor laughed, clapping an arm about Lorcan's shoulders and startling him out of his thoughts. "Fear not, I am not mad enough to make the attempt quite yet. Sadly, I must ensure I have complete control over my dynasty here in Otherworld before I attempt any business venture in the earthly realm. I cannot risk any rogue factions interfering with my plans and allowing their bloodlust to overcome them in the mortal world."

"I can see how that might be bad for business." Lorcan eyed him in fascination.

"Indeed. But perhaps you are the very person to help me to quash my rebellious underlings? It had not occurred to me until now, but a powerful necromancer may be just what I need."

"Sorry, I've another big task ahead of me right now. Jethro is your man if you want a necromancer who is for hire." Lorcan spoke without thinking, but the prince's intent expression was an instant reminder of recent history. Silently, he cursed his unruly tongue. *Go, Malone. Draw the vampire overlord's attention to your friend, why don't you?*

"Ah, Jethro de Loix." Tibor's voice was like cream mixed with honey. "How I look forward to meeting him again. You do not happen to know his current where-abouts, I suppose?"

"He's never been one for leaving a forwarding ad-dress."

"I was sorry it had to end that way with Dimitar. A bad business all round." It would be easy to believe Tibor was genuinely regretful.

"Did it have to end that way?" Dimitar had served Tibor faithfully for many years. Lorcan still couldn't see why he had to die just for wanting his freedom.

"But of course. What sort of leader would I be if I let my human servant leave me for another without extract-ing a painful retribution?" The question hung between them for a minute, reminding Lorcan once again that be-neath the cultured surface there lurked a dangerous mon-ster. The glinting smile returned to Tibor's face. "So tell me, what brings you to my humble home? What is this favor I can do for you?"

It was a not-so-subtle reminder to Lorcan that he had placed himself in the vampire ruler's power. "I have come to request safe passage to sail through the waters around the Vampire Archipelago, Highness."

"Do you travel alone?"

Damn. That was the one question Lorcan had hoped to avoid. If he said he was on his own and Tibor sub-sequently discovered he was lying, the vampire prince would have no hesitation in sending out the word to have him captured. He very much doubted a necromancer would get a fair trial in vampire territory. He might as well offer Tibor his throat now. He stifled a sigh. "No, I am traveling with a companion."

"And who accompanies you on your journey?"

Lorcan drew a breath. "The Crown Princess Tanzi of the faerie dynasty."

If he didn't have Tibor's full attention before he spoke those words, he certainly had it as soon as they left his lips.

Tanzi upended the bag she had brought with her when she fled her father's palace in search of Lorcan. She hadn't looked at its contents since Lorcan had retrieved them from the imps, and the items spread on the bed belonged to another time. How long ago it seemed, that foolish flight when she had no idea of where she was going or how she would find Lorcan. *I'm glad of the naïveté that led me into that mad, headlong dash. No matter how much I deplore the way it must end, I can't regret this time with Lorcan. Now, did I pack anything suitable for dinner with the Prince of the Vampires?*

When she emerged on deck, she wore a sleeveless, white lace shift dress that skimmed her thighs. Intricately tied sandals on her feet and simple pearls in her ears perfectly matched the color of the dress and complemented the pale sheen of her skin. Her hair hung in loose, gold waves almost to her waist. Lorcan stared at her for a very long time.

"Is something wrong?" she asked at last.

Slowly, he shook his head. The look in his eyes turned her insides to liquid. "You look good enough to eat. Which is a worry considering who our host will be."

"Must we go?" The thought of meeting Tibor again unnerved her. It was a link to her father—to the past life she thought she had severed completely—that she didn't want. All she wanted to do—right now and for always—was be alone with Lorcan.

"He was most insistent. You know Tibor. All charm, but the subtext was clear. If we want our safe passage, I must bring you to dinner tonight."

"Is it a trap?"

"There's only one way to find out." His headlamp grin flickered. "We have to walk into it and see what happens."

"I wish you'd find another way of detecting a trap," she grumbled, as he handed her into the dinghy.

"Sure, aren't I just a simple Irish lad with no guile about me?" His accent was more pronounced than ever.

"No, Lorcan, you're not." She gave him a stern look and he met it with an innocent gaze. Even though he poured himself into her with a passion that scorched and astounded her, and afterward held her in his arms each night while—she strongly suspected—watching her as she slept, he remained unfathomable. Since that one occasion when he had told her he was an immortal hybrid, there had been no more confidences. She sensed he regretted that one. But, because she loved him, she knew much more about Lorcan than his words could ever tell her. She knew that behind the laughter there was immense sadness. Something had damaged him and he was determined to keep whatever it was hidden and secret. Most of the time he was very good at it. Now and then the mask slipped and the hurt in the clear blue depths of his eyes made her heart ache.

Lorcan explained that Tibor had instructed him to take the dinghy around the headland and into the hotel's private bay. "Which is a bonus. One climb up those steps in a day was quite enough."

He stretched his long legs out in front of him with a grimace. Although he wore jeans and boots, he had graced the occasion by donning a crisp white shirt that enhanced his muscular chest and biceps. His freshly washed hair flopped forward and he tossed it back in a characteristic gesture. Tanzi's chest constricted with love.

"Don't look at me like that in front of Tibor, *Searc*."

"Like what?" Her voice was slightly husky.

"Like you want to rip my clothes off."

"I always want to rip your clothes off."

Lorcan gave a soft groan. "What are you trying to do to me? Let's save this conversation for later, when we can see it through to a satisfactory conclusion. The story I've told Tibor is that I'm escorting you on a mission on behalf of the Alliance. We're going to the Isle of Spae, one of the largest and most remote islands of Otherworld. The inhabitants rarely engage with anyone outside of their own shores, but Cal wants to discover if they want representation on the council. To reach Spae, we must pass through Tibor's territory."

"You came up with that tale very quickly. I didn't even know the Isle of Spae existed. It's not on any of the maps Cal left us."

"That's the way the Spae prefer it." His face was turned away from her, his expression curiously closed. If they'd had time, she would have liked to ask him more about his connection to the Spae.

The dinghy appeared tiny alongside the sleek yachts in the marina below the castle walls. Once Lorcan had tied it up and helped Tanzi onto the quayside, a dark-suited figure appeared as if from nowhere and bowed low before her. "Your Highness. I am Nicu, attendant to the prince. It is my honor to serve you."

Ignoring Lorcan, Nicu led the way along the quayside and into the grounds of the castle. The message was clear. Only one of Tibor's guests was important enough to warrant any attention. Tanzi cast a rueful glance in Lorcan's direction. Although he made no comment, his eyes twinkled and one side of his mouth lifted in an appreciative half smile.

The inside of the castle was every bit as elegant as its

exterior. White marble floors, gold-colored upholstery and antique furnishings were complemented by vast crystal chandeliers and exquisite paintings. Tibor was waiting for them at the foot of a sweeping staircase, and one look at his face was enough to confirm Tanzi's fears. His feelings had not changed. His light eyes blazed with the same passion they always had when he looked at her, only now his smile held a hint of triumph that she found unnerving. Why should he feel triumphant? She had no qualms about meeting his gaze. He could not bind her with his vampire stare any more than she could enchant him with her faerie glamor.

"Princess." The word was a caress as he raised her hand to his lips. Tanzi risked another swift glance in Lorcan's direction. All trace of the smile had vanished and she was instantly aware of his alert expression, the lithe, coiled strength of his body. It was going to be a long night.

She tried to dredge up a memory of that other Tanzi, the one who existed before the day when Moncoya made his fateful announcement about her forthcoming marriage to the devil. How would *that* Tanzi have acted in this situation? To her shame, she suspected the other Tanzi might have flirted with Tibor, even encouraged his advances. "I was honored to receive your invitation, Tibor."

"The honor is all mine." Lorcan cleared his throat impatiently and the sound served as a reminder to Tibor that he was still holding Tanzi's hand. He released her, bowing slightly and indicating a room on his right. "Shall we?" His smile deepened as Lorcan made a move to follow them. "There will be no need for your bodyguard to accompany us. I am more than capable of looking after you." His silken tone became dismissive as he faced Lorcan. "Nicu will escort you to the kitchens, where the cook will provide a meal for you."

"I am not leaving the princess's side." Lorcan folded his arms across his chest. It was a statement of intent.

"Such devotion to duty." Tibor's eyes narrowed slightly as they took in the unyielding look on Lorcan's face.

Tanzi debated the situation quickly. They needed this safe passage from Tibor. If he refused them, they would be forced to turn back. She would be driven into hiding and, even with Lorcan at her side, she didn't like her chances of staying concealed with Moncoya and Iago—not to mention Satan himself—on her tail. Turning to Lorcan so that her back was to Tibor, she tried to convey her thoughts to him with her eyes. At the same time, she uttered the words he didn't want to hear. "You may leave me with the prince."

For a moment she thought he would refuse. His jaw was rigid and she could see the internal battle he was waging. Willing him with her eyes to comply, she bit her lip. Eventually, he drew a ragged breath before nodding curtly. "Call me if you need me."

Turning on his heel, he strode away. Watching the proud set of those broad shoulders, Tanzi felt suddenly, overwhelmingly sad.

Tibor ushered her into an informal dining room, where a table had been set for two. "Alone at last."

He really was such a cliché. Just not a stereotypical vampire, she thought, as he held out her chair with old-fashioned courtesy. Tibor was more her idea of a mortal playboy prince. Strikingly handsome with razor-sharp cheekbones and a square, sculpted jaw, he wore his white-blond hair so short that the stubble on his head was the same length as the neat beard framing his surprisingly full lips. In contrast to his Nordic coloring, his skin had a light gold hue. Beneath his perfectly fitting designer suit, his body was hard and toned. Although he had never shown her anything other than courtesy, Tanzi knew his reputation. His control over the vampires was absolute, and he was ruthless when crossed.

Tibor indicated the array of silver salvers that were arranged on the table. "My chef has prepared your favorite dishes."

His words jolted her. *He remembers the foods I like?* Having an admirer who was the vampire overlord was one thing. This felt uncomfortably like stalking. His eyes on her face did nothing to alleviate her unease. His expression was...*hungry.* For the first time ever, Tanzi could have sworn she glimpsed the white gleam of his fangs as he turned aside to pour wine into her glass. Usually, Tibor was completely in control. Suddenly, it seemed he wasn't. Perhaps sending Lorcan away had not been such a good idea, after all. Despite her strength and Valkyrie training, Tanzi knew she would be no match for a vampire. *He doesn't want to fight you,* a little voice inside her whispered. *It might be better if he did,* another one snickered.

Although he was unable to eat any of the food, Tibor insisted on serving her himself. "We don't want interruptions."

He sat back in his chair, watching her as she made a pretense of enjoying the exquisitely prepared food. Her mind insisted on making contrasts. *I don't want a man who can't eat anything. I want a man who can share pizza and beer with me. I don't want a man who has been measured for his hand-stitched suit. I want a man who doesn't care if his boots are worn and his jeans are frayed. I don't want a man who looks at me as if I'm a precious jewel. I want a man who hauls me into his arms and shows me how much he wants me by taking me first roughly then tenderly. I don't want to make polite conversation. I want to flirt and laugh and whisper nonsense after we've made love. I don't want a prince. I know exactly who I want.*

"Have you heard from your father since his exile?"

The abrupt question made her choke slightly on her wine. It seemed Tibor was not so lost in love that he couldn't spare time for a little business. She shot him a sidelong glance under her lashes. It was a difficult question to answer, since she had no idea whether Tibor himself was still in touch with Moncoya. Otherworld politics were a complex affair.

In the end, she opted for a noncommittal approach. "Now, how am I supposed to answer that? If I say yes, I am guilty of treason against the Alliance. If I say no, you will see me as a disloyal daughter."

"You are learning to be a diplomat." His smile was genuinely charming.

"Merlin Caledonius is a good tutor."

"This mission to the Spae is an odd one. With only the Irish necromancer for company? Hardly in keeping with your royal status." He leaned back in his chair, deceptively casual. She was reminded of an inquisitor waiting to pounce as soon as she slipped up.

Tanzi kept her voice light. "The Spae are known for their dislike of ceremony." Was that true? She hoped so. "It was felt a low-key approach was best."

"The food is good?"

The change of subject caught her off guard. "Um, yes. Delicious." She set her knife and fork down. "But I'm full. Thank you."

Without warning, he caught hold of her hand, raising it to his lips once more. This time, there was no mistaking the glide of fangs over her flesh. It took every ounce of Tanzi's self-control to stop herself from shuddering. "You know how I have always felt about you. Let me offer you a return to the lifestyle you lost with your father's defeat."

That explained the triumph. He thought she was so shallow that she would want her royal status back at any price. *Let's face it, Tanzi, that's exactly the person you used to be.* "My family is disgraced. I am no longer a fit person to rule alongside you."

His eyes narrowed to chips of blue ice. "Let me be the judge of that. Or are you telling me you do not wish to be my wife?"

Oh hell. How was she supposed to answer *that* and get out of here with a safe passage? Lowering her eyes, she tried to keep her voice shy and soft. "These past months have been so difficult, Tibor. The battle lost, the faeries overthrown, my father disgraced, my sister injured… and now I am charged with this new role of envoy to the Alliance."

"You are saying you need time to consider?" She risked a glance at his face. His expression was a combination of incredulity and suspicion.

Appeal to his chivalrous nature. Not a rule she ever thought she would apply to a vampire, but Tibor was no ordinary vampire. "You have always been so understanding." She sighed. She decided against a flutter of the eyelashes. That might be a step too far.

He bowed his head in acknowledgment. "Very well. I will be patient awhile longer. Next time we meet, however, I will expect an answer from you, Tanzi." This time, when he smiled, he made no attempt to disguise his fangs.

Chapter 15

If he hadn't been so worried about how Tanzi was faring with her bloodsucking admirer, Lorcan might actually have been able to enjoy himself. It wasn't often he got to set a roomful of vampires on edge with his very presence. The servants' quarters occupied the entire basement of the castle, and it was apparent that word of his arrival had spread like wildfire. As if he was the monster in an old-fashioned freak show, every one of Tibor's attendants wanted to get a look at the necromancer, even though he clearly struck fear into their hearts. *The rumors are true, guys. I can turn each of you into a statue with a single word.* Lorcan got the feeling if he said "boo" loudly enough, they would all run screaming to their master. It was worth bearing in mind. That would be one way to interrupt Tibor's amorous plans for Tanzi.

"How did you get to be such a good cook when you can't eat anything yourself?" he asked the chef, as the man skittered around him serving plates of delicious food.

"Before my transformation, I trained at the finest hotel in Paris."

The only other person who ate anything was Nicu. The man was obviously Tibor's new human slave. Dimitar's replacement. The thought took him back to that night in Tangier. "Why would a human servant switch allegiance?" Lorcan tilted his chair back, startling a young vampire housemaid who had sneaked closer to him.

"Stupidity." A sneer accompanied the word.

Lorcan decided he didn't like Nicu. "Seriously. I thought you guys were bonded to your vampire master for all eternity."

"We are. In the mortal realm we are the daylight eyes, ears, hands and voices of the master vampire we serve. Becoming a servant gives us immunity to the mind control of other vampires. Unless one more powerful than our own master wills us."

Lorcan shook his head. "That's not what happened with Dimitar. Jethro is not a vampire and he didn't command Dimitar to leave Prince Tibor. In fact, he was as surprised as everyone else when he suddenly acquired a human servant."

Nicu shook his head dismissively. "Not possible."

Lorcan was tired of the man's sour expression. "Have it your way." He glanced at the clock that hung over the vast industrial cooker, although the action was pointless. Time meant nothing to vampires. The clock was for decorative purposes only. Its hands were frozen in position at midnight. The witching hour.

Nicu followed Lorcan's gaze. "My master likes to take his time over affairs of the heart."

"I'll just bet he does." Telling himself his feelings were rooted in his dislike and distrust of Tibor, nothing more, Lorcan scraped back his chair and rose to his feet.

"Unfortunately for the prince, time is one thing I don't have much of."

"You will not dare disturb him!"

"Won't I?" Lorcan made for the door. He threw a challenging look back over his shoulder. "Care to watch me?" None of the vampires moved.

Nicu was hard at his heels as Lorcan sprinted up the flight of stairs that led back to the palatial entrance hall. *Touch me and Tibor will be looking for yet another human servant.* Desperate for an outlet for the pent-up anger that had been fizzing inside him ever since Tanzi had dismissed him earlier, he willed Nicu to try something. Perhaps Nicu sensed it, for, although he stayed with him, he kept his hands to himself.

Shit! Which room had they gone into? He threw open two other doors before bursting into the dining room, where Tanzi was seated with Tibor.

"I tried to stop him, master..." Nicu's voice was a high-pitched wheedle.

"Unsuccessfully, I perceive."

Tibor's tone sent a slight shiver down Lorcan's spine. It didn't bode well for Nicu later. He scanned Tanzi's face. She returned his probing gaze with a reassuring smile. "Have you come to tell me we must go if we are to complete our journey in the allotted time?"

"If you like." Her eyes widened in warning. Lorcan shrugged a response. He was no longer in the mood to be conciliatory.

Tibor rose to his feet, his suave manner unruffled. "So we must part company again, Princess." He turned to Lorcan. "You have my word that you will be safe in my waters, my friend."

"Thank you." Lorcan did his best to sound gracious. It was difficult through clenched teeth. He could keep telling himself this wasn't about jealousy. He might even succeed in convincing himself.

"There is one small problem, however." *Wouldn't you just know it?* Tibor beckoned Lorcan and Tanzi over to a large, gilt-framed map that occupied most of one wall. It was a chart of the islands of the Vampire Archipelago, more detailed than those Cal had provided for them. The prince tapped one manicured fingernail against the northernmost island. "I cannot vouch for the obedience of the inhabitants of this island."

"Who are they?"

"The Loup Garou."

Lorcan raised his brows. "I am surprised to learn any of their number reside within your jurisdiction, Highness."

"They are a bloody nuisance." The civilized veneer slipped slightly as Tibor's frustration showed. "As you know, the Loup Garou have the body of a wolf, but the fangs and bloodlust of a vampire. They are also possessed of magical powers akin to those of a warlock. Several centuries ago, a breakaway group decided they wished to be classed as vampires, not wolves. After lengthy negotiations, I ceded them this island, now known simply as Garou. In recent years their descendants have decided they no longer wish to accept my authority."

"I suspect they will come to regret their defiance."

Tibor's smile was enough to give a grown man nightmares. "Your suspicions will be proved correct. Unfortunately, that will not happen in time for the completion of your journey." He traced a route between the island of Garou and a larger body of land with his fingertip. "This the Wallachia Channel. You will be forced to traverse it in order to reach the open seas. The Loup Garou have been known to cause problems for travelers along this passage."

"Thank you for the warning, Highness."

Tibor bowed over Tanzi's hand once more. "Remember what I said, Princess."

"What *did* he say?" Lorcan demanded as soon as the dinghy was skimming across the bay and they were safe from prying ears. He cringed at his own neediness. *I sound like a jealous teenager whose prom date has just danced with another guy.* The large flashlight he had placed in the bottom of the small craft lit up Tanzi's face. Her expression was serene, and her long hair blew out behind her like a streamer.

"That he still wanted to marry me. He made me promise to answer him next time I saw him."

"I see." He bent over the engine, pretending it needed his attention. Anything rather than let her see the hurt in his eyes.

"No you don't." Tanzi caught hold of his arm, forcing him to look at her. "Don't you dare be all agonized and noble about this, Lorcan. How could you possibly think I would say that to Tibor and *mean* it? I said it to buy us time, to get our safe passage. For God's sake, we both know I'm never going to see Tibor again."

"I'm sorry." He placed an arm around her shoulders and drew her close. "I just can't bear the thought of that leech putting his hands anywhere near you."

"He didn't touch me. Well, only to kiss my hand once or twice. Although—" she cast him a sidelong glance "—he couldn't hide his fangs."

The corners of his mouth turned down in a brief expression of disgust. "The vampire equivalent of a raging hard-on. Fucking pervert." He turned away, watching the sleek, white outline of *Igraine* loom closer in the darkness. Drawing a breath, he asked the question that had been bothering him all night. "Although…is Tibor such a poor deal? Wouldn't marriage to him be preferable to life as a Valkyrie?"

She didn't answer and he wondered if she'd heard him. When he turned to face her, she was looking away so he was unable to read her expression. When she finally did speak, her voice was low. "I don't love Tibor."

"I thought you couldn't feel love?"

She shifted position so that her face was turned up toward his. It made no difference. He still couldn't tell what she was thinking.

"Turns out I was wrong about that."

Lorcan viewed the Wallachia Channel with misgivings. Although the entrance to the passage was wide, he could see far enough along its route to observe how it rapidly narrowed. High cliffs rose like sheer walls on each side so that it looked as if he would be able to lean over *Igraine*'s side and touch the rocky surface as they passed. Although the water out here in the open was calm, within the strait it churned wildly like the inside of a washing machine. He might as well don a blindfold and take the boat into a cave. He had no idea what might be waiting for them around each twist and turn of the tight channel.

"Can't we sail around the island of Garou?" Tanzi came to stand beside him.

"I checked the charts again this morning. Tibor is right. To get to the open seas to Spae, we must navigate this channel. All around the coastline of Garou there are hidden and treacherous rocks. They'd rip *Igraine*'s belly out if we risked it."

"I don't understand why we must actually go to Spae.

I thought that was a story you thought up on the spur of the moment to tell Tibor?"

"It was, but do you seriously think he won't check up on us?" He gave Tanzi a moment to assimilate the question and shake her head. "Besides, the Spae are the very people to help us with the rest of our route."

And with my search for the true King of the Faeries. With any luck, they would tell him King Ivo's mystery descendant had never existed or was dead. That way he could forget this needle-in-a-haystack quest of Cal's and shake off the feeling that he was betraying Tanzi's trust.

"Have you met with the Spae before?" Tanzi looked surprised. "I thought they were an insular race."

"They are." He hoped she wouldn't notice the way he avoided the question. All the other times he'd been to Spae, his approach had been a damn sight easier than this. He'd taken the direct route straight through a portal from the mortal realm to the Isle of Spae. He viewed the channel again. Was he really going to take them in there with no idea of the depth of the water, the wind speed or what hazards lay in wait for them? His stomach tightened with a combination of nerves and excitement. "Grab yourself a life jacket, *Searc*, this is going to be a white-knuckle ride."

Lorcan approached the channel slowly, maneuvering *Igraine* into the entrance with care. The boat met the harsh slap of the first waves valiantly as he guided it between the looming rocky walls. From his experiences in the fishing boats as a boy, he knew there was a difference between this and meeting steep waves out in the open. Even the most minor miscalculation on his part could send *Igraine* crashing into the cliffs. Once they had entered the passage there was no turning back.

"Okay?" He had to shout to Tanzi to be heard above

the rush of sound all around them, and she nodded, clinging to the back of the seat, her face strained as she stared ahead at the roiling waters. The waves slapped the boat's sides and the channel acted as a funnel for the wind, driving the spray into their faces and robbing them of their breath. *Igraine* mounted each wave, running down the crest and gathering speed as she prepared to meet the back side of the next wave. Burying her bow in the oncoming wave, she was slewed hard by the resistance of the wall of water and would have veered sharply off toward the cliffs if Lorcan had not maintained an iron grip on the wheel. The deeper into the channel they went, the more of his strength it took to keep them on a straight course.

Tanzi's hand grasped his arm hard. Although her lips moved, any sound she made was whipped away by the wind. She pointed up at the cliffs ahead of them. Half closing his eyes against the spray, he followed the line of her finger. Dark shapes were crouched on rocky outcrops that hung low over the water. The Loup Garou were watching their progress. Could this day get any worse?

It seemed it could. As they drew level with the first of the Loup Garou, the wolflike figure swung himself down from the rock, landing easily on the deck.

"You've done this before, haven't you, big guy?" Lorcan asked, observing the way the loup's body rolled easily with the motion of the boat. Fangs the thickness of Tanzi's wrist flashed in something close to a grin. Not wanting to worry Tanzi unduly, Lorcan weighed up the situation. The Loup Garou were undead, meaning he could control them. But in order to do so he would need to concentrate solely on them. Not an easy task while he was trying to stop the waves from battering *Igraine* against the rocks.

As these thoughts were passing through his mind, another of the Loup Garou dropped onto the deck.

"You keep hold of the wheel. I'll take care of these two." Tanzi had to press her lips up against his ear to be heard. Then she was away, doing what she did so well. Gripping the mast for added leverage, she swung both feet off the ground, catching the first loup firmly under the chin. Staggering back, he looked mildly surprised, but didn't go down. Instead, his wolfish smile deepened as he beckoned Tanzi closer.

"Bring it on, little girl." His growl was loud enough to be heard over the clamor. "You want to play rough? We like it rough."

"Tanzi, get back over here!"

Whether she didn't hear him or chose to ignore him, Lorcan didn't know. He muttered a curse—several curses—as Tanzi clambered onto the back of the bench seat and launched herself at the grinning loup. He knew what her tactics would be. Eyes and balls. Street fighter tactics. By the way the loup was reeling back, she'd managed to implement part one of the plan and, clinging to him like a limpet, was already gouging at his eyes. Would she have time to get him down and kick him in the balls before his companion got to her? Lorcan's nerves were strained to the point of breaking as he tried to watch what was going on while at the same time steer the boat through the ever-narrowing channel. Despite his annoyance at her determination to place herself at risk, he felt a fierce sense of pride. God, she was amazing. His little warrior princess was bringing that huge wolf to his knees. Sure enough, her foot connected solidly with the loup's groin. Lorcan gave a wince of male solidarity, even as he applauded Tanzi's strategy. The loup collapsed in a groaning heap on the deck. From his posture and the way he was clutching between his legs, he wouldn't be getting up again anytime soon.

Just then, the boat lurched through a particularly high wave, distracting Lorcan and throwing Tanzi off balance. She stumbled against the deck rail and was caught in the grasp of the other Loup Garou. Having seen what had happened to his friend, this one was taking no chances. Holding her at arm's length by the back of her shirt, he shook Tanzi as easily as if she was a rag doll.

"Stay at the wheel!" Tanzi's cry told Lorcan she knew exactly what he intended.

The end of the channel was in sight. He could see the calmer, open waters ahead. If only Tanzi could hold out against the loup who now had her pinned up against the cabin wall by her throat. Lorcan could see her hands flailing wildly as she tried to grapple with him.

"Oflinnan." In desperation, he hurled the halt command at the Loup Garou. But his focus was impaired by everything else that was going on and the word had no effect. As the loup smashed its fist into Tanzi's ribs and she screamed in pain, Lorcan knew he had no choice. He released the wheel. "Hang in there, *Igraine*, sweetheart."

With yards left before they reached the end of the channel, he grabbed a coil of rope from the deck and skidded across the wet boards. Snagging a loop of rope around the neck of the loup, he pulled it tight. It worked like a charm and the loup instantly released Tanzi. She dropped like a stone onto the deck while the creature tore wildly at the rope around its neck with both hands. Preoccupied as he was with keeping a grip on the rope, Lorcan still had time to notice Tanzi's pallor and the fact that she stayed down rather than coming to his aid.

"Oflinnan. Do it now, you loup bastard." Usually when he issued the command, he made sure to keep his voice

level. This time he could feel the rage trembling through every syllable. Obediently, the Loup Garou froze.

Shaking with a combination of rage and relief, Lorcan fell to his knees beside Tanzi. She was alive, but her breathing was shallow and he could see the angry red imprints of the loup's fingers on the tender flesh of her throat. As he cradled her against his chest, she opened her eyes.

"The wheel…" It was a whispered croak, but it made him look up and take stock of what was happening around them.

He was just in time to see *Igraine* give a final bound through the last waves as she broke free of the channel and crashed out into the open sea beyond. It was almost as if the boat had listened and obeyed him when he urged her on. But even Cal couldn't do that. Could he? There was no time to ponder the matter. Scooping Tanzi up into his arms, he carried her down into the cabin, depositing her carefully on the bed.

"Give me one minute. I need to get rid of our uninvited guests, then I'll be back to take care of you."

It probably took less than a minute to tip the two Loup Garou over the side of the boat and run back down the steps into the cabin. Nevertheless, while he was gone, Tanzi had managed to get up and go into the bathroom so that she could examine the damage to her ribs. Lorcan felt cold, impotent fury rip through him again as he viewed the angry red marks ravaging her pale skin. Without the protection of her life jacket, she'd probably have been killed.

He soaked a towel under the faucet and held it against her side. Tanzi sucked in her breath sharply, catching her lower lip between her teeth. "I'd like to go and drag those two back out of the water just so I could make them pay for every bruise."

"Could you get me a glass of water instead?" Her voice still sounded as if she'd gargled with broken glass, but she managed to smile. "And then maybe help me out of these wet clothes?"

It was only much later, when he sat on the bed next to her as she slept, that he paused to examine his feelings in that moment on the deck when he didn't know if she was alive. It had felt as if his chest was being cut open with a rusty saw and his heart torn, still beating, from the cavity. *And I'm going to do it all over again by voluntarily letting her go when we reach Valhalla. What kind of idiot does that make me?* He already knew the answer. *The worst kind.*

Chapter 16

The Isle of Spae was a patchwork of gold and green, an enchanting landscape of rocky hillocks, dazzling white sands and wind-tossed turquoise waters.

"What awaits us here?" Tanzi viewed the blue-and-white bird-filled skies with a feeling that was as close to fear as she ever came. Nowhere could live up to the perfection this place promised.

"Hopefully, a chance for you to rest and recuperate." Lorcan steered the dinghy into the secluded bay. Springing lightly onto the stony shore, he reached out a hand to assist her. Tanzi followed him, aware of every aching muscle. Although two days had passed since her encounter with the loup, the bruises to her ribs were still painful and her throat, although healing, remained raw.

"No wolves?"

"No Loup Garou. But there are real wolves in the forests." He smiled, drawing her to his side and pressing his lips to her temple. Gratefully, Tanzi leaned against him, enjoying his strength and the muscular warmth of his body. He released her so that he could haul the boat farther up onto dry land. Grabbing the bag he had packed, he took Tanzi's hand. "Come on, they know how to look after their visitors on Spae."

They followed the rugged sweep of the beach, their progress watched by stags on the hillside, otters gamboling at the edge of a small lake and golden eagles swooping down from the higher crags. When they reached the far side of the bay, Lorcan took an inland route toward rolling hills. As their path led them into a deep valley, Tanzi caught a glimpse of white-walled, thatched cottages in the distance. Drawing closer, she could see horse-drawn carts in the fields, barefoot children playing on the grassy square in front of the houses and women carrying pails of water. Laughter, happy chatter and the smell of cooking filled the air.

"Welcome to the Isle of Spae." Lorcan was watching her face.

She felt the tension ooze out of her body. "Who are these people?"

"They are the Spae folk."

"I hadn't heard of them until you spoke of them a few days ago." There was a tangible sense of community about the place. The women were the focal point. Working together to prepare and cook a meal over a large open fire in the center of the green, they managed to watch over the children, issue instructions and tend the livestock at the same time. Their clothing belonged to another century, and there was no sign that the trappings of modern life had encroached upon their village.

"They are the descendants of the ancient Celtic race of Spae-wives, women who possess all the supernatural wisdom and power, but lack the malevolent spirit, of witches. They were persecuted in the mortal realm, hunted and burned as witches during medieval times until they were forced to take up refuge here in Otherworld. They keep to themselves here on Spae, refusing to interact with, or swear allegiance to, any of the dynasties. This is a matriarchal clan. The women are in charge. They are skilled in medicine and surgery. They deal in healing, dreams, foresight and second-sight, and in preventing the influence of evil and witchcraft."

"It sounds like heaven." Tanzi spoke the words with feeling. After the tension of their visit to Tibor followed by the skirmish with the Loup Garou, Spae seemed like a haven of peace that was almost too good to be true.

They had reached the edge of the village green now, and one of the women looked up as if sensing their approach. "Lorcan!"

She cast aside the vegetables she had been chopping and, gathering up her long skirts, ran to greet him. Throwing her arms around his neck, she hugged him tightly, kissing him first on one cheek then the other, over and over. Before long she had been joined by several other women and most of the children. Tanzi found herself in the middle of an excited, chattering group.

Laughing, Lorcan looked at her over the head of the woman who was still embracing him. "Tanzi, if she ever lets me go, I'll introduce you to Ailie."

If anyone noticed what he had called her, they didn't mention it. Suddenly, in this tranquil place, it didn't matter. She could just be Tanzi, with no baggage attached to her name. After only a few minutes in their company, she knew that no one here would care who her father was, or what crimes he might have committed. They wouldn't judge her by her clothes, or her hair or her ability to converse with kings and princes. The only thing that would matter to these people was what was in her heart. Fervently, Tanzi hoped hers would make the grade.

Ailie finally released Lorcan. "If you stopped by more often, maybe I wouldn't need to hug you quite so hard whenever I do get to see you. Did you ever think of it that way, Lorcan Malone?"

Her face was youthful, but Ailie's dark blond hair was tinged with lighter strands of gray and there were fine lines at the corners of her brown eyes. She turned around and, although her expression was kindly, Tanzi got the impression she was being carefully scrutinized. After a few moments Ailie gave a decisive little nod.

"Sure, it's grand to welcome you here, Tanzi. You'll be needing time to rest and heal those injuries."

Tanzi's gaze flew to Lorcan's face in surprise, and he laughed. "The Spae are known for their perceptiveness. And Ailie here, as the leader of the Spae-wives, has more than her fair share of intuition."

"Let me show you to your cottage and then I'll see what I can do about those bruises of yours while the others get on with preparing dinner." Ailie held out her hands so that Tanzi was on one side and Lorcan on the other. As she led them along with her, the other women and children followed behind. Tanzi had the feeling of being swept along on a relentless but benevolent tide. It was one of the most welcome things she had ever experienced.

"The men are returning with the day's catch." One of the young girls pointed to where a group were approaching the village along the path Lorcan and Tanzi had taken.

Tanzi felt Lorcan stiffen and saw his eyes narrow. She followed the direction of his gaze and saw two familiar figures among the fishermen.

"What the fuck are you two doing here?" Raimo and Ronab had been laughing and joking together, but the laughter died on their lips when they saw the tall figure with his arms folded across his chest barring their way.

"Hello, Lorcan." Raimo licked his lips nervously and glanced over his shoulder as though seeking a means of escape. "You told us to come home and find a new master."

"You know very well I meant go back to Ireland, not come here to Spae."

"You weren't specific." The imp's voice became a whine.

"Ah, will you have done with intimidating the imps, Lorcan? They've made themselves useful while they've been waiting for you, so they have." Raimo cast a grateful glance in Ailie's direction.

Lorcan's frown did not diminish. He jerked a thumb in Tanzi's direction. "This is the lady you robbed in Barcelona. She's a faerie." The imps took several shocked steps back. "That's right. Be afraid, guys. Step out of line and I'll let her loose on you."

"Lorcan is happy here." Tanzi spoke quietly and Ailie followed the direction of her gaze. Lorcan was sitting on the rocks with the other men, chatting as he worked at mending one of the fishing nets. His chest was bare, his hands busy and, as they watched, he threw back his head and laughed at something that was said to him. In that instant, Tanzi wanted nothing more than to be able to give him the gift of having a future in which every day was like this one. No fighting monsters, no uncertainty, no raising the dead, no sadness in his eyes. Just peace and sunlight and laughter.

"I think so, but I have not seen him elsewhere." She was aware that Ailie took care with her answer.

"It is as if this is where he belongs." Tanzi tried not to phrase it as a question.

The older woman's face remained neutral. Then she sighed. "It is not my story to tell, Tanzi. If he wants you to know—and I don't see why he would not, since he clearly cares about you very much—Lorcan will share it with you in his own time."

They had been in the island for a week, and Tanzi's injuries were almost healed. She wasn't sure if Spae itself had some therapeutic qualities or whether the potions Ailie applied and the massages the other woman gave were responsible for the speed of her recovery. Or perhaps it was the unique way of life here. There was a sense of serenity and community that she had never known, or dreamed existed until now. Whatever it was, Tanzi felt a sense of well-being that was disproportionate to the knowledge that they must soon be on their way again.

"Tell me what lies in store for us when we leave here."

Ailie turned her face to the sea, looking beyond the seen into a distance only she could perceive. At first, Tanzi had been unsettled by this strange extra sense the Spae possessed. She had quickly grown used to it and found it curiously soothing. "The Isles of the Aesir are not what they seem."

"What does that mean? Are they even more dangerous than we have been led to believe?" The lack of information on the charts was frustrating. It would be useful if Ailie could tell them what to expect.

"Sometimes, what we are led to believe may simply be an illusion." Tanzi waited patiently, but Ailie shook her head. She gazed out at the line where the sea met the sky. "I cannot see more. All I know is that the Isles of the Aesir lie beyond that horizon. Yet none of our people, no matter how far from Spae we have strayed, have ever seen them. That in itself is strange, is it not?" The group of men had dispersed and Lorcan was coming toward them. Ailie rose to her feet. "I do know you will be tested again when you leave here, Tanzi. Perhaps not physically next time. Trust your heart. It already knows the answer."

That's exactly what I am doing, Tanzi thought as she watched Ailie pause and exchange a few words with Lorcan. *If only my heart wasn't in agreement with my head. They are both telling me there is only one solution.* She looked at the point on the shimmering horizon where Ailie had stared for so long. *Next stop, Valhalla.*

"Come on, *Searc*." Lorcan's appearance beside her tugged her away from her thoughts. "Ailie tells me there's a grand feast planned for tonight. Let's go home."

Home. Lorcan didn't know what he'd done to her with that simple word. How could he? He slipped an arm around her shoulders and they walked in silence to the two-roomed cottage they had shared since their arrival on the island. The interior of the tiny dwelling was half the size of Tanzi's bedroom back at the faerie palace. The front door didn't quite fit, so a fierce wind whipped straight off the ocean and rattled the window frames. There was no bathroom or kitchen, so they had to share the communal village facilities. But it contained her big, beautiful Irishman, and that made it home. The only home she had ever known. The only one she ever wanted.

"You're quiet this evening, *Searc*." Lorcan threw his long frame down onto the sofa that almost filled the living room and patted the seat next to him.

Tanzi sat down, curling her feet under her and resting her head on his shoulder. "I've been thinking about the Spae. You told me that they judge others only by what is in their heart."

"Yes." He ran his hand down the length of her hair.

"That is how you have always judged me. You looked beyond the pampered sidhe princess and found the real me." The hand stilled and she lifted her head so that she could look at him.

His eyes on hers were the endless, unreadable blue of a summer sky. "It is what I always try to do."

"When you were injured fighting the zombies, you healed almost instantly." He didn't respond. "Are you of the Spae, Lorcan?"

Pain replaced the blue, like rain clouds scudding across the heavens. "Once I was."

He turned away, his bent head and hunched shoulders conveying unspeakable anguish. Knowing that words would not do, Tanzi slid her arms about his waist from behind and rested her cheek between his shoulder blades. He remained stiff and still in her embrace for a long heartbeat before a sigh racked his whole body.

"My mother was one of the original Spae-wives. My father was an Irish fisherman. When they wed, she chose to live a mortal life."

Turning, he drew her into his arms, seeking her lips in a kiss that seemed to draw the very soul from her body, until Tanzi could no longer tell where she began and he ended. "I need you so badly right now."

"I'm here."

"I don't want to hurt you." The words were a groan against her lips.

"I'm all healed, Lorcan." She stood up, pulling her sweater over her head and moving to unbutton her jeans. "And I need you, too."

When she stood naked before him, he gripped her waist, drawing her to him and holding her between his knees. He moved his mouth to claim one already stiff nipple, grasping it with his teeth and sending a thrill through her entire body. Tanzi's primal moan echoed around the tiny room as he suckled her with slow, teasing motions, alternating the softness of his lips with the roughness of his teeth.

She sank to her knees between his legs, tugging his fly open. His cock sprang free of the restraining material and Tanzi dipped her head, licking along his shaft. Lorcan jerked in his seat. As she eased her lips over the head of his cock, he groaned and let his head fall back. She relaxed her mouth, working him deeper. When he struck the back of her throat, Lorcan tangled his hands in her hair, easing out of her mouth.

"Too much." His voice was hoarse.

He stood up, his jeans sliding farther down his hips, and gripped Tanzi under her arms. Lifting her so that her upper body rested on the sofa while she knelt on the floor, he positioned himself behind her. Tanzi couldn't wait any longer. As she felt his thumb caress her back passage, she let her hips rock back. His cock, huge and throbbing, filled her immediately.

So many sensations filled her that Tanzi was begging him for more before he'd even moved. Lorcan stayed still, hilted deep within her. The only movements were Tanzi's own grinding motions, and she pleaded with him, gasping out her longing. When Lorcan finally began to drive in and out, it was with slow and precise motions, his pelvis thrusting, his hips rotating against her as his thumb continued to tease her. His other hand reached around to stroke her clitoris. He was in complete control, circling the throbbing nub in time with his thrusts.

The deeper he drove, the less restrained he became. Jolts of pleasure shimmered up and down Tanzi's spine, and her cries of pleasure mingled with Lorcan's groans.

She heard him grunt above her, thrusting in even harder. He tightened as he pushed into her once more before a growl escaped his throat and he came inside her. Tanzi whimpered, taking him as far inside her as she could and gripping him tight to hold him there. Lorcan held on to her hips, grinding his pelvis against her, making her feel every last jolt that ran through him. His powerful orgasm, together with his fingers teasing her clitoris, rocked her over the edge and she screamed as her own climax tore through her.

With his body still shuddering, he pulled out of her, sitting on the floor and cradling her in his lap. "Ah, shit, Tanzi. You know what just happened? I was so mad with wanting you, I forgot to use any protection."

She wrapped her arms around his waist, her own voice shaky. "*We* forgot. We were both part of that wonderful madness."

The feast was over and the villagers sat around the campfire, talking quietly or drinking as they gazed into the flames. Tanzi's eyelids were drooping with tiredness, and Lorcan kissed the top of her head. "Go to bed, *Searc*. I'll be with you soon."

Nodding sleepily, she waved a hand to the group before making her way across the green to their cottage. Ailie watched her progress, a thoughtful expression on her kindly face. "What do you want to talk to me about?"

Lorcan laughed. "I never could hide anything from you, could I? Can we go to your cottage and talk there?"

"Things must be serious if you need privacy from the rest of the village." Nevertheless, she rose and walked with him to her cottage, which was set back slightly from the edge of the green. She gestured him to a chair next to the fireplace and pulled up a stool, seating herself close to him. "I don't like secrets, Lorcan. And you are storing up trouble for yourself if you don't tell Tanzi everything. She is not just any girl."

"I already know that." He ran a hand through his hair. "But you've no idea how complicated this is. I'm hoping you'll simplify one part of it at least. That way I may not have to keep a secret from her after all."

"I'll do my best." She placed a hand on his knee. "I care about you. It would do me good to see you happy at last."

He couldn't explain it to her. It would take all night and he wouldn't know where to begin. He couldn't very well blurt out the truth, could he? *I never knew what happiness was until now. But this is fleeting because in a few days I have to hand the woman I love over to the Valkyrie and walk away from her forever.* Instead, he did his best to give Ailie a reassuring smile. The troubled light in her eyes told him he'd failed miserably.

"What do you know about the true King of the Faeries?"

She looked startled. "Moncoya?"

"No. He is not the rightful king." Briefly he outlined the story Cal had told him about the baby boy who had been spirited away during the massacre of King Ivo and his family. "It is said that he grew up with no idea of who he really was. I want to know if he is still alive and where I can find him."

"Does Tanzi know you are searching for him?" Trust Ailie to get straight to the heart of the matter. Trust her to know who Tanzi really was.

"No."

"I understand now why you wanted to be private. It's clear that Tanzi has no great love for her father, but the discovery of a challenger for the crown will have an overwhelming effect on the faerie dynasty. It will rip them apart. And, knowing her, I can tell that is something about which she will care greatly."

Lorcan didn't need any reminders of how much his actions would hurt Tanzi. His own conscience told him often enough. "Will you help me?"

With a nod, Ailie closed her eyes. Lorcan had seen so-called seers at work in the mortal realm. Their tricks and convolutions always amused him. The Spae had no need of crystal balls or cards. Ailie did not need to go into a trance or utter an incantation. She could simply discover what she wanted to learn by turning her thoughts inward. When she opened her eyes again a few minutes later, her expression was distant. "He is still alive."

"I wish him no harm, but you've no idea how much I wanted to hear that he wasn't." He tried to say it in a light-hearted tone, but it wasn't funny. Of course he wanted Moncoya defeated. He just didn't want to feel he was the one betraying Tanzi.

"That thought does you no credit. Merlin Caledonius is correct. This is the man who can restore the faerie dynasty to its former greatness. He has both strength and a fierce sense of what is right, although at present he may not always use them wisely. If anyone can defeat Moncoya, he can."

"So who is he? And, more to the point, where can I find him?"

Ailie shook her head. "I can't answer either of those questions. I gained only a vague impression of your challenger. All I can tell you for sure is that he does not look like a faerie."

"How the hell does that work, since he was born a pure-blood faerie?"

"I can only tell you what I see." Ailie reached up a

hand to pat his cheek. "Don't hide yourself from her, Lorcan."

He smiled. "Sure, in a cottage that size, wouldn't it be impossible to play those sorts of games?"

She shook her head, a trace of sadness in her eyes. "You know what I mean."

Chapter 17

Tanzi came slowly awake when the mattress dipped as Lorcan joined her in the bed. He fitted his body to hers, spooning her from behind, and she murmured appreciatively as he lifted her hair and kissed the back of her neck. His hand moved over her breasts and down to her hip, so that he could pull her back against him. Tanzi wriggled with pleasure and then gasped when his erection pressed between her naked buttocks.

"Hold on to that thought."

He moved away and she heard him grab a little foil wrapper from the nightstand. Lightning fast, he had the condom on and returned to wedge his shaft between her cheeks. He lifted her knee and shifted position so that the head of his cock was pressed up against her entrance. Tanzi pushed back against him and she was already so wet that he slid into her. He felt so good. Rock hard, filling her completely. When he could go no farther, he lifted her hips to settle her closer to him while his hands reached around and stroked her breasts and stomach.

They writhed slowly in unison. When Tanzi tried to encourage him to go harder and faster by squirming against him, Lorcan held her still. "Oh, no you don't." His chin was pressed between her shoulder and her neck. "This time, we're going to take it nice and slow."

Obediently, Tanzi stilled and he pumped himself gently into her with tiny movements. The slick little sounds of their bodies moving in time made her crave more. She ground her teeth together, determined to do as he said and enjoy the exquisite agony.

Lorcan's fingertips moved lower over her stomach until they reached the point where his cock moved in and out of her. Holding her outer lips apart, he ran a finger lightly between them, coaxing the swollen bud of her clitoris. Sensation sparked through her. It was no good, she could stand only so much.

"Faster, Lorcan. Please."

His fingers increased their speed in response to her plea.

"More." Tanzi gasped as his touch became rougher, his cock moving in time with his fingers.

Tanzi clenched her muscles hard around him, her body succumbing to the spasms of electricity that surged through it. She gasped, then cried out, her orgasm hitting as his thrusts and fingers coaxed more from her. At the same time, Lorcan shuddered. Tanzi clasped him tight inside her and they plunged together over the edge of ecstasy.

When they drew apart, Lorcan nuzzled the back of her neck and shoulders gently. Tanzi turned to face him so that he could draw her into his arms.

"Why did you leave the Spae?" The words hung in the darkened air between them.

He held her close so that she could tuck her head into the curve of his neck. "I've never been able to talk about it. Even to Cal, and he already knows most of it. Somehow, telling you about it now feels right. Not easy…just right." His chest hitched with an indrawn breath. "I grew up in a small fishing port on the west coast of Ireland. Home was a cottage a lot like this one. We were poor, but my childhood was a happy one."

"Were you an only child?"

"Yes. My mother, as I've already told you, chose a mortal life with my father. The Spae women usually inherit the powers. It is rare for them to pass to a male child, but, when they do, they are more concentrated. I inherited my mother's ability. She used to say I was special, even for a Spae. Very early, she recognized that I could become a great sorcerer, so I was sent to the monks in a nearby priory to learn to read and write. It was through them that I came to Cal's attention. I was twelve when I left Ireland and went to Camelot to study with him. I suppose I was his sorcerer's apprentice. My father was mortal, and he aged at a normal rate. He died when I was fifteen. I remember him, even after all this time, as a good man."

"Like you." Tanzi held him close, feeling the rigidity in his frame as the story unfolded.

"Perhaps. Along with my abilities, I inherited immortality from my mother, of course. Once I reached adulthood, the aging process slowed so that it was infinitesimal. My mother was the wise woman of our village, the healer, the one people consulted when there was a problem. That was back when magic was accepted, even welcomed, by mortals. But things changed. Over the centuries, fear of witchcraft became rife. Suspicion set in. My mother had to leave our home village and keep moving. I went back to Ireland to see her regularly, and each time she told me a new story of persecution. There was a refusal to accept that foresight and second sight were not indicators of witchcraft. Ironically, had the church elders only acknowledged her as a force for good, my mother would have been the very person to assist them in preventing the harm done by witches. In the same way that she managed, for a long time, to control the mischief done by that bloody pair of imps she adopted and tried so hard to rehabilitate." He gave a shaky laugh. "Anyway, I was getting concerned about the danger she was in, so I asked Cal to come with me on one of my visits. It seemed as though they were targeting my mother, and I wanted his opinion. While we were there, the witch finder arrived in the area—"

He broke off, and Tanzi wrapped her arms more tightly around him. "It's okay. You don't have to go on if it's too painful."

"No, I do. Now I've started, I have to tell it all. My mother was imprisoned. She was subjected to the usual flawed tests. Cut with a blunt knife and the fact that she didn't bleed was said to be proof that she was a witch. Thrown into the river and when she swam to shore, it was said that the devil had come to her aid. She was sentenced to death. Nothing I said could sway the witch finder. Then I hit on the idea of asking some of the other Spae-wives to come and give evidence. If they could just persuade him that my mother only ever used her powers for good, not evil, I reasoned, surely the witch finder must see she wasn't a witch."

"Did the Spae come?"

Lorcan shook his head. "Although the Spae originated

in the mortal realm, they, too, had faced terrible persecution there. By that time, they had settled here on their own island in Otherworld. They refused to get involved. On the day of the trial, I was still hopeful, but no one turned up. My mother was found guilty and sentenced to be burned at the stake the following day."

Tanzi reached up to touch his cheek. "I'm so sorry."

He caught her hand to his lips and kissed her palm. "I was half-mad with grief and rage. I sought an audience with the witch finder. I pleaded—I actually went down on my knees and begged—for my mother's life. The witch finder offered me a deal."

Tanzi lifted her head, even though she could not see him in the darkness. "What sort of a deal?" She knew she wasn't going to like the answer.

"One I couldn't take. The witch finder would release my mother if I would provide him with information that Cal was guilty of practicing witchcraft. The deal was a straight swap. Cal would be executed in my mother's place."

Tanzi was outraged. "My God! Who was this man? Weren't the witch finders government officials? How was it possible for him to offer you a deal like that?"

"I don't know. The thing was, he shouldn't have known Cal was there...or even that Cal was still alive. You know the story of how Niniane, the sorceress known as the Lady of the Lake, imprisoned Cal in a cave at Darnantes and that the mortal realm believed—still believe to this day—that he died there?" Tanzi nodded. Her father had enjoyed recounting the story of his half brother's downfall. "Only, of course, he didn't die. He was freed by the Dominion, the angels of the fourth choir, on condition that he went to work for them and kept his identity secret. Well, my mother's trial took place centuries *after*

Cal's release from Darnantes. He was no longer known as Merlin Caledonius. He wasn't with me in Ireland openly, he was in disguise. So the witch finder should not have known who he was. Since then, I've been over and over it in my mind. But at the time, I wasn't exactly thinking straight. I told the witch finder in no uncertain terms what he could do with his deal."

Tanzi had to ask the question in her mind, even though it might cause Lorcan pain. "Could it all have been a ruse to get to Cal?"

"That's one of the things I've wondered ever since. I'll never know for sure, of course. In my desperation to free my mother, I even went to the Dominion and told them about the witch finder's offer. I explained that my mother was being used as a pawn to get to Cal and pleaded with them to intercede. They refused." Tension quivered through him. "I couldn't save her. I couldn't do the only thing the witch finder would agree to. Even though she was my mother, how could I deprive the world of Merlin, its finest sorcerer, one of the greatest sources of good the mortal realm would ever know? On the day of the execution, I stormed into the town square and tried to drag my mother from the stake. The witch finder's guards seized me and I was tied up next to her. They were starting to light the fire beneath me when Cal came to my rescue. It was too late for my mother."

Tanzi held him in her arms for a long time until the trembling in his limbs ceased. "You never told Cal about the deal you were offered." It was a statement, not a question.

"How could I? It was over and he'd have felt guilt about something over which he had no control. No, I turned my back on my past life, and renounced the Spae. I vowed never to have anything to do with the Dominion—Cal often wonders why I hate the angels—and took to wandering. That's why I'm a renegade. The only constant in my life since then has been Cal."

"You renounced the Spae, yet Ailie greeted you like one of her family."

"If I don't come here now and then, my immunity to illness and my ability to heal start to wear off. Being here is still one of the best and yet one of the hardest things I ever do. Ailie knows my story and she's a good friend, but I avoid this place if I can."

Tanzi frowned. "But you appear to be so happy here."

"This time I have been." He didn't elaborate further, simply sighing like a man who had just put down a heavy burden he had carried for many miles. "I'm glad I told you, *Searc*."

"I'm glad there are no more secrets between us."

She wondered if he was about to say something more. Were there more confidences to come? Instead, Lorcan pulled her closer into his arms and pressed his lips to her forehead. "Let's get some sleep. Tomorrow we need to get *Igraine* ready for the journey."

When the time came to depart, the whole village accompanied Lorcan and Tanzi to the beach. Ailie had packed up enough provisions to feed them for a week, despite Tanzi's laughing protest. The older woman hugged her close before holding her at arm's length, her kindly eyes scanning Tanzi's face. "This thing you feel compelled to do…if you change your mind, or it proves too difficult, come back to me and I will do all I can to help you."

For a moment, Tanzi couldn't speak, such was the force of emotion that swept over her. Sharp tears stung the back of her eyelids and burned her throat. If only she could take Ailie up on that offer. The thought lasted only seconds before she resolutely pushed it aside. These people had chosen a way of life apart from Otherworld with all its fighting, wars and politics. If Moncoya discovered her here, he would rip the peace of Spae apart, bringing chaos and bloodshed in his wake. And once this beautiful land had been conquered, what would happen to the Spae folk and their culture? No, Tanzi could not be responsible for bringing this idyll to an end.

"I wish it could be different."

"Wishes are all very well. Sometimes we have to fight to make them come true." Tanzi followed Ailie's gaze across to where Lorcan was saying his farewells to the men. Even if the dual threats of Moncoya and Satan were removed tomorrow, she had no way of knowing what her future held. Ever since Lorcan had told her the story of how he became a renegade, he had seemed lighter of heart and yet more distant. It was as if one barrier around his heart had been broken down only to find another raised in its place. Perhaps he was simply preparing himself for the moment when they must say goodbye. Maybe she should do the same.

"Ready, *Searc*?"

The compulsion to throw herself into his arms—to beg him to stay here with her, to fight her father at her side—was almost overwhelming. Instead, she nodded brightly and placed her hand in his. With one final wave over her shoulder, she walked with Lorcan down the beach to the dinghy.

As soon as they were on board *Igraine*, Lorcan started the engines and soon the faithful boat was skimming across perfect blue seas toward the mysterious horizon Ailie had deliberated about.

"I told you about my mother. Tell me about yours."

Lorcan's words surprised her and Tanzi, who had been standing at the deck rail, looking out across the water, came to sit close by him on the bench. "I can't. I don't know anything about her."

"You know she was a Valkyrie."

"I learned from Vashti when I last saw her that our mother wasn't born a Valkyrie. She was a faerie who joined the Valkyrie ranks…just as I intend to do."

"I thought all Valkyrie were descendants of Odin."

Tanzi shook her head. "It is true that the original Valkyrie were Odin's daughters, but, over time, their ranks have been widened to include warriors from other races who prove themselves worthy."

"So Odin could still turn you away if he thinks you aren't worthy?" His eyes were fixed on her face, his expression impenetrable.

Tanzi's exclamation was one of outraged pride. "Why would he think that?"

Lorcan shrugged. "Just thinking out loud. Back to your mother. So you never knew her?"

"No, she left my father when Vashti and I were babies. We assume that she returned to the Valkyrie, but we don't know that for sure."

"Moncoya must have done something pretty outrageous to make her up and leave her own children."

"You've met my father." The thought hung between them.

"True. So, when we get to Valhalla, what happens? You just walk up to Odin—or Zeus, Jupiter, Manannán or whatever the hell other name you give him depending on which part of the world you live in—and ask to undergo a test to become a Valkyrie?"

Tanzi laughed. "Because of my mother, I have always called him by the old Norse name of Odin, even though my father is descended from the Celtic sidhes, who call him Manannán. But you and I are not important enough to enter Valhalla. Only the Valkyrie, Odin himself and his chosen heroes may enter the great hall. No, when we arrive at our destination, I will go to the great palace of Gladsheim and seek an audience with Brynhild, the Valkyrie leader. I will ask her if I may undertake the required initiation tasks."

"Will you also inquire about your mother?"

Tanzi looked out across the endless blue expanse once more. "I don't know. How would I feel if I finally got to meet her? After all, no matter how compelling her reasons, she left us to be raised by a monster."

It was early morning and Lorcan emerged sleepily from the cabin when Tanzi, who had been on the deck for some time, called his name for the third time. They had dropped anchor overnight in the shallow bay of a small island that was not marked on any of their maps or charts. Tanzi was practically hopping with impatience as she pointed out to sea. "Look."

Lorcan came to stand behind her, wrapping his arms around her waist and resting his chin on the top of her head. "What am I meant to be looking at exactly?"

"Wait a minute." He slid his hands inside her shirt, claiming her breasts as his lips moved lower to graze her neck. "Concentrate or you'll miss it."

"I am concentrating," he grumbled, raising his head again. "And on something far more interesting than miles of ocean."

"There!" Tanzi's voice was triumphant as she kept her finger trained on the horizon. "Can you see it?"

"Bloody hell." In the distance, an island shimmered into sight as though hovering just above the water. As

Lorcan stared at the phenomenon, its outline became clearer. "When did you first see it?"

"About half an hour ago. At first, I thought I was imagining things, because it stays in view for a few minutes and then disappears." Tanzi turned in his embrace. "Can it be what I think it is?"

He frowned, unwilling to accept the evidence of his own eyes. And yet, there it was. Where there had been nothing just minutes ago, there was now a large, mountainous island, wreathed in mist and stretching across the expanse of horizon. And, as Tanzi's words implied, there was only one place it could be. "You mean, is it Avalon? I don't know. I've only heard of it, never seen it."

"I wasn't sure if Avalon existed at all or if it was a mortal myth."

"Oh, it exists all right. But the only person I know who's been there is Cal, and then only once. All he's ever said of it was that it was somewhere between a dream and a nightmare." Lorcan looked back at the island. "The outline fits the description he gave of it. Three pointed peaks like cathedral spires, with the tallest in the center." As they watched in fascination, the island began to fade once more from view.

"This reminds me of something Ailie said. She said that no matter how far beyond their own horizon the Spae strayed, they had never seen the Isles of the Aesir. What if that is because, like Avalon, the isles cannot always be seen?"

Lorcan frowned. "You've lost me, *Searc*."

"What is the legend that mortals tell about Avalon?"

"Ah, don't we need Cal here for the exact wording? He's good at this sort of thing. Let me see, it goes something like this… *On Avalon will be found the last bright hope, a memory of what once was before the darkness snuffed the flame.* And there's another bit about *in the bleakest hour, the mists of will lift for those whose sight is clear.* It was always thought to mean that King Arthur, the one true king, will rise again when the mortal realm needs him most." A thought—outrageous and fleeting—crossed his mind. It was gone before he could fully grasp it, and Tanzi was claiming his attention once more.

"That legend suggests that Avalon cannot always be seen. Perhaps Avalon is one of the Isles of the Aesir. If all the isles have the same qualities—" she waved a hand toward the now empty horizon "—that would explain why the Spae have never seen them."

Lorcan furrowed his brow. "It's a theory...but a pretty flawed one. Why can we see Avalon and the Spae can't?"

"Because we are meant to and they aren't?" Tanzi hazarded.

"Why?" Lorcan persisted.

"I don't know. Work with me."

"I'm going to need a lot of coffee and some serious persuasion before you get me to listen to any more of this theory."

"What sort of persuasion?" She was already laughing at the mock lecherous expression on his face.

"Why don't you come a little closer and find out?"

As the day wore on Tanzi's theory was beginning to look less far-fetched. They sailed onward, passing more islands that first appeared and then gradually faded from sight. These varied in size from tree-covered rocks to vast mountainous landscapes that shimmered in and out of view for several hours. Captivated, Lorcan watched in silence as the raw, natural beauty of hundreds of islets, coves and reefs unfolded and retreated before their eyes.

"How will we know which is the one we seek?" Tanzi's whisper was awestruck as she nestled close against his side.

"I'm guessing that the gateway to Valhalla will be unmistakable."

"I thought we would be prevented from entering these waters."

"Let's not get complacent." He had to concede that Tanzi was right. It all seemed too easy. Lorcan too had imagined they would have to battle their way across the waters surrounding the Isles of the Aesir, yet this surreal journey had so far been completely free from strife. The only life forms they had seen were a few birds and some dolphins that had followed the boat before tiring of the game and swimming off.

The sun had been shining brightly all day, but now a chill breeze cut through the air as though a storm was looming, even though the sky was clear and the sea calm. Within minutes, the blue of the water had turned to gunmetal gray and the sky darkened abruptly like nightfall in the tropics.

"We spoke too soon." Lorcan eyed the sudden changes with misgivings. Already, the waves were rising, their white crests standing out against the stormy backdrop. Spray slapped over the sides of the boat and the wind dragged at Tanzi's hair, then whipped it across her face.

"We must be approaching Valhalla." Tanzi had to raise her voice over the soaring wind.

Sure enough, ahead of them, another island began to take shape through the gloom. And there it was at last. Snow-peaked mountains rose so high they appeared to be reaching into the heavens. A lush green shoreline that, even with the storm obscuring the view, shone with a glint of pure beauty. There was no doubt in Lorcan's mind that he was looking at Odin's legendary home.

Tanzi gripped his arm, drawing his attention away from the island and up into the sky. Thick, black clouds—so low he felt he could reach out a hand and touch them—had gathered. Now they began to swirl and change shape. Within the billowing vapor, Lorcan could see figures beginning to form.

"What are they?" Tanzi watched the strange phenomenon with a mixture of absorption and trepidation.

"I don't know, but I'm guessing they're not our welcome party." Lorcan knew his feisty little faerie all too well by now, and decided a word of warning was needed. She might be the most formidable fighting machine he had ever seen, but she'd taken a nasty beating from the Loup Garou and, despite her assurances to the contrary, he wasn't sure she was completely healed. "Tanzi, if you try to fight these things single-handed, I'm going to take you down to that cabin and tie you to the bed."

"Why don't we save that particular fantasy for a more appropriate time?" She flashed him a look that, even in the uncertainty of the moment, caused molten heat to shoot straight to his groin at an alarming rate. It was scary how easily she could make him lose control. He loved it.

Dark, tormented faces appeared in the clouds, mouths stretched wide in endless silent screams. Huge hands reached down to them, giant, grasping fingers threatening to pluck the boat from the waves and hurl it into oblivion. Within the howling of the wind a new sound, a soft, imploring incantation, tugged at the edge of Lorcan's sanity.

"Even I can't fight those things." Tanzi viewed the huge shapes with a combination of awe and disgust. "There is no substance to them."

"They want us to go with them."

"Where to?"

"Anywhere. I don't think it matters. Their job is to turn us away from here. Either by scaring us or luring us." Tanzi's face showed her confusion. "That chanting is imploring us to follow them."

"I don't hear any chanting." Tanzi cocked her head. "No, nothing."

Lorcan released the wheel, gripping the sides of his head. "It's inside my head. Hurts like hell," he muttered.

Tanzi took charge. "Give me the wheel. They are working on us on two levels. Trying to scare us and at the same time preying on our empathy. If you can hold out, they won't get any sympathy from me. I'm immune. And they sure as hell won't scare me."

"Has anything ever scared you?" Lorcan sat on the bench, keeping his head in his hands. It was easier if he didn't look at the cloud shapes. Easier again if he could focus his thoughts on something other than that haunting refrain.

He couldn't see Tanzi's face, but her voice was curiously expressionless. "Only one thing." She turned the subject quickly. "I think it must be worse for you because you are so perceptive to the feelings of others."

Lorcan couldn't respond. He couldn't speak. The crooning voices were trying to take control of his mind. The sobbing, pleading and begging of a thousand broken souls sent pure agony pulsing through his head. It felt as if someone was systematically hammering at his skull with an ice pick. There was only one way to make it stop. Looking up, he could see Tanzi through the fog of his pain. She stood straight and proud. A tiny, defiant figure against a backdrop of gigantic snarling, jeering faces and clutching claws. The closer they got to the island, the wilder the onslaught became and the more intense the siren song inside Lorcan's brain. He rose to his feet, staggering to Tanzi's side.

"Take my hand." If she could face them, so could he. With a supreme effort, he squared his shoulders and lifted his chin. Pain so violent it nearly knocked him off his feet jolted from the base of his skull to the top of his head and back again. "They are not real." He said it as loudly as he could, but it was little more than a whisper.

When the chanting changed and became a bellow, then a scream, he thought he'd misjudged it. Falling to his knees at the assault on his senses, Lorcan almost let go of Tanzi's hand, but she retained a tight grip on him.

"You're right." Her voice was stronger than his, and she was able to tilt her face skyward. "They can only hurt us if we let them."

The voices faltered, before attempting to resume their song. It no longer touched Lorcan's sympathy in the same way. The tone changed. No longer a lullaby craving compassion, it became a self-pitying wail. The cloud shapes lightened and began to disperse.

"You can't stop us." His voice was stronger now and he twined his fingers more tightly with Tanzi's, drawing on her strength. "We won't turn back."

A final melody, a last wheedling plea. The clouds faded from gray, to white, to nothing. Lorcan's head, like the skies above the boat, cleared. He gave a whoop of delight and lifted Tanzi off her feet, twirling her around. "You are a little miracle. When you said only one thing had ever scared you, what was it?"

"This." As he set her back on her feet, she burrowed closer to him.

He drew back slightly, frowning down at her. "You didn't appear scared at all. And it must have been a bloody good act because those cloud monsters, whatever they were, didn't pick up on your fear."

Tanzi shook her head and he sensed frustration emanating from her. He could tell she wanted to say something more, and that whatever it was really mattered. Her lips parted, then she seemed to think better of it. Laughing, she lifted her face to his once more. "I had you all fooled, didn't I?"

Chapter 18

The island resembled a tropical paradise, edged with sand as white as a mountain snowdrift and dotted about with enticing coral caves. Brightly colored seaweed and shells with the sheen of pearls lined their path as they hauled the dinghy up the beach and into the shelter of a cluster of palm trees.

Tanzi looked around, drinking in the golden sunlight, the little sandpipers running back and forth across the beach and the seabirds gliding in the air above her head. Waves swished against the rocks in a soothing rhythm, gulls cried a mournful tune and summer breezes murmured through the trees. It would be so tempting to pause awhile. Just sit on the rocks by the shore, and watch the seals bask in the sunlight or feed the beautiful swans.

Swans? Tanzi blinked and shook her head slightly to clear it. It made no difference. There really were swans. Dozens of them, gliding serenely on the crystal waters.

Out of place and yet a clear message. She pointed them out to Lorcan.

"Yeah, that must mean we're in the right place." He eyed the swans in fascination. "Swans and Valkyrie. I guess the stories are true."

Once they were clear of the beach, the landscape changed dramatically. Hills, lined with green grass and bright flowers, rose up sharply from the narrow strip of coast. Above them, huge rocky peaks reached into the clouds, signaling that the island's interior was the land of ice and snow they had been seeking. Tanzi pointed again, into the far distance. A rainbow spanned the highest peaks.

"Bifröst, the rainbow bridge. It is supposed to link Valhalla to Asgard, the city of the gods."

Lorcan's expression was unreadable as he studied the mountains. When his eyes returned to her face, she detected something there that she hadn't seen before. She had seen pain in those blue depths many times, but this was something sharper and deeper. This was close to agony. Before she could ask him what was wrong, the look had vanished. Lorcan had forced it away and in its place was the Irish-charmer smile he showed the world.

"I'd say that's your final destination then, wouldn't you, *Searc*? Let's see if we can find this grand palace they call Gladsheim."

Still troubled by that look, Tanzi followed him onto the lower slopes of the hillside. On the boat, when Lorcan asked what frightened her, she was glad he'd misunderstood her. She'd come so close to blurting out the truth. To saying the words aloud. *Loving you. Losing you. Nothing comes close to the fear of never seeing you again.* Her feelings were a mirror of what she'd just seen in Lorcan's eyes. *This wasn't meant to happen. When did*

*we start to care so much? When did this—us—become
all that mattered?*

It was just as well they had arrived here at last. The
sooner Tanzi could undertake her induction and Lorcan
could get back to his wandering, the better. *We'll both
look back on this as a pleasant interlude, nothing more.*
As Lorcan himself would say…sure we will.

The hillside quickly changed from gentle slope to
steep incline, and they had to scramble to climb it. Their
efforts were rewarded when they paused and looked back
at the view below them. The island was stunning and the
other isles, all clearly visible now, were spread out across
the turquoise and cobalt waters like jewels scattered on a
velvet cloth. Although all around them the wildlife was
plentiful, there did not seem to be any signs of civiliza-
tion on this particular island.

"This *must* be the island we seek," Tanzi said. "The
signs are all here."

As they gazed in frustration at the landscape around
them, sunlight struck the higher peaks. And there it was.
On a perpendicular cliff, hundreds of feet above their
heads, loomed the palace of Gladsheim. It was a huge
structure built from the same burnished red sandstone
as the mountains surrounding it. Imposing, invincible
and yet with a strange haunting beauty, the fortress was
deftly camouflaged so that it appeared to be part of the
mountain range itself.

"How will we climb up there?" Tanzi wondered.

"Carefully."

As they drew nearer, it was clear that the approach to
the palace would be easier than it initially looked. Steps
had been carved into the stone and, although these were
narrow and treacherous, they were preferable to the alternative of attempting to climb the sheer rock face. Over an

hour later, they arrived at the huge, gilt-decorated gates that marked the entrance to the palace. Their way was barred by two guards wearing horned helmets and carrying huge, long-handled axes.

Lorcan suggested in a whisper that Tanzi should do all the talking. "Sure, aren't you good at that whole looking-down-your-nose-and-being-royal thing?"

"I am the Crown Princess Tanzi of the faerie dynasty. I seek an audience with Brynhild." The words might be regal, but she wasn't sure how convincing she appeared with her face flushed bright red and her breath coming in short, sharp bursts after the strenuous climb.

One of the guards looked her up and down. Mostly down, since he was at least a foot taller than her. "Brynhild is not in residence."

It was hardly the response she had been hoping for. Nevertheless, Tanzi drew herself up to her full height. "Then we will await her return. Be so good as to stand aside."

Lorcan's intuition proved correct. Something in her manner swayed the encounter in her favor. Nodding, the guard gave a signal and the gates swung open, allowing them to step inside.

"Nice going, *Searc*," Lorcan congratulated her. "You even had me a bit intimidated there."

They stepped into a central courtyard that resembled a bustling market square with hundreds of people going about their daily business. Tanzi gazed around in confusion. "How are we supposed to know where to go from here?"

As if in answer to her question, a young woman emerged from the crowds. Her plump face broke into a smile of delight as though they were honored guests and she had been expecting them. "I am Flora. I am Brynhild's maidservant, and it is my job to care for her guests. Please come with me."

Tanzi threw Lorcan a look of surprise as they followed in Flora's wake. "I wasn't sure we would be made welcome."

Flora glanced over her shoulder, her hearing obviously keen enough to pick up Tanzi's whispered words. "My mistress believes that anyone who braves the Isles of the Aesir in order to seek her out deserves an audience. Once she has heard what they have to say, that is when Brynhild will decide whether they are worthy of further notice."

"What happens to those who are not worthy?" Lorcan asked.

Flora appeared to have been afflicted with sudden deafness. Lorcan grimaced at Tanzi and she returned the expression before trying a different question. "When will Brynhild return?"

"Oh, very soon. The Valkyrie have been sent into battle in the mortal realm. My mistress leads the ride. She is Odin the Allfather's chosen shield maiden, and she will bring back those warriors who must take up their place in Valhalla. Brynhild never stays away from Gladsheim for long."

Flora led them through the throng and toward the castle entrance. Once they passed through the palace doors, the contrasting silence after the bustle of the exterior made Tanzi feel she had entered a sacred sanctuary.

"This is the Hall of Pearls." Flora paused to allow them time to admire the grand, highly ornamented reception room. It was easy to see where the name came from, since the surface of the walls had a seashell-like luster. Oil lamps glowed from every alcove. Light bounced off the gold filigree ceiling and reflected the colors of the stained glass windows. The effect enhanced the sensation of celestial tranquility.

"The women's quarters are this way." Flora gestured to a corridor to her right. She turned to Lorcan, forestalling him before he could follow them. "Wait here and someone will escort you to a room in the men's area of the palace."

Tanzi directed an apologetic smile his way. "What will you do to make sure you don't get bored while we await Brynhild's return?"

His answering smile made her stomach do the strange flipping motion that only he could inspire. "I'll think of something. Although—" he lowered his voice so that even Flora with her supercharged hearing couldn't eavesdrop "—my preferred option for passing the time doesn't generally involve you being in a different room."

If she had been offered a choice, Tanzi would have taken life on board *Igraine* or on the Isle of Spae—as long as those options included Lorcan, of course—over life as a Valkyrie. But she had to admit that sinking into a gold-plated bath filled with steaming, scented water had its compensations. When she emerged, she found that Flora had taken her clothes away to be washed and had left an ivory silk robe and gold-colored sandals in their place. This was the lifestyle she had once taken for granted, she thought with a smile, as she fastened a gold cord belt around her waist. How quickly she had left it behind. And how little she missed it!

A soft knock on the door signaled Flora's return. "I will escort you to the grand hall for dinner."

The grand hall sounded promising. She might see Lorcan again. *You are pathetic,* she scolded herself as Flora led her along a series of ornate corridors. *If you are missing him this much after one hour apart, how will you cope with forever?* Since she already knew the answer to the question, she felt her spirits sink even further. To distract herself, she glanced around at her surroundings. They were crossing an open courtyard, bordered on all four sides by a high tower. In one of these, a young woman was leaning on the parapet looking out across the mountain scenery. Her waist-length red-gold hair caught the dying rays of the evening sunlight and, even across the distance, the haunting sadness of her demeanor communicated itself to Tanzi.

"Who is she?"

Flora sighed, her reluctance to discuss the matter obvious. "That is Silja, the youngest of Odin's daughters. Before she was banished to a prison in that tower, she was my mistress and the most favored of the Valkyrie."

"What was her crime?"

Flora glanced over her shoulder as though afraid someone might be listening. "Silja broke the Valkyrie code with a *man*. And, to make things worse, he was a mere mortal." Her voice dropped to a horrified whisper. "The code is clear. The Valkyrie must remain pure in heart and body."

Tanzi felt color flame in her cheeks. *If that is the case, I might have a similar problem. I can hardly claim, by Valkyrie standards, to have been "pure of body" lately!* In the circumstances, she decided it might be best not to mention her relationship with Lorcan during the induction process.

Her eyes traveled upward again to the tower where the lonely figure of Silja continued to gaze out across the darkening hillside. "How sad."

"Yes, my poor young mistress was foolish. She spoke to this man, rescued him from the battlefield and tended his wounds. When Brynhild discovered her treachery, she was outraged and went straight to Odin with the story. Silja was banished to that tower for the rest of her days, never to ride again with the Valkyrie."

"Wait a minute." Tanzi stopped in her tracks, unable to quite believe what she was hearing. "Silja was imprisoned just for *helping* a man?"

"Yes. What did you think…? Oh!" Flora covered her mouth with one hand. "You thought I meant—" she made a helpless gesture "—she had been intimate with him? Oh, good heavens, no! *That* would have led to certain death. Odin would not allow a Valkyrie to disgrace her calling so."

That clinched it. *I will definitely not mention Lorcan.* Although the thought instantly angered her. It also made her want to seek Lorcan out and drag him off to bed. *Why shouldn't I? I'm not a Valkyrie yet. To hell with their code. I'll follow it once I reach Valhalla. In the meantime, what I do is my business and no one else's. And my heart is pure and true. It belongs to Lorcan…*

"You look quite fierce. Is everything well?" Flora's expression was alarmed.

Tanzi attempted a laugh. It almost worked. "I'm fine." *As fine as someone can be when she is wondering if she is about to make the biggest mistake of her life.* "Where is the grand hall?"

Flora indicated for Tanzi to precede her across the courtyard and into another wing of the palace. When Tanzi cast a final glance back over her shoulder, Silja had turned away. Life imprisonment for helping a wounded soldier. Brynhild certainly lived up to her fearsome reputation.

When they entered the grand hall, it was full of people, all of whom were seated on cushions on the marble-tiled floor. Lorcan was already there, sitting with a group

of men. The familiar smile lit his eyes when he looked
up and saw her. Some of the heaviness around her heart
lifted and she made a move toward him, but Flora's hand
on her arm restrained her.

"It is forbidden for the men and women to mingle."
Flora's voice was laden with condemnation.

With a regretful look in Lorcan's direction, Tanzi took
a seat on the opposite side of the hall. The meal, which
consisted of a number of courses—all of which were
delicious—seemed to take forever, and Tanzi had to be
content with watching Lorcan across the room as he con-
versed with his companions. Now and then their eyes met
and Tanzi felt the full force of her love for him ignite inside her like an out-of-control forest fire. Only his touch
could quench it and, since that was not to be forthcoming, she was forced to let it rage wildly. Unable, and unwilling, to follow his lead and make small talk, she ate
in silence, desperate to get away from the oppressive atmosphere of the hall.

"I can find my own way back," she told Flora, when
the meal was finally over. Ignoring the look of hurt the
maidservant gave her, Tanzi stalked out of the hall on
her own. The courtyard was in darkness, lit only by an
occasional pool of golden light from torches set high in
the sandstone walls. As she neared the entrance to the
women's wing, a hand shot out of the gloom and grasped
her by the arm. She was hauled into a dark corner and
pinned against the wall by a warm body.

Before she could protest, a familiar voice murmured
in her ear. "I thought I'd go mad if I had to spend another
minute not being able to touch you."

Tanzi melted against Lorcan's muscular chest. "We
are not supposed to mingle."

His laughter turned to a husky groan as her lips

found the pulse at the base of his throat. Lorcan's hands smoothed the slippery silk of her gown over the curve of her buttocks. "I want to do a lot more than mingle with you, *Searc.*"

As if on cue, Flora's disapproving voice called out across the courtyard. "Your Highness?"

"Ignore her." Lorcan pulled Tanzi deeper into the shadows.

"The Valkyrie have returned. Brynhild will see you now."

Tanzi didn't know the meaning of the Gaelic words Lorcan muttered under his breath, but she got the impression they were not complimentary toward Odin's eldest daughter.

"Go to my room. I'll be there as soon as I can."

Pressing a swift kiss onto his lips, she emerged from the darkness and crossed the courtyard to where Flora was waiting for her.

The coats of the horses shone like satin and the steeds plunged and reared with restless energy even after their long ride. Each horse unfurled giant wings in preparation for the flight back to the stables. Brynhild, all-powerful leader of the warrior maidens, dismounted and strode out at the head of her armor-clad troop. Noted for their beauty, each Valkyrie was possessed of fair, silken skin, impossibly blue eyes and flowing, golden tresses. They were dressed in identical silver helmets adorned with white wings, and scarlet corsets over which they wore fish-scale breastplates. Over their battledress they wore cloaks made of the purest feathers from the whitest swans. Each Valkyrie carried her own shield and spear and wore a short sword at her side.

Brynhild paused in front of Tanzi, looking her up and

down. Signaling for the other Valkyrie to enter the grand hall ahead of her, she took Tanzi's arm and led her into a small reception room.

"What was your mother's name?" No preliminaries, no greeting. Tanzi bit back smile. It was like being with Vashti.

"Enja. She was a sidhe who became a Valkyrie, until she married my father." Tanzi drew a breath. Now for the hard part. "He is Moncoya, King of the Faeries." Brynhild gave no sign that she knew the name, so Tanzi continued with her story. "When my twin sister and I were babies, she left and we always believed that she returned here."

Brynhild gave her a sideways glance. "I remember Enja."

"You do?" Tanzi had not been prepared for her own reaction to those words. Sharp tears stung her eyelids and then spilled over. "I'm sorry. My father always forbade any mention of her, so I've never met anyone who could tell me about her. What was she like?"

Brynhild smiled. "Like all Valkyrie. Beautiful, brave, true of heart. You look like her."

"I've always wondered how she met my father."

"In battle, of course. It was one of many in the endless war of supremacy for Otherworld. Enja was one of the Valkyrie sent to gather the fallen. She never returned."

Tanzi frowned. "You make it sound strange."

"That's because it is. It is the sworn duty of a Valkyrie to bring the bravest of the fallen to Valhalla that they might serve Odin. That is why I remember your mother so well. It is the only time a Valkyrie has failed us."

Although Brynhild's tone was neutral, Tanzi sensed censure in her manner. She thought of Silja in her lonely prison tower. The fate of a Valkyrie who stepped out of line was not one she wanted to dwell on. "She must have loved my father very much if she was prepared to break the Valkyrie code for him."

Did she imagine it, or was the look Brynhild gave her one of pity? "Either that or there was some other incentive—or constraint—so great, she was unable to return to us."

Tanzi frowned, puzzling over the words. Was Brynhild trying to say that her father had forced Enja to leave the Valkyrie and stay with him? It would be almost impossible to believe…if they were not discussing Moncoya. "I take it we were wrong and she is not here now?"

Brynhild shook her head. "Wherever Enja went when she finally left your father, she did not return to us." There seemed to be a number of messages in Brynhild's words, and Tanzi felt she needed time to analyze them. Brynhild was moving on. "And now you wish to follow her and become a Valkyrie yourself?"

"If you'll have me."

"Why?" That blue gaze was sharp and inescapable, pinning her in place.

Tanzi had prepared a speech. Every word went out of her head. In that instant she knew that only the truth would do. "Because my father has arranged for me to marry the devil and I have nowhere else to go."

Brynhild was silent for a long, heart-stopping moment. "Come to the Valkyrie Hall tomorrow at noon so that we can begin your induction."

Chapter 19

Tanzi ran back to her room on feet spurred by Brynhild's words about her mother coupled with the need to see Lorcan. Fortunately, when she whirled through the door and slammed it behind her, he was lying full length on her bed with his hands clasped behind his head.

"How did it go?"

She inhaled deeply to calm herself, even though her ragged breathing was due to tension rather than exertion. "I am to begin my induction at noon tomorrow."

The shutters instantly came down on his expression. "So this is 'goodbye'?"

That was a question she could never answer. How could she ever bring herself to say that word to him? Instead, Tanzi replied with a question of her own. "Have you seen the tower that holds Odin's youngest daughter?" Lorcan shook his head, his eyes still fixed on her face. "They imprisoned her there because she spoke to a man. All she did was help him when he was injured during a battle." Her voice rose slightly on a note of panic.

Lorcan rose from the bed and came to her, running his hands down her arms. "You're shaking. What has happened to upset you so much?"

His touch stilled some of the trembling in her limbs. Even so, she couldn't tell him of her fears about her mother's fate. "The Valkyrie are ruthless. Their code does not allow for any interaction with a man."

"So I take it you have decided to keep 'us' a secret from Brynhild?"

Tanzi tilted her head back, desire—an instant, molten antidote to any other emotion—flooding through her as she looked up at him. "Is there an 'us,' Lorcan?"

Since she was in the act of undoing his fly and freeing his erection from his jeans, she supposed Lorcan could be forgiven for the look of surprise he shot her way. "I don't know about you, but this feels a lot like an 'us' to me."

"Can we talk about this later?" As she spoke, she sank to her knees, her lips closing over the silken head of his cock. The breath left Lorcan's body in one long hiss and he leaned back, propping his shoulders against the door for support. Tanzi took his helpless shudder to be a sign of agreement. She felt his groans reverberate through her as she sucked him as deep and hard as she could. Cupping his sac in her hand, she commenced a sweeping rhythm, taking in his full length, then licking the sensitive underside of his cock as she pulled back again.

"I need to be inside you." Lorcan pulled her to her feet.

As soon as Tanzi had slipped her underwear off, Lorcan hoisted her dress around her waist and lifted her so that she could wrap her legs around his body. Holding her with her back against the wall, he drove into her so hard that she cried out. Keeping her still with his hands gripping her buttocks, he impaled her, each thrust sending an electric current of pleasure up and down her spine.

"You're so hot and tight. Let me feel you come."

She closed her eyes as his words tipped her over the edge and she tightened and convulsed, squeezing him hard with each contraction of her muscles. Every nerve in her body felt the impact of her orgasm and she moaned and shuddered. Lorcan joined her, his cock pumping rhythmically inside her. He kissed her, drawing her tongue into his mouth and sucking it gently as he pulled out of her and lowered her to her feet.

"This can't be 'goodbye.'" He murmured the words against her lips. Tanzi could hear her own anguish echoing in his voice and see it reflected in his eyes.

She wrapped her arms around his neck. "It isn't. We have until noon tomorrow."

Lorcan watched Tanzi as she slept. She was sprawled across the bed, doing her usual starfish impersonation, relegating him to a small corner. Every muscle in his body ached, and he stretched. Since this was their last night together, they'd made it a good one. He managed a reminiscent smile, even though the expression was at odds with his mood. All he really wanted to do was lock that door and make sure Tanzi was forced to stay with him forever.

His mind went back to a time before he got to know her, when she'd been Moncoya's condescending daughter instead of his lover. He shook his head as if to clear it. Lorcan had spent his whole life fighting. Battling monsters and saving lives for the resistance had become something he did to keep from warring with the demons inside himself. Moving from one fight to the next was all he'd ever known. After his mother's death, there had been nothing in his life worth putting down roots for, nothing worth keeping. He'd always thought his heart was damaged beyond repair. Now he knew it was simply that nothing had ever managed to breach the walls he had built up around his emotions. Until Tanzi came along. He almost laughed. *Who'd have thought I could fall so hard, fast and gloriously for the high-and-mighty, untouchable faerie princess?*

I won't say "goodbye" to her. The thought was so sudden and decisive that he sat bolt upright. *I can't let her walk away. I love her too much for that.* A sigh of relief shuddered through him. *It's about bloody time, Malone. What took you so long to get here?*

He made a move to wake her, to tell her the jumble of emotions that was coursing through him, but before his hand could connect with her shoulder, there was a furious hammering on the door. Tanzi's eyes flew open, her fae instincts overcoming any trace of slumber so that she was instantly alert.

"Who is it?" She clutched the bedclothes around her naked body.

"It is Flora. I must speak with you immediately."

"Have we been discovered?" Lorcan cocked an inquiring brow in Tanzi's direction. "Will Brynhild try to have you locked away in that tower with her youngest sister?"

"The tower would be too good for me. Stay here and behave," she whispered, tugging her gown from the previous night over her head. Going to the door, she opened it just wide enough to allow herself to see Flora, but used her body to block the view so that the maidservant could not see into the room. "What is it?" The regal tone that worked so well was back in her voice.

"The Norn have asked me to take you to them."

Tanzi paused, and, from his position on the bed, Lorcan saw her expression change as she regarded Flora with suspicion. The Norn were the three Goddesses of Fate, said to control the destiny of every mortal from birth to death. "I am not mortal. What can the Norn possibly want with me?"

He sensed a shrug from Flora. "I am merely the messenger. It is rare these days that the Norn ask to speak with anyone. They are independent of the other gods and cannot be commanded, although it is well-known that Odin wishes he *could* order them to obey him because they annoy him intensely. They please themselves, keeping to their own tower in the palace. Nevertheless, they were most insistent. They told me they have something to tell you that you will want to hear. It concerns the future of the entire faerie dynasty."

Tanzi appeared to think for a moment. Lorcan knew anything that concerned the fate of the faeries would gain her attention. She nodded decisively. "Give me ten minutes to wash and dress." She closed the door, leaving Flora waiting in the hall. Turning to Lorcan, she cast an apologetic glance in his direction. "This sounds like something I need to hear."

"Cal has no time for the Norn. He's met the three old crones who sit at their spindles spinning the threads of human destiny. He thinks they enjoy meddling and like making mortals suffer." Cal had said it often enough. Lorcan didn't think the Norn could do any real harm. How much could they actually know of the world beyond their tower and their spinning wheel?

"But I don't see how they can hurt me, since I'm not mortal." Tanzi's confusion showed on her face. "One thing I do know about the Norn is that they cannot lie. Whatever they are about to tell me must be the truth."

She bit her lip, her expression troubled. "Even so, my instincts are telling me not to go, to stay with you."

His gaze was warm on her face, his voice gently mocking. "Listen to you, the faerie princess who doesn't do emotion suddenly discovering her intuition. Go and see what they want. I'll wait here for you. I need to talk to you when you get back. The Norn might have something to say to you, but what I want to tell you is much more important."

If the Norn wanted to tell her something that affected the future of the faerie dynasty, there was someone else Tanzi wanted involved in the forthcoming conversation. Although Vashti couldn't be present physically, Tanzi hoped she could use their psychic bond to her advantage. As she hurried along the labyrinthine corridors in Flora's wake, she felt for the acorn that she had slipped into the pocket of her jeans.

Vashti? There was no response. *Vashti, can you hear me?*

Nothing. Perhaps Vashti was wrong about the fact that they could communicate no matter how far apart they might be. Tanzi rolled the acorn between her fingers. A faint but unmistakable noise reached her ears, and she turned her head, seeking its source. A smile touched her lips. The sound was inside her head. Vashti's gentle snores were rhythmic and reminded her of when they were children. She had heard that noise a lot during her early years. It had been a constant source of exasperation to Rina. Her twin had always been difficult to wake up.

Vashti, listen to me!

They were mounting a staircase now, nearing the top of the tower that housed the reclusive Norn. Tanzi was reminded of childhood tales of secrets and attics.

Would they find a sleeping princess or an evil goblin? Her thoughts were interrupted by a sleepy voice inside her own head.

Tanzi? Do you know what time it is? It was Vashti's familiar early-morning grumble, and Tanzi felt her heart expand with love and relief.

I need you to listen in on a conversation.

A soft chuckle echoed in her mind. *Whoa. If this is between you and your Irish stud, leave me out of it.*

Flora held open a door and Tanzi stepped inside, her eyes narrowing in an attempt to adjust to the gloom.

Just stay with me, Vashti. This could be important.

The attic room was cluttered, filled with the remnants of centuries of abandoned memories. Motes of dust hung in the air and tickled Tanzi's nose, and the only source of light was a high window covered by a graying lace curtain. Three figures were huddled in the center of the room. Even in the poor light, it was easy to see why Cal called them "crones."

"The goddesses are Clotho, spinner of the thread of life, Lachesis, who decides on the length of the yarn, and Atropos, whose responsibility is to make the final cut." Flora made no move to enter the room as she made the introduction.

"You may leave us." Clotho addressed Flora, who followed the order with relief. She quickly closed the door behind her. Clotho gestured for Tanzi to come closer, and she stepped forward. "Your journey has been one of highs and lows, Princess. Yet Lorcan Malone has not yet shared with you the true reason for his involvement in this quest."

Tanzi felt a sudden chill. She didn't want to hear this. "He came with me to take care of me on my journey to Valhalla."

Lachesis spoke up, snickering behind her hand. "And he has taken care of you very well." She looked Tanzi up and down suggestively.

"Hush, sister." Clotho seemed to be in charge. "Lorcan Malone came with you because he has been given the task of finding the true heir of the faerie dynasty. The one who can challenge your father for the crown."

Tanzi frowned. "I don't know what you are talking about."

"Then Lorcan Malone has carried out his mission well. It is well-known that his loyalty lies with Merlin Caledonius, and he alone. The sorcerer swore him to secrecy."

Tanzi felt an icy hand begin to close around her heart. "Are you telling me that Lorcan had another reason for making this journey? One that was nothing to do with me?"

Clotho nodded. "Your sorcerer has woven his spell to great effect. You were so blinded by his charm, you could not see past the blue of those eyes."

"That isn't true." Tanzi lifted her chin higher, trying to ignore the horrible, sick churning of her stomach. "We both knew our time together was a pleasant diversion. Nothing more."

Lachesis laughed again, the sound—a high-pitched cackle—making Tanzi wince. "Really?" She caught her sister's glance and subsided, muttering under her breath.

"The identity of the true heir is irrelevant now." Clotho's tone was dismissive. "Lorcan Malone already knows who he is."

Irrelevant? Tanzi felt as though the ground beneath her feet was shifting. Lorcan had lied to her. All along, he had used that Irish charm to dupe her into believing he cared about her so that she wouldn't question what he was really doing. He had been seeking this challenger to her father's crown. Someone who would rip the faerie dynasty in two. Even though she no longer felt any loyalty to her father, Lorcan must have known how she would react to the news of what he was planning and what it would do to her people. Of course he knew. That was why he hadn't told her. Even though there had been plenty of opportunities. Such as every night when they lay in bed together...

"You have gone very pale. Do you need a seat?" Lachesis asked, her voice filled with gleeful concern.

"I'm fine." The words came out mechanically through lips that were stiff with tension.

"Of course you are. It is far too soon for your condition to have any effect."

Tanzi frowned with an effort to concentrate. "Condition?"

Clotho sighed. "My sister gets ahead of herself sometimes. But she is right. Although you are a faerie, Lorcan Malone is half mortal, so we can see his future. You are carrying his child."

"Congratulations." Lachesis gave her a sly smile.

"Now I do need to sit down." Tanzi groped for a rickety chair and flopped into it, sending a cloud of dust into the air. She looked from serious Clotho to smug Lachesis and across at sad, silent Atropos—who examined her colored threads before making an occasional snip—with a feeling of unreality. *Why did I decide to come here this morning when my instincts told me to stay in Lorcan's arms?* "Are you sure?"

"The child was conceived on the Isle of Spae. You will give birth to a healthy boy. We are never wrong." There was a touch of hauteur in Clotho's tone. She turned away, hunching a dismissive shoulder over her spinning wheel.

"You may tell Merlin Caledonius that the truth about the challenger can be found on the Isle of Avalon."

"That's it?" Tanzi rose to her feet. Her legs trembled and she held on to the chair back. "You brought me here so that I could pass on a message to Cal?"

"The sorcerer will not listen to us. He prefers to believe that mortals make their own fate."

Tanzi drew herself up to her full height. "I will not see Cal again. You will have to find another way to deliver your message. My induction begins at noon."

Clotho's smile was a mix of triumph and sympathy. "You think so?"

It was Vashti's voice in her head that answered the question. *The old witch is right, Tanzi. Brynhild will not admit a pregnant woman into the ranks of the Valkyrie.*

Tanzi didn't know how long she sat on the stone bench in a secluded corner of the courtyard. All she knew was she couldn't go back to her room. She was afraid that if she saw him again her resolve would crumble and she would allow Lorcan to talk his way out of this. Even now, part of her was trying to reason away what he had done. Did it matter? She could go to him, spend the next few hours in his arms and let him think she was going to join the Valkyrie at noon. Lorcan need never know what the Norn had told her. She had no reason to tell him she knew he had duped her. He didn't need to know about the child or the fact that she would be unable to join the Valkyrie. She could let him walk away from Gladsheim while she dealt with the aftermath alone. If he could pretend, so could she.

Except I can't. Her pride was hurt beyond measure. Not because he had used her journey as the reason to search for the challenger. As a betrayal of her trust, that was bad enough. But why did he have to make her believe his love for her was pure? Because she had believed it. That had been a cruel trick. He had let her believe she had found someone who was truly honest, trustworthy and good. Someone who was the complete opposite of her father. That was what hurt so much, what caused this awful burning feeling deep inside, this restless ache that made her want to see him, to fling all her pain at him, then collapse in his arms and sob until he said all the right things to make it go away. Because she had no doubt he would be able to do that. He was the ultimate charmer, the man to whom she had given her heart. A lovable rogue who could make any woman believe anything he wanted. *I am one of many to fall for love-'em-and-leave-'em Malone. Just another poor fool whose heart litters his path.*

And that was why she couldn't go to him. Her pride wouldn't let her. That was why she sat curled on her seat, wrapped in her pain and her thoughts until the sun was high overhead and she judged it was time to make her way to the Valkyrie Hall to face Brynhild. Unwinding her limbs from the stone bench, she left her quiet corner and made her way back into the palace. *Even though I may have to confront my father once I do, I will be glad to leave this hateful place.*

"Tanzi!" Lorcan's voice halted her in her tracks as she traversed the gilded corridors toward the Valkyrie Hall. "I've been looking everywhere for you." She wanted to keep walking, but, knowing he would only catch up to her, she stopped and turned to face him. "You didn't come back." His eyes scanned her face, a frown tugging his brows together. "My God, what did the Norn say to you?"

"It doesn't matter." The effort of trying to make her

voice sound normal made her head ache. Even so, the deepening frown in Lorcan's eyes told her the attempt wasn't working. "I have to go. Brynhild will be waiting." Keeping her head down, she walked toward the double doors emblazoned with the swan insignia beyond which only the Valkyrie could pass.

"No, wait." Lorcan caught hold of her arm. Tanzi halted and turned to face him. He might be able to stop her, but he couldn't make her look at him. "That's what I wanted to talk to you about."

"I have to go."

"Do you?" He ducked his head, trying to look at her face. "I've been thinking about it. I've thought about nothing else lately. When we started out on this journey, it seemed like the only way. But now I think there might be another future for you...for us. Look at me, Tanzi." In spite of everything, she was powerless to resist him. She lifted her head. His smile was heartbreaking and almost shy. What a pity she knew it was all a facade. "What I'm trying to say is I love you. And, if there's the slightest chance you might love me, too—and I think you do— then maybe we can go away from here and keep doing what we've been doing these last few weeks. Just be together and love each other." He tried to draw her closer, but she resisted. The frown pulling his brows together deepened further. "I'll keep you safe, Tanzi. I swear it. Moncoya won't touch you while you're with me."

His words only served to sharpen her hurt into an anger that was already razor-edged. But the source of its peak surprised her. She wanted to scream at him. *Why couldn't you have said this a few hours ago? When I was still a blissful, loved-up little fool who didn't know how she'd been betrayed? Then I could have thrown myself laughing into your arms. I'd have gone with you to the*

*ends of this realm and the next, Lorcan Malone, secure
in your love. Now I know my hopes and dreams are nothing but a sham.* Lorcan had taught her to how feel but he
had also taught her how to hurt. Drawing deep within
herself, she found the tattered remnants of her pride and
drew them about her like a royal mantle.

Stepping away from him, she managed to tilt her chin
slightly. "I'm sorry, Lorcan." Why was she the one apolo-
gizing? Her resolve hardened. Her voice came out stronger and harder than she'd believed it could. "I don't feel
the same way. I don't love you."

He shook his head. Whatever she had expected from
him, it wasn't disbelief. Although, given his track record,
perhaps that's exactly what she should have expected.
"No. I don't know why you're saying this, but I know
you love me. When you're in my arms, when I'm inside
you, that's when I know it for sure. That's when there's
no place for denial, Tanzi."

The pain in his eyes almost undid her resolve. She
forced herself to focus. So he did love her. She could
see it was true. It should assuage her pride a little, but it
wasn't enough. It couldn't excuse his behavior. He had
used her. She had been his excuse, his passport to start his
journey across Otherworld, his reason to try to find the
man who could destroy the faerie dynasty. Her people.

"I'll admit we've had fun, but joining the Valkyrie
was always my plan. We both knew it. All good things
come to an end, as they say. Now, if you'll excuse me…"

"Don't do this, Tanzi. Please."

It took everything she had to turn her back on him and
walk away. But she did it. It was only at the entrance to
the Valkyrie Hall that her resolve crumbled. She looked
back over her shoulder at him. If Lorcan had been standing there, still gazing at her with that same bewildered

expression in his eyes, she knew she wouldn't have been able to continue. She would have run to him. But he was walking away. His shoulders were set, his stride determined. He was gone forever. Choking back the hoarse sob that rose like a solid lump in her throat, Tanzi continued through the doors.

Brynhild and the other Valkyrie maidens were waiting to greet her. Brynhild held her arms wide in welcome. "My sister. My fellow Valkyrie."

Tanzi took a deep breath. "Before you say any more, there is something you should know."

Chapter 20

Lorcan's journey back to the palace took considerably less time than the one that had taken him to Valhalla, probably because he didn't linger and he had a clearer idea of his route. He also didn't care if Moncoya was on his tail. In fact he'd have welcomed a confrontation with the evil little bastard, but none was forthcoming. He went about the task of handling the boat in a methodical, mechanical way, waiting almost impatiently for the numbness to go and the pain to kick in. When it finally came, it was so bad he lay down in the prow of the boat, curling into a fetal position, helpless to do anything.

The irony of it was that he had been so sure he *couldn't* love. He had truly believed for centuries that his heart was untouchable. Now he wished he could rip it still beating out of his chest and cast it aside. Anything to stop the burning, aching longing that wouldn't leave him. The worst part of it all was that he knew Tanzi loved him in return. He couldn't understand what had changed in those few hours between her lying warm and wanting in his arms and the cold, hard fury he had seen in her gaze before she walked through the doors of the Valkyrie Hall. The Norn had told her something that had made her feel differently about him, and he suspected whatever it was it might be connected to his quest to find the true King of the Faeries.

"If I ever do find that guy, so help me, he's going to have some serious explaining to do," he muttered.

It didn't matter what the Norn had said. Nothing mattered except that Tanzi had voluntarily entered the Valkyrie Hall rather than stay with him. Lorcan hadn't been able to watch her take the final step. He had turned and walked away. He hadn't looked back, but something told him Tanzi might have cast a final glance in his direction. Whether it was his extra sense, his vanity or his desperate longing, he didn't know. He decided the wisest course was to ignore them all. It was too late. Tanzi was gone. She couldn't leave the Valkyrie Hall now of her own free will. The only way for her to get out would be if Odin himself granted her permission to leave. Would that happen? Could it? For now, all Lorcan wanted was to get back to the only person who might be able to give him an answer to that question. Cal would know. Cal knew everything.

He steered *Igraine* into waters that took him dangerously wide of Spae, not wanting to risk seeing the fishermen. He couldn't face Ailie and her well-meaning questions. The Strait of Wallachia held no fears for him this time. The Loup Garou assumed the same menacing positions high on the rock, looming over him.

"What are you waiting for, you loup bastards?" Even though he challenged them, they made no move to board the boat. Perhaps they remembered the gutsy little fire-ball who had taken on two of their number last time. Or maybe they sensed his desperation. If Moncoya wasn't around, he was ready for a fight with a wolf instead. Either way, the loup bared their teeth, but remained in place, content to watch him pass.

Lorcan thought of Tibor as he passed the Vampire Archipelago. The prince was whiling away his time, still believing that one day he would win the hand of Crown Princess Tanzi. Lorcan raised his coffee cup in salute as he sailed past the high-class resort. "We both have it bad, my friend. But there's a difference between us. You love the image, the perfect face and the gorgeous body. I love the funny, fiery, fearless reality behind the princess."

It was dusk when he anchored *Igraine* close to the cliffs below the faerie palace and set out in the dinghy for the beach. When he drew closer, he could see a tall figure on the sands. As he reached the shore, Lorcan recognized Jethro de Loix.

"What brings you here?" Lorcan asked, jumping ashore.

"You do. Well, you, Cal and Stella to be exact. I've been hearing some strange stories about a sorcerer who is out to get the four of us at all costs. Moncoya's new weapon. Apparently he's something to do with Niniane. Anyway, I thought I'd come and check it out, see what Cal has to say."

"Iago." Jethro raised his brows and Lorcan continued. "That's his name, but I've no idea why he's after us or what his connection is to Niniane. And Cal doesn't know. I already asked him."

"I'm hearing bad things about this one, Lorcan." Jethro helped him pull the dinghy up onto the sand. "It may be more Moncoya propaganda, but there's a rumor this guy is a real chameleon. He can disguise himself in pretty much any way he wants." Jethro's irrepressible grin appeared. "We need to watch our backs. At least I know what my other enemy looks like."

"On that subject, I saw Prince Tibor recently."

"Am I forgiven?"

"I wouldn't count on it."

Together the two men made their way up the steps in the cliff, past the lake and over the manicured lawn toward the castle entrance. They were within a few yards of the vast oak doors when something solid hit Lorcan hard between the shoulder blades, causing him to stagger forward.

"What the—?" He swung around to find the something solid that had hit him was a small, determined faerie princess. Vashti launched herself at him again, fury blazing in the icy depths of her eyes. Lorcan was less worried about that and more concerned with the dagger she held in her hand. He tried to sidestep and catch hold of her by the wrist, but Jethro was faster. Coming up behind Vashti, he caught her unawares. Jethro lifted her off the ground and held her against his own body with his muscular arms wrapped around her waist, pinning her own arms at her sides.

"Let go of me!" She squirmed wildly in Jethro's hold.

"So you can kill my friend? I think not."

"What the hell is this all about?" Lorcan regarded Vashti in astonishment.

"I warned you what would happen if you did not take care of my sister, necromancer."

He held up his hands in a helpless gesture. "Vashti, you know it was Tanzi's own decision to stay with the Valkyrie."

She continued to struggle to break free. Her efforts

were futile. As Jethro's biceps bulged with the strain of containing her, Vashti looked tiny in the circle of his arms. "But she couldn't, could she? All because of you!"

Lorcan frowned. "What do you mean 'she couldn't'? I watched her enter the Valkyrie Hall. I didn't leave until she was inside."

"Once she was there, Tanzi had to confess the truth to Brynhild." Vashti was so agitated, she was panting.

"What are you talking about? What truth?" The dagger forgotten, Lorcan took a half step toward Vashti, ready to shake her into talking sense if need be.

"She couldn't join the Valkyrie. Not after the Norn had told her she was carrying your child."

"What?" Lorcan could hardly believe what he was hearing.

"Yes, my sister, the faerie princess. Carrying the child of a hybrid sorcerer! A renegade with no people of his own. How proud she must be." Vashti's lips drew back in a sneer.

"Wait…are you telling me she *hasn't* joined the Valkyrie?"

"Of course not. Do you think they would take a pregnant warrior? Brynhild told Tanzi she must leave Gladsheim at once, before Odin learned of her effrontery."

Lorcan ran a hand through his hair, his brain refusing to fully process what he had just heard. "My God, you mean she's out there somewhere, all alone?"

Jethro spoke in Vashti's ear. "If you drop the dagger I'll let you go." She debated her options. Muttering a curse, she let the knife fall to the floor. Releasing her, Jethro bent to pick it up before turning to Lorcan. "I'm not even going to pretend I understand any of this, but what danger is Tanzi facing right now?"

"Moncoya will go after her. He wants her to marry the devil."

"So we have to find her before he does?" With his usual quick wits, Jethro managed to sum up the situation in a few succinct words.

Lorcan threw him a grateful look. "Not a minute to lose."

Vashti stepped closer, her burst of temper forgotten. "I'm coming with you."

"Daddy's little spy? I don't think so." Jethro shook his head.

Vashti's eyes narrowed dangerously, but Lorcan intervened before she could respond. "She might be useful. Vashti and Tanzi can communicate telepathically." He glanced up at the castle. "If Moncoya is after her, there's one other person we need."

Jethro nodded. "The sooner we get Cal, the sooner we can set off."

When Tanzi explained why she could not join the Valkyrie, Brynhild had surprised her. The Valkyrie leader's expression had taken on a faraway look, as though she was recalling memories of her own.

"You are not the first, and you won't be the last woman to be faced with a choice between love and duty. I envy the outcome you have reached." A gleam of humor had entered her eyes. "But the Allfather will not be as sympathetic, so you must leave Gladsheim as soon as possible."

When Brynhild offered her an escort to take her anywhere she wanted to go, there was only one place Tanzi could think of. It was dawn when the boat Brynhild provided arrived at Spae, and the island looked as inviting as ever with the sunlight dispersing the early-morning mists. Tanzi had been slightly worried that Lorcan might also have chosen to come here, but she remembered his words. This was the one place he avoided if he could. She drew in a cleansing breath of sea air as the sand crunched under her feet. *This is where I want to raise my child...if my father will only leave me in peace to do so.*

Ailie greeted her with a hug and a mug of steaming tea. The older woman listened in silence as they sat on the grass on the village green and Tanzi told her story. Only when she had finished did Ailie speak. "Lorcan spoke to me of this challenger for your father's crown when you stayed here. It was eating away at him that he had not told you of it."

"So why didn't he do so?"

Ailie sighed. "It was the age-old story. A secret gone too far. At first he didn't tell you because you were never going to need to know. You would be gone from this world before it mattered. By the time he realized how important you were to him, the secret had become too big to tell." She gave Tanzi a sidelong glance. "Men don't always get it right, you know."

"But the Norn told me he knows the identity of the challenger. If that's the case, he must have been working hard behind my back to discover it. And then he kept it hidden from me."

Ailie shook her head so hard that her curls flew wildly about her face. "He does not. I know nothing about the Norn, but I know Lorcan. He didn't put much effort into finding the challenger precisely because he knew it would hurt you. He has not discovered who the true heir is." She patted Tanzi's hand. "And I know how much he loves you. And, for Lorcan, love is not something that came easily. Or something that might ever have come at all."

Tanzi felt sharp tears sting her eyelids. "Ailie, what does *Searc* mean?" It was a question that had occurred to her on the journey from Valhalla. Lorcan had been so insistent about his love for her. That speech he had made begging her not to join the Valkyrie had really mattered, she was sure of it. At the time, through the haze of her damaged pride, the depth of his emotion had had not penetrated her hurt. Now doubt buzzed away in her consciousness like a persistent wasp.

Ailie wrinkled her nose. "*Searc?* It means nothing. Not on its own. *A chéadsearc*, that means 'my first love,' and *a rúnsearc* means 'my secret love.'" She looked at Tanzi in alarm. "Why are you laughing?"

Tanzi shook her head, unable to explain. Lorcan had called her *Searc* back in Barcelona. Had she been his first and secret love even then? *It doesn't matter. I sent him away. I told him I didn't love him in return. I broke his heart all over again.* The laughter turned to tears. She leaned on Ailie's shoulder and cried as though her own heart would break, as well.

"There will always be a home for you and the child here on Spae."

Drying her eyes, Tanzi sat up straight. "I wouldn't wish my father on you. He will come looking for me now I no longer have the protection of Cal's spells. A visit from him would rip this island apart."

Ailie was looking beyond her—at the path that led from the beach—her eyes widening. "I think it may be too late."

Tanzi turned her head with a sense of dread. As out of place as an orchid in a field of wildflowers, Moncoya was striding toward them. Even in his haste, his sartorial flair had not been forgotten and he wore pristine white riding breeches tucked into highly polished black boots. A long-tailed coat of burgundy velvet hung open over his signature ruffled shirt and his mane of hair streamed behind him in the breeze. From the expression on his perfect features, Tanzi surmised he was not happy to see her.

"My daughter." His jaw was rigid with anger. "You have added to my difficulties of late with your elusiveness. Let us talk in private."

Ailie rose to her feet. "That may not be what Tanzi wants."

Moncoya glanced at her in the manner he used toward any woman with neither beauty nor power enough to interest him. "And you are?" The ice in his tone made Tanzi shudder, but it appeared not to affect Ailie.

"Your daughter's friend." Ailie stood her ground, appearing very small even though Moncoya was only a few inches taller.

The ring of fire in her father's eyes blazed brighter than ever and Tanzi decided it was time to intervene. "I will talk to my father alone, Ailie. Is there somewhere we can go?"

"You can use your own cottage." Ailie nodded across the square to the little house Tanzi and Lorcan had shared. "Call me if you need me." The message was clear. She watched them walk away with her hands on her hips.

Once inside the cottage, Moncoya glanced around him with a disbelieving curl of his lip. "You, my Tanzi? Living here?"

Tanzi wasn't prepared to play his games. "What do you want?"

"I think you know the answer to that question. I have a boat waiting to take you away with me."

She shook her head. "No." His perfectly shaped brows rose in surprise, but, before he could speak, she plunged on. "It is too late for your plan. I am carrying another man's child."

Something darkened in the depths of Moncoya's eyes. She knew that look. It usually heralded a burst of temper. "Is this a lie? A pathetic attempt to get out of the marriage?"

She laughed. "If so, you will find me out in a little less than nine months' time."

He took a step toward her, his lips white with fury. In the past, this was the point when she would have run from him. Instead, she stood her ground. If she was ever going to step out of the shadow of her fear of him, now was the time to do it. "Who is the father?"

"That is none of your business."

"My sources tell me you took refuge with the Irish necromancer, Lorcan Malone. Tell me you have not stooped so low."

Tanzi felt her temper flare and she welcomed it. She had never been brave enough to defy Moncoya, even verbally. Now, for the first time, as he dared to insult Lorcan, she saw him for what he was. An arrogant bully. A dangerous one, it was true, but she was ready to take him on. As she drew herself up to her full height, she saw something shift in Moncoya's expression. "Why did my mother leave you?"

For a moment, the question threw him off balance. Then Moncoya gave a mocking laugh. "You don't seriously think I would ever allow *any* woman to leave me, do you?"

"Stella did. She chose Cal instead of you."

The laughter vanished from his eyes. "For now. The necromancer star will come to regret that decision."

Tanzi swallowed the nervousness caused by the venom in his voice. "So if my mother didn't leave you, what did happen to her?" He regarded her in silence. "I know she didn't return to the Valkyrie as we always believed. She couldn't because she had disgraced herself by leaving them for you in the first place. Did you kill her?"

He shrugged. "She had a choice. Stay with me or face the consequences."

"That's the same sort of choice you gave her when you kidnapped her and refused to let her return to the Valkyrie. She had to stay with you and submit to a forced marriage. She had nowhere else to go."

His eyes narrowed dangerously. "You've been listening to stories about me."

"Is it untrue? Are you telling me my mother was in love with you and that was the reason she was the first Valkyrie to defy Odin and betray their warrior code?"

He remained silent for a moment, regarding her from under lowered brows. His silence told her everything she needed to know. Her worst fears had been right all along. Tanzi had long ago stopped believing she and Vashti were the result of a loving relationship, but this was so much worse than anything she could have imagined. "You know nothing of such matters. A conversation about your mother is not what I came here for."

"No, you came intending to bully me into returning with you so that you could force me into marriage with the devil." Tanzi folded her arms across her chest. "Now I've told you that's not going to happen, you can leave."

Moncoya regarded her speculatively. "I have an alternative proposition for you. One that gets you neatly out of the marriage contract and disposes of this inconvenient child at the same time."

Chapter 21

With Cal on board, *Igraine* flew across the waves faster than ever. Even so, they were not covering the miles quickly enough for Lorcan. Could he trust his instincts? *What if she hasn't gone to Spae?* Lorcan forced the thought away. *If she's not there, then I'll keep looking until I find her.* When the outline of the island came into view, he wanted to yell at Jethro, who was at the wheel, to speed up. Cal, sensing his mood, came to stand at his side.

"We're almost there."

"What if Moncoya has already found her?"

Cal's eyes scanned the horizon, as though searching for some sign of his hated half brother. "From what I know of Tanzi, I'd say she's pretty fearless."

Lorcan smiled reminiscently. "In most things, yes. But Moncoya terrifies her, and he's had his spies out looking for her ever since we left Barcelona. It was only your warding spells that kept her safe while she was with me."

They were approaching the bay now, and he pointed to the cluster of fishing boats bobbing on the waves. To one side of them there was a sleek yacht. It was unfamiliar and out of place among the simpler craft belonging to the Spae. "Unless I'm very much mistaken, I'd say that means Moncoya's already here."

Waiting while they dropped anchor, got into the dinghy and reached the beach was pure agony. Once they reached the shore, Lorcan didn't wait for the others. He took off at a run along the path that took him in the direction of the village. When he arrived all was ominously quiet, and he paused on the green in the center of the houses, glancing around as he caught his breath. Was he too late? Had Moncoya already seized Tanzi and taken her somewhere else?

He was about to seek out Ailie and ask for her help, when he heard Tanzi's voice raised in protest. His heart rate kicked up another notch. Following the sound, he approached the cottage they had shared during their stay on the island.

"Never!" Tanzi's exclamation was filled with horror.

As he recognized the soft, coaxing tones that answered her, Lorcan froze, pressing his body against the cottage wall. "Think about it. The child you carry will mean nothing to you. A foolish mistake, an error of judgment. We all make them. It is the prerogative of royalty. When the time comes, hand the bastard hybrid over to me. Satan will be happy to accept it as a substitute for begetting a child with you, especially as this one is likely to inherit the necromancer's powers. You will be free to walk away from the pact I made. You can marry whom you choose. Prince Tibor is so smitten he will still take you, even though you can no longer offer him purity."

Lorcan risked a glance through the open window. Tanzi was turned toward her father, her face pale with anger, her jaw rigid. Even across the distance that separated them he could see that her whole body was trembling, although he soon realized she was shaking with anger, not fear. She held one hand over her flat stomach in a protective gesture. "Listen to me, Moncoya—"

"You are my daughter. How dare you use my given name?" His voice was like a whiplash as he interrupted her.

"You lost the right to call me your daughter when you tried to sell me to the devil. Now, listen to me and listen good. This child is mine. Mine and Lorcan's." She enunciated every syllable clearly. "He was conceived in love. And he will be loved. I wronged his father by sending him away, but I will do right by this child." She drew in a breath. "And the very first thing I will do is make sure he has nothing to do with you and your evil schemes."

The mocking note in Moncoya's voice became more pronounced. "You are a sidhe princess. You cannot feel love, and certainly not toward a common necromancer."

"You are wrong. I love Lorcan Malone with all my heart. I always will. Through my foolish pride, I tossed aside any chance we had at a future. But Lorcan taught me how to love…and he is a better man than any prince or king will ever be." No one hearing Tanzi in that moment could have doubted her ability to feel. Each word thrummed with raw emotion.

Deciding it was time to announce his presence, Lorcan strolled through the door. "Sure, couldn't you have said all of that back at Gladsheim instead of playing hard to get in such a spectacular way?"

He was sent staggering back several paces as Tanzi hurled herself into his arms. He caught her against his chest with one arm and managed to press a swift kiss onto the top of her head while keeping his eyes fixed on

Moncoya. Even on his own, the faerie king was a dangerous opponent. Lorcan's powers of necromancy were useless against Moncoya. Faeries weren't dead, but they were vicious fighters and cunning as hell. They seemed to be hardwired to make up for their lack of inches by fighting dirty. Biting, kicking and gouging were all part of the sidhe repertoire. And Moncoya hadn't risen to the top through his tact and diplomacy. It was also hard to believe he had been arrogant enough to come to Spae alone. Lorcan fully expected a group of sidhe bodyguards to be lurking close by, just waiting to come to the boss's aid. *At least I've a couple of powerful allies of my own to call on.*

"You will never get to call me father." The familiar sneer was back on Moncoya's face.

"Too fucking right I won't." The thought made Lorcan shudder. "I can't imagine anything worse. No matter how much I love your daughter, I don't see this ending with us all playing happy families."

A footstep inside the door made him turn his head. "Sure, isn't that a shame?" The woman who entered the cottage had a pronounced Irish accent and a smile as wide as the Emerald Isle itself. "Just as I was looking forward to getting myself a new grandchild."

"What the—?" Lorcan gasped for breath, unable to believe his eyes.

"Who is this?" Tanzi reached for his hand, clearly able to sense the waves of shock emanating from him.

"Aren't you going to introduce us, son?"

Lorcan shook his head in an attempt to clear it. "You can't be." He glanced at Moncoya, who was leaning against the wall with his arms folded across his chest. A smile played about his lips as he enjoyed the show. "You bastard. That's not my mother."

"He's too good for us, Moncoya." The voice changed,

became familiar, even though he couldn't quite place the masculine tone while it was still coming from his mother's lips.

As he watched, the figure in front of him shimmered and changed. It was like watching a magician's illusion performed in double time. One second his mother stood before him, the next, her expression changed to one of fear and pain as flames engulfed her. Before he could move, the image had faded and Lorcan was staring into the face of the witch finder who had killed her. Under his horrified gaze, the witch finder changed to briefly become the tearstained face of Iphae, the murdered dryad. An instant later, Lorcan was looking at the smiling features of Iago.

The next moment Cal and Jethro erupted into the room with Vashti hard on their heels. "You are very welcome, my daughter, but this place really isn't big enough for any more of these muscular necromancers," Moncoya drawled.

"Shall I shut him up?" Jethro's voice held a trace of longing as he cracked his knuckles.

No one answered. Everyone was staring at the small, bearded man at Moncoya's side.

"Have you figured out who I am yet?" Iago spoke directly to Cal.

"I know who you look like. But you can't be who I first thought you were." Cal was gazing at Iago as if he'd seen a ghost. "Mordred died at the battle of Camlan."

"Who is Mordred?" Tanzi whispered to Lorcan, twining her fingers more tightly with his. The tension in the room was so thick he felt he might choke on it.

"King Arthur's illegitimate son with Morgan le Fay."

Tanzi wrinkled her brow in confusion. "I thought Morgan le Fay was King Arthur's sister?"

"It's complicated."

"You are very certain that Mordred is dead." Iago seemed to be enjoying himself now he was the center of attention.

"I should be." Cal's expression was grim. "I killed him myself right after he injured Arthur."

Iago's smile turned nasty. "At least you are not denying the rumor that you were my father's murderer."

"Iago, of course. That's where I've heard the name. You are Mordred's son?"

Iago bowed slightly in acknowledgment. "I was raised by my grandmother Morgan le Fay and her half-sister Niniane—whom I think you know only too well—on the Isle of Avalon. Between them, they taught me everything they knew. In other words... I'm your worst nightmare, Merlin Caledonius."

"Wasn't Morgan le Fay a faerie?" Tanzi whispered to Lorcan again.

"Faerie. Witch. Or the worst possible combination of both. Whatever Morgan was—or possibly still is—none of us, not even Cal, would want to mess with her. If your man there really is her grandson, I'm thinking we're all in big trouble."

"You sort out the faerie, Cal. I'll take the new guy. Lorcan can have a rest and sit this one out." Jethro was beginning to sound impatient.

"You must be Jethro de Loix." Iago turned to him with a smile. "I heard you liked to talk yourself up. It's a shame we haven't got all four of Niniane's murderers here, so I can finish you all at once. But I don't imagine your little necromancer star will pose too many problems once I've dealt with the three of you."

"Leave Stella out of this." Cal's features hardened further.

"For God's sake, can we all stop talking now and get

on with kicking the shit out of these two?" Lorcan made a move to grab Iago by his shirtfront.

To his surprise, the sorcerer sidestepped him. He hadn't imagined Iago would be particularly brave when it came to a physical confrontation, but after all that bluster, Lorcan thought he might at least attempt to fight back. What happened next was even more bizarre. Iago and Moncoya moved closer together in a choreographed movement, almost as if they were about to embrace or step into an old-fashioned dance. When they were facing each other only inches apart, both men extended their arms to shoulder height and began to spin wildly on the spot, moving so fast that they became a blur of motion.

"It's obviously a private thing. Let's give them a moment." Jethro regarded the phenomenon in disgust.

Gradually, the spinning slowed and then stopped. When it did, they were faced by two identical, smiling Moncoya figures, both clad in the same burgundy-and-white clothing. "Hell. Now we don't know which evil bastard is which." Cal ran a hand through his hair.

"Go for the face. The one who squeals like a girl is the real Moncoya," Lorcan said.

"Ahem." Tanzi gave him a you've-totally-said-the-wrong-thing look.

"Sorry." He grinned apologetically. "The one who squeals like a faerie king with chipped nail polish is the real Moncoya." Becoming serious, he lowered his voice. "Take Vashti to Ailie's cottage and keep her there. I want you out of this." He hoped she'd understand the subtext, which was that he didn't want Vashti adding her strength to that of Moncoya and Iago.

She nodded. "Just be careful."

"I will. Now I have you, I've too much to lose to be anything else."

Cal waited until Tanzi had dragged a protesting Vashti out of the cottage. When he spoke again, his voice was as cold and hard as a steel shutter slamming down. "I don't care which one is which. I'm taking one or both of you back with me to stand trial."

"Two against three." One Moncoya grinned at the other. "I like those odds."

"Make that five against two." Raimo and Ronab sidled into the room and arranged themselves on each side of Lorcan. "When our master fights, we stand with him."

"I didn't know you had yourself a couple of imps." Jethro regarded Lorcan in surprise.

"Nor did I." Lorcan's tone held a trace of weary resignation. "Welcome to the team anyway, guys."

He was tired of waiting. With a practiced movement he knew Cal would follow, he lunged forward. He figured Iago would be the easiest target, and he knew Moncoya would fight dirty. But which was Iago? He took a chance, delivering a swift kick to the gut of one opponent while Cal brought his elbow up hard under the chin of the other. They both went down. Too easily.

Raimo and Ronab rushed forward. "It's a trick. Stay back," Lorcan ordered, but the warning came too late.

There was a flurry of activity, during which one of the burgundy-clad figures vanished. The other lashed out with a lethal-looking blade, striking Ronab in the neck. The imp toppled forward, hitting the floor with a thud. The Moncoya figure sprang back, distaste spreading across his features as the imp's blood gushed over his white breeches.

"That's the real one." Lorcan rushed him. "Take care of Iago."

"We would if we could see the fucker," Jethro called back.

Lorcan didn't have time to respond. He threw himself onto Moncoya, pinning the faerie king to the floor with his superior size and slamming his fist repeatedly into the other man's face. Moncoya writhed beneath him, but couldn't break free. All the fury and resentment that had been burning through him toward Moncoya for his treatment of Tanzi found an outlet now that he finally had Moncoya in his power, and Lorcan was only vaguely aware of what was happening around him.

Nearby Raimo was cradling Ronab's lifeless body in his arms while the other side of the room suddenly erupted into a maelstrom of violence and cursing. Lorcan paused, his arm suspended in the air on its way to Moncoya's face again as he assimilated what was happening. Cal and Jethro had found Iago. The sorcerer had transformed himself yet again, becoming a full-sized male tiger. He was tearing up the room in an attempt to get at Cal and Jethro, who were holding the table between them and using it as a makeshift shield.

Lorcan dealt a final blow to the faerie king, rendering him unconscious. "Raimo, get Moncoya out of here and lock him up. Make sure he can't go anywhere."

"I can't leave Ronab." The imp's side-to-side eyelids fluttered.

Lorcan felt for a pulse in Ronab's neck. Raimo watched him, his hopeful expression fading pathetically when Lorcan shook his head. "There's nothing more you can do for him."

With a gulp and a nod, Raimo released his friend's body. Giving Moncoya's unconscious form a sharp kick in the ribs, he grasped him by the wrists and dragged him out of the cottage. Lorcan grabbed the bloody knife that was still protruding from Ronab's neck. With a sharp twist, he pulled it out of the imp's flesh and wiped it on Ronab's shirt.

"Sorry I'm a bit late to the party, guys." Lorcan sized up the situation. The tiger's teeth were bared in a furious snarl. "One of us needs to get on its back."

"It's not a fucking fairground pony," Jethro muttered as the huge cat lunged again.

Ignoring him, Lorcan tossed the knife to Cal before circling the tiger. The animal sensed his intention and followed his movement, snarling and lashing at him. Cal and Jethro distracted it by shouting and banging on the table and, when it turned their way again, Lorcan threw himself onto it, clinging to the thick pelt of its back for all he was worth. The tiger roared in fury, lunging and rearing as it attempted to throw him off. Lorcan managed to stay on and get a hand up so he could reach for its eyes.

Cal and Jethro smashed up the table and were coming at the tiger using the wooden legs as clubs. Cal also had the long-bladed knife extended in front of him. Slowed by Lorcan's weight on its back, and his fingers gouging its eyes, the tiger promptly vanished, leaving Lorcan sprawling on the floor.

"Tricky bastard," he muttered. "What's his next prank going to be?"

They didn't have to wait long to find out. Seconds later, Jethro jerked uncontrollably before dropping to the floor clutching at his throat. As Lorcan and Cal hurried to his aid, Iago materialized again. The smaller man was holding his hands around Jethro's throat and, as they watched, their much larger, more powerful friend shook him off and grappled with him. As the two men rolled around on the floor, Lorcan struggled to see what was happening.

"He's doing it again," Cal pointed out. "He's transforming himself into Jethro, so we can't figure out which one is which."

Sure enough, when the two beings on the floor separated, they were identical. Twin Jethro figures started to get to their feet, eying each other in horror. "This is taking showing off to a whole new level," one of them commented in a long-suffering voice.

That was good enough for Lorcan and he drop-kicked the one who had spoken in the side of the head before he could rise any farther. The fake Jethro toppled to the floor in a heap.

"How did you know I was the real one?" Jethro pointed to the figure at his feet. "That could easily have been me."

"He looked like you, he even sounded like you. But he couldn't do pissed off and sarcastic the way you can."

Iago groaned and then promptly disappeared. "For God's sake, what next?" Cal asked. "Even Niniane wasn't this slippery."

"Over there. That's what." Jethro pointed.

A huge falcon, Cal's own animal familiar, appeared on the step just inside the cottage. Spreading its wings wide, it cocked its head jauntily, as though mocking them, before taking flight. They watched it soar off into the blue sky, where it circled the village once in a defiant gesture.

Lorcan turned to Cal. "Will he go after Stella?"

"He might try, but she's not at the palace. I didn't want to leave her there without me, so I sent her away. He won't be able to get at her." Cal studied the sky again, watching as the falcon became a distant speck before disappearing. "Not this time. But something tells me we haven't seen the last of Iago."

Dusk had fallen when they finally sat around the open fire on the village green, eating Ailie's delicious stew and drinking her home-brewed beer. Moncoya was securely locked up in one of the empty cottages, and the plan was for Cal and Jethro to take him back to be imprisoned in his own palace dungeons on the following morning. There he would stand trial for his crimes and, if found guilty, he would be executed.

"I will arrange for Ronab's funeral to take place here in the village burial ground." Lorcan shook his head. "It's hit Raimo hard. They were inseparable. He'll find it difficult to commit as many crimes on his own."

Tanzi decided it was time to bring up the topic they were all avoiding. "What will you do about King Ivo's heir?" she asked Cal.

He threw her a grateful glance. "Now I know he exists, I can't just ignore him. As the leader of the Alliance, I have to take that information back to the council members. I think we should make a push to find him. He may be the very person we need to restore peace to the faerie dynasty and, at the same time, to Otherworld."

With a furious sound, Vashti threw her plate down on the grass and stomped off into the lowering darkness. "It is harder for her to visualize the end of Moncoya's reign," Tanzi explained. "She has not been directly on the receiving end of my father's villainy as I have. I know from experience she is best left alone in this mood."

"We still have the problem of how to find the challenger," Lorcan said.

"The Norn said you already know who the true heir is," Tanzi reminded him.

"But I don't." Lorcan ran a hand through his hair in a gesture of frustration. "I swear it. If I knew who he was, I would tell Cal. I learned nothing of him on my journey."

"Yet the Norn cannot lie."

"No, they can only bloody interfere." Lorcan's mouth thinned to a hard line and he slid his arm around Tanzi's shoulders, drawing her close. "When I think how close I came to losing you because of them, *Searc*."

"Yes, they are good at meddling." Cal nodded his agreement. "Nevertheless, because of them, we *are* slightly closer to the true heir. If we accept that the Norn must be telling the truth, then it has to be someone known to Lorcan."

"Could be anyone." Lorcan shrugged. "Although there is something else. I almost forgot. Ailie told me he doesn't look like a sidhe."

"Great." Jethro started to laugh. "How old are you, Lorcan? We just have to get you to remember everyone you've ever met over the centuries and eliminate those who look like sidhes. Anyone who is left is a possibility."

"The Norn said the truth would be found on Avalon," Tanzi said.

"Oh, yes. I was forgetting. The most dangerous place in either world." Cal's voice took on a reminiscent note. "Home to Morgan le Fay and, if he's telling the truth, our delightful new acquaintance, Iago the Trickster. I won't be going back there in a hurry."

Lorcan held up his hands in a warding-off gesture. "Don't look at me either."

Jethro grinned. "What you guys need is a mercenary. A powerful sorcerer who's seen what Iago can do and isn't afraid to stand up to him. Now, where will you get yourselves one of those, I wonder?"

Cal laughed, clapping him on the shoulder. "I'll put it to the council. In the meantime, after all this excitement, I need a good night's sleep."

Cal and Jethro made their way to the guest cottage Ailie had made ready for them. Lorcan rose to his feet, reaching down a hand to help Tanzi up from the grass.

He held her against him for a moment, resting his cheek on her hair.

"I don't know where to start."

She tilted her head so that she could look at him. "You got it wrong."

"I know—"

She silenced him by placing her finger on his lips. "I got it wrong, too. We don't need to analyze it." She stood on the tips of her toes so that she could replace her finger with her mouth, kissing him long and hard. "Let's try not to do it again. Now, tell me how much you love me."

His laugh was shaky. "That could take some time."

"We've got forever."

"That's just it. Before you, I had forever and it meant nothing. All those empty years, but I wasn't really living them. You've shown me what it is to be alive, Tanzi. Other people would have looked at me and said I was happy. Although I put on a good act, I was dead inside. You've taught me how to smile, what to say, how to love. I found my heart again because of you." His eyes were earnest as they searched her face. "I'm just scared all I have won't be enough for you."

Sharp tears prickled the backs of her eyelids. "Until I met you, I was a china doll, caught up in a world where all that mattered were looks and status. I didn't know how to feel even the simplest emotions. Now I have my love for you, and that means more than any material belongings. When you say my name, when you take my hand, when you hold me close at night…those are my precious possessions. Our future together, this child we have made… that is my silver and gold. All I want is you." She took his hand. "Now take me home."

Chapter 22

Vashti sighed. It was no good. She couldn't sleep, and it wasn't just because the mattress was hard and a quarter of the size of her own bed at home in the faerie palace. No, it was the thought of her father locked up like a common criminal just yards away.

She accepted now that the stories about him must be true. Even if she hadn't heard the accounts of his war crimes and atrocities against the faeries who opposed him, what he'd attempted to do to Tanzi proved beyond doubt he was a monster. *But he's* my *monster. Can I let him go to his trial, probably to be executed, without at least hearing what he has to say?* She decided not. Throwing aside the blankets covering her legs, she slid from the bed and hurriedly threw on her clothes. Aware that Jethro and Cal were sleeping in the next room, Vashti tiptoed carefully past their door and out into the inky darkness of the Spae night.

Tripping and stumbling over boulders and tree roots, she made her way to the isolated cottage where they had imprisoned Moncoya earlier that night. Aware that Raimo was guarding the front of the building, Vashti made her way around to the rear of the property. The wooden shutters over the window could be unlatched from the outside. Holding her breath in case the slightest noise alerted the imp guard, she found the window itself was easily pried open. Was Tanzi really considering coming to live in such a primitive society? The thought of her sister, feted and admired Princess Tanzi of the designer clothes and celebrity lifestyle, living in this backwater made Vashti choke back a derisive laugh. Love! They said it made you blind. She hadn't realized until now that it also rendered you stupid.

"My father?" Vashti whispered the words as she wriggled through the window and then dropped into a crouch in the darkened room on the other side. Had Cal posted a guard inside the cottage, as well? She could take out the imp or one of the Spae with a single punch. Jethro or Lorcan might be more of a problem. Either way, brawling with her father's captors in the middle of the night wouldn't look good. Remembering she was the faerie representative on the Alliance could be such an inconvenience at times.

A chain clanked, and Vashti felt cold fury spike through her veins. They had dared to chain the King of the Faeries?

"Vashti?" She followed the sound of Moncoya's answering murmur. These cottages all had the same unimaginative layout. He was in the small bedroom. By the light of a candle, she could see him sitting on the narrow bed. His hands were tied behind his back and there was an iron shackle around his left ankle. This was attached to a short length of chain that had, in turn, been secured to the leg of the bed. Even in these circumstances and in spite of his swollen and bruised features, Moncoya managed to look broodingly handsome. A smile lit his eyes when he saw her. She pressed a finger to her lips and he kept his voice low. "It is good to know that one of my daughters, at least, still remembers her duty to me."

A wry smile lifted one corner of Vashti's mouth. Even after everything he had done, his charm was irresistible. "You are fairly unforgettable."

"Your sister appears to think otherwise."

"To be fair, you have just attempted to marry her off to the devil. When that didn't work, you tried to persuade her to give her unborn baby to Satan instead. She's hardly likely to be thinking warm fuzzy thoughts toward you right about now."

Moncoya frowned. "If Tanzi had been dutiful, none of this would have happened."

Vashti shook her head. He would never change. He couldn't accept his own faults. Would never admit he had a fault. It was that arrogance that was likely to get him executed in the near future. "Tanzi said you killed our mother."

His eyes narrowed. There was a beat while he considered her statement. Then Moncoya gave a regretful shake of his tousled head. "She said that?" He tried to squirm into a more upright position. "Will you do something for me? These bonds around my wrists are so tight they are cutting off the circulation. Can you loosen them?"

Vashti regarded him suspiciously. Moncoya returned her stare without blinking. It couldn't hurt to do as he asked, could it? As long as he was tied up, there was no reason why he had to be in pain. Moving around so that she was behind him, Vashti knelt on the floor beside the bed so that she could see the ropes that bound his wrists.

It was difficult in the flickering candlelight. Moncoya didn't help the situation by straining to look over his shoulder at what she was doing.

"Whoever tied these knots knew what they were doing." Vashti found it difficult to get a grip on the thick twine.

"It was that bastard half-breed."

"I take it you are referring to your brother, Merlin Caledonius?" One of the knots was beginning to give and she worked determinedly at it.

"In a moment of madness my father lay with a mortal woman. The sorcerer who is the result of that mania may call me brother, but it is not a connection to which I will ever own. Can't you go faster?"

"Almost done. There. Just hold still while I—" The words froze on her lips as, lightning fast, Moncoya freed his hands from the loosened restraints and caught hold of her, his hand encircling her upper arm. Vashti shook her head as he rose to his feet, hauling her with him. "No, letting you go was not part of the deal."

"Too late, my daughter." His face was inches from hers, his smile mocking. "Are you going to fight me? Try to tie me up once more?"

Vashti swallowed hard. "If I have to."

"I would advise against it." Reaching into his belt with his free hand, Moncoya withdrew another slim-bladed knife similar to the one he had used to kill Ronab. Looking into the eyes she knew so well, Vashti knew for certain he wouldn't hesitate to use it on her. *He would slit my throat without hesitation or regret. He would kill me as easily as he did the imp...and our mother.* Because she knew now what Tanzi had told her was true. If she had ever really doubted it. "Help me get free of this chain."

"I don't have a key." Vashti's mind darted wildly

through her options. She could cry out to the imp guard. But if he came running in here Moncoya would kill them both and still get away. If she called to Raimo to fetch Cal, her father would still have time to use the knife on her before escaping. Could she contact Tanzi telepathically? That would require all her concentration...

"Lift the end of the bed so that I can slide the chain off."

"It will still be attached to your ankle."

"Stop arguing and do it! Once I am free of this cursed island I'll worry about getting rid of the unfashionable ankle bracelet."

Conscious of the knife close to her throat, Vashti did as he ordered. Moncoya slid the chain off the leg of the bed. As she lowered the bed once more, the grin she knew of old lit his features. "So they thought they could tether the greatest leader Otherworld has ever known? Fools." He gestured with the knife. "Lie facedown on the bed. Don't look so nervous. I'm only going to tie you up."

Within minutes, Vashti was trussed up in his place, her hands secured behind her back. Moncoya removed the pillowcase and stuffed its corner into her mouth. Then with the loose end of the chain slung casually over his shoulder like a scarf, he made his way out of the bedroom. Vashti heard him climbing out through the same window she had used to enter.

Tanzi! It was no good. Her thoughts were too panicky, her mind still focused on what Moncoya was doing and not on her sister. She pictured him sneaking through the outskirts of the village, taking the path down to the beach, wading out to the point where he had left his dinghy and looking back with a gloating smile as he sailed away. She tried wriggling her hands around to see if she could loosen the rope, but Moncoya had made sure there was no possibility of her getting free. *Lie still. Concentrate on Tanzi.* Just as she was trying to force herself to do that, a voice outside caught her attention.

"All quiet in there?" It was Jethro. "Prisoner behaving himself?" She didn't hear Raimo's reply. "Really? That doesn't sound like him. I think I'll take a look just to be sure."

Vashti felt her cheeks flame with humiliation. Why did it have to be *him*? Why couldn't Cal, or even Lorcan, have been the one to come along and find her in this position? She tensed, waiting for the outburst. Jethro's footsteps approached the bedroom, the door opened and he paused on the threshold. She felt his gaze on her, even though she couldn't see him.

"I suppose this was to be expected."

"Mnnnf?" Vashti craned her head at a painful angle. All she could see was a pair of long, muscular thighs encased in black denim.

"Daddy's precious princess taking his place while he gets away. Quite a masquerade. We should have foreseen it and locked you both up together."

Vashti made a furious sound into her gag and struggled wildly against the restraints.

"Sorry, I don't have time for conversation. I've got a dangerous criminal to recapture."

Was he leaving her? Vashti couldn't quite believe it was happening, but—sure enough—Jethro walked away. She heard his voice again, giving instructions to Raimo. Rage, pure and undiluted, flooded through her. How dare he treat her like this? And how dare he make assumptions about her? One thing was for sure… Jethro de Loix was going to be very, very sorry for tonight's actions.

Before long, there were signs of activity outside the cottage. Vashti heard voices and sounds of people running. It was evident a search was under way. Some minutes later, another footstep sounded inside the room and Vashti recognized Tanzi's voice in the startled exclamation her sister gave. Tanzi hurried over and removed the gag from Vashti's mouth before untying her hands.

"What happened?"

Unaccustomed tears pricked the backs of Vashti's eyelids and she blinked them hurriedly away. "He tricked me."

"Jethro thought..." Tanzi trailed off at the blaze of fury that made Vashti bound up from the bed.

"Jethro! Just wait until I get my hands on that slimy bastard. I'll rip his heart out, stuff it down his throat, then make him take back every judgmental word."

"To be fair, with his heart in his throat, he might find it difficult to talk."

"Don't you dare laugh at me, Tanzi." Vashti had started to pace the small room like an enraged wildcat, but she paused to glare at her sister.

Tanzi held up her hands in a gesture of surrender. "I wouldn't dream of it."

Vashti bit her lip. "Did he get away?"

Lorcan walked in at that moment. "Looks like it," he said in answer to her question. "His boat is gone."

Vashti's cheeks flamed. "Can you go after him?"

"That's what Cal and Jethro are debating. Jethro's inclined to go for it, but Cal's wary. We don't know what firepower Moncoya's craft has, how many sidhes are waiting close by or where Iago is. *Igraine* is fast, but she's not equipped for a fight." He cocked his head at the sound of approaching voices. "Looks like Cal prevailed."

Suddenly, the room appeared even smaller as the other sorcerers entered. Cal and Lorcan were both tall and muscular, but the sheer rippling power of Jethro's frame had a tendency to make Vashti's breath catch slightly. It was a reaction that annoyed her. *I refuse to be dazzled by him.* Tonight, she was even less inclined to find him impressive. She stormed up to him, stopping with the point of her finger pressed deep enough into his chest to leave an indentation. "Apologize."

"Why? For believing you could be trusted?" His eyes, dark as midnight, but lit with flecks of lighter gold, gazed into hers briefly. It was a contemptuous expression that made her blood reach boiling point in an instant. "Yeah, that was dumb. I'm sorry we fell for it."

Vashti made a strangled sound in her throat and launched herself at him. She was prevented from attacking him by Cal, who caught her deftly by her upper arms. "Let's just cool things down here, shall we? Moncoya would like nothing more than to see us at each other's throats."

"Make him take it back." Vashti could barely recognize the snarling, panting sounds her own voice made. No one had ever roused her to anger as quickly and easily as Jethro, and the fact that he managed to do it while staying calm himself infuriated her further.

"Jethro?" Cal looked across at where the mercenary was now leaning his broad shoulders against the wall. His arms were folded across his chest, and he was regarding Vashti with a combination of amusement and scorn.

"Oh, come on. Why would she come here in the middle of the night if not to help Daddy Dearest get away?"

Every eye turned to Vashti. She felt the weight of their stares. Why *had* she come here? "I wanted to hear it from him...about our mother." She looked directly at Tanzi.

"And did you?"

"Not exactly. But I know it's the truth. I know he killed

her." Vashti swallowed hard. "He would have killed me tonight if I'd resisted."

Cal risked releasing his grip on her arms and she stood still, her frame trembling with a different sort of tension now. "Can we draw a line under these allegations?" Cal raised a brow in Jethro's direction.

Jethro shrugged. "You're the boss."

"That's not an apology." Vashti felt some of her strength seeping back alongside her renewed indignation.

"Best you're going to get." White teeth flashed in a grin. It was the one that made him look like a pirate. The one that made her want to smash her fist into his mouth. Over and over.

"Subject closed." No one did authoritative better than Cal. "I suggest we all try to make the most of what's left of tonight by getting some sleep. In the morning, we can talk further about what needs to be done." Cal stretched and yawned, before heading off in the direction of the other cottage.

Lorcan slid an arm around Tanzi's shoulders. "Play nice, guys." He waved a hand at Jethro and Vashti before he and Tanzi drifted off into the darkness.

Determined not to walk with Jethro, Vashti dawdled behind him in the moonlight. He reached the cottage just ahead of her and paused at the door, awaiting her approach.

"Just so you know—" she felt his eyes scanning her face in the darkness "—no matter what Cal says, I don't buy in to the innocent act. I think you colluded with Moncoya to let him get away. It's not up to me, but if it was, I'd take you back to the palace in chains and make you stand trial in his place." When she drew in an angry hiss of breath, he gave a soft laugh. "Sleep well, Princess."

* * *

There was nothing they could do. That was the gist of the conversation over breakfast. They were back to where they started, with Moncoya returning to control his terrorist forces from his hiding place. Lorcan had been with Tanzi when she'd gone to Cal and told him where she had visited her father. Lorcan, aware of what it cost her, held her hand while she blurted out details of the location of Moncoya's secret headquarters on the Silver Isle.

Cal shook his head sadly. "I appreciate your loyalty to the Alliance, Tanzi, but we received intelligence some time ago from another source that he was there. The peacekeeping force went in, but he'd already moved on."

Tanzi let out a shaky breath. "I know it sounds strange, but I'm relieved. I want him captured. I just don't want to be the reason."

Cal regarded her with curiosity. "He can still inspire that sort of loyalty, even after everything he's done?"

"It's difficult to explain his magnetism. The closest I can come to explaining it is to call it faerie glamor." She laughed. "Which my father would hate, since he despises the old ways." She turned to Lorcan. "I will leave the two of you to say your farewells."

She walked away and the friends regarded each other. "So it's a life among the fishing nets for you?"

"Ah, don't be telling me you're not jealous as hell."

Cal laughed. "I am. I told you I've no wish to be a politician. Just promise me the wedding won't coincide with an Alliance meeting."

"You have my word. Although you do have other things to worry about, big feller."

Cal wrinkled his brow. "You mean how to stop Jethro and Vashti from killing each other on the journey home?"

"I'm not going to bet against that, although my money

would be on Vashti. No, this is worse. Has Prince Tibor ever discussed his plans for a luxury vampire resort in the mortal realm with you? Apparently, he wants to show the earth-born that vampires can be nice guys."

Cal's expression was a picture of incredulity. "You have got to be kidding me."

"Does this look like the face of a man who is joking?"

"How the hell am I going to police that?" Cal draped an arm around Lorcan's shoulders. "Especially without my right-hand man."

"I can recommend another right-hand man to you. A young faerie by the name of Aydan. He currently works for the resistance, and he's loyal, hardworking and—as an added bonus—he hates Moncoya." Lorcan looked across at the group who had gathered on the beach. "I can also let you have Raimo for a small price. Ah, what the hell. For you, I'll part with him for nothing."

Cal started to laugh. "I'll look up Aydan when I get back, but you can keep your imp."

Lorcan became serious. "This may be a long shot, but something occurred to me when Tanzi and I saw Avalon. You know more about the Arthurian legends than anyone, but it was the one that states, *'On Avalon will be found the last bright hope, a memory of what once was before the darkness snuffed the flame.'* For centuries we've all believed it meant King Arthur would rise up and come to the rescue of the mortal realm when he was needed. What if that's not what it means?"

Cal frowned. "Go on."

"What if the last bright hope in the legend of Avalon is not Arthur, but the faerie challenger? And the darkness that snuffed the flame is Moncoya, not Mordred?" Lorcan looked at Cal's stunned face. "You think I'm mad."

"I think that regularly, but I also think there's even more reason to send someone to Avalon to find out."

"Jethro?" Lorcan looked at the mercenary, who was hauling the dinghy to the water's edge.

"He's fearless enough, but who goes will be a decision for the council." Tanzi was walking back toward them, and Cal nodded in her direction. "This is everything you've ever wanted."

Lorcan smiled. "I just never knew it until I met her. All this time, I thought I was a wanderer and a renegade. Turns out, I was just searching for the right person and a place to call home." As Tanzi drew level with him, he slid an arm around her shoulders. "From now on, I'm not alone. It's the two of us."

"Soon to be three," she reminded him. "Or four."

"Whoa. Twins?"

"I was thinking of my inner cat. The one you've become so fond of."

"Four it is then."

"Five if you count Raimo." Tanzi ran a coaxing hand down his chest.

"The cat can stay, but I draw the line at the imp who beat you up in a back alley."

"He did also fight Iago for you, and he's lost his best friend."

Lorcan waved a hand in the direction of Cal and Jethro, who had come to say goodbye. "Make sure you get yourselves back here for the wedding."

Lorcan scooped Tanzi up into his arms, preparing to continue the conversation about Raimo as they made their way home. Jethro's bemused voice followed him.

"He didn't even notice us. How are the mighty fallen."

Cal laughed in reply. "Falling is a good way to describe it. But it's very pleasant. As you'll find out when it happens to you."

Jethro snorted. "Not me. No way. Never..." His protests faded from Lorcan's hearing as he made his way up the path to the village.

"About Raimo." Tanzi drew his attention back to her.

He sighed. "You win. The imp can stay, but he gets his own cottage. Is there anyone else you want me to adopt? Perhaps you'd like Lisbet to come and brighten up our lives with her sunny personality, or Tibor to add a touch of aristocratic class to the village? I know, maybe we should get ourselves a Loup Garou and take it for walkies along the beach."

Tanzi chuckled and tucked her head into his shoulder. "I do love you, Lorcan Malone."

As he hugged her closer, Lorcan knew he would never get tired of hearing those words. Words that were made sweeter by all the years of wandering and heartache.

"And I love you, my first and not-so-secret love. My *Searc*."

* * * * *

MILLS & BOON®

Mills & Boon have been at the heart of romance since 1908... and while the fashions may have changed, one thing remains the same: from pulse-pounding passion to the gentlest caress, we're always known how to bring romance alive.

Now, we're delighted to present you with these irresistible illustrations, inspired by the vintage glamour of our covers. So indulge your wildest dreams and unleash your imagination as we present the most iconic Mills & Boon moments of the last century.

Visit **www.millsandboon.co.uk/ArtofRomance** to order yours!

MILLS & BOON®

Why shop at millsandboon.co.uk?

Each year, thousands of romance readers find their perfect read at millsandboon.co.uk. That's because we're passionate about bringing you the very best romantic fiction. Here are some of the advantages of shopping at www.millsandboon.co.uk:

* **Get new books first**—you'll be able to buy your favourite books one month before they hit the shops

* **Get exclusive discounts**—you'll also be able to buy our specially created monthly collections, with up to 50% off the RRP

* **Find your favourite authors**—latest news, interviews and new releases for all your favourite authors and series on our website, plus ideas for what to try next

* **Join in**—once you've bought your favourite books, don't forget to register with us to rate, review and join in the discussions

Visit **www.millsandboon.co.uk** for all this and more today!